MOONLIGHT PREDATOR

GRAHAM SHARPE

A Sid Harta publication
This edition published in 2023 by Sid Harta Publishers,
23 Stirling Cres, Glen Waverley VIC 3150, Australia

Copyright © Graham Sharpe 2023
Cover design and typesetting: Luke Harris, WorkingType Studio

ISBN: 978-1-922958-48-8

The author on safari, 1956.

ABOUT THE AUTHOR

Graham Sharpe has led an adventurous life, starting when he served with a "crack" special forces battalion and army intelligence unit. He has travelled the world extensively, lived in several countries, including Kenya, where his eldest daughter was born. He worked for organisations varying in size from multinationals, where he rose to be managing director and chief executive, to his own small company, where he was everything from chairperson to  "chief bottle washer". Now he lives quietly, having been widowed, after many years of marriage to "the most gorgeous girl in the world!".

BY THE SAME AUTHOR

Caroline Dalglish is a young freelance features writer, recently widowed when her husband, a brilliant Oxford historian, dies in an accident.

She had been quietly adjusting to life without John when she is approached by the UK Government, which offers her funding to undertake research for an article about The Foundation, a suspicious organisation based in San Francisco. The new assignment pulls Caroline into an exciting romance and puts her life, and that of her new love, in danger.

LOVE, DANGER AND SHADY DEALS...
TOUCH AND GO
GRAHAM SHARPE

This novel's story and characters are fictitious. Although certain long-standing institutions, agencies and public offices are mentioned, the characters and situations involved are wholly imaginary.

For Family and Friends.

ACKNOWLEDGEMENTS

My daughter Belinda, for acting as my literary agent, Kerry and the excellent team at Sid Harta Publishing, Jenn, for her editing skills and Luke for his dynamic cover design.

CHAPTER 1

He exploded through the scrub like an express train out of hell. Frothing at the mouth with spittle flying in all directions, he looked exactly like what he was—wild and extremely dangerous.

We were seconds from disaster; it was simply a matter of life or death.

No time to bring my rifle up to my shoulder; I just had to take a shot from the hip.

The double-barrelled Rigby.450 thundered as I squeezed off the first shot.

The buffalo was coming straight at us with his head slightly tilted to one side and his eyes locked on us. My shot hit him where I intended, passing straight through his muzzle, it entered his chest.

Okay, it stopped him, but only just; the velocity of the bullet pushing him back onto his haunches. He was on his feet again in a split second and coming straight for me. By now I had my rifle up into my shoulder but that wasn't going to make much difference, there was still only one place to put a bullet. For such a big beast, at such a close range, you would think there were more options but his massive horns, which would deflect even a .450 bullet, gave him a lot of protection. So, I just squeezed off and let him have the contents of my second barrel in the same place as the first one.

Without taking my eyes off the buffalo for a second, I broke my Rigby and slammed in the two cartridges that I had between the fingers of my left hand. A very good trick this as it allows the hunter to get off four shots in the shortest possible time.

The beast bellowed and tried to roll over and then started to get back on his feet. He was dead, he'd got to be with two .450 bullets in his chest from a range of 15 to 20 feet, but he was a Cape buffalo so he wouldn't accept the fact.

I was desperately trying to move round beside him to get in a finishing shot.

For a second, I wondered if it would be my last safari,

as I couldn't move, my feet being well and truly stuck in the swamp mud.

Then out of the corner of my eye I saw Mkamba move up beside the buff and give it the coup de grace with two shots from the Holland and Holland .500 he was carrying.

There was no time to even say thanks to him as all hell was immediately let loose.

There were buffalo in all directions. They were not looking for us, it was just they didn't know what had happened or where they should be going. With the elephant grass and swamp bushes, they couldn't see us.

It was still a very dangerous situation.

I shouted, 'We must let them see where we are. Get on the dead buff's back.'

I stood on his back and waved my rifle in the air, shouting like a lunatic. Mkamba and Kidogo did the same. But not William. I could see him still standing in his original position. What was the matter with the bloody man? Was he paralysed, scared out of his mind or just brain dead? I was about to go back to him when Kidogo very bravely got off the buff and went and stood beside William with his Jeffreys .475 at the ready. Not a good situation but it showed me once again that Mkamba was right when he said Kidogo was a very good man to have along.

For a few more minutes it was like being in the middle of Piccadilly during rush hour. Then suddenly it was deathly quiet.

What a relief.

I gave Mkamba's shoulder a pat and said in Swahili, 'Well done, my friend, and many thanks. That's another one I owe you.'

He just gave me a grin. We had known each other for such a long time and so well that words were not really necessary between us.

We got down off the buff's back and moved to join the other two. I said in Swahili to Kidogo that he had done well.

Then I turned to look at my illustrious client, Sir William Evans. He was even whiter than usual and visibly shaking. I couldn't really blame him. It had, after all, been a few very scary minutes.

'I'm sorry about that, William, are you all right?'

'Yes, thank you,' he replied in a rather breathless, halting way.

Looking at him, I could see it had really knocked the stuffing out of him, not that he had much to start with.

'I'm sorry I poached your beast, but I didn't really have any alternative. If I had waited for you to take a shot, I think one, or more of us, would now be rather indisposed. In any case, not to worry too much as I see this old boy had a broken horn so he would not have made a good trophy for you.'

'Don't apologise, I thought you were splendid. I couldn't even have hit him, let alone stopped him.'

William was trying to get a grip of himself but not very successfully. I needed a diversion to give him a few minutes more before we moved off.

'William, I think it would be nice to have a photograph of you and Mkamba with the buff. We've got a camera in the pack. Now, let's have the two of you sitting on his head with your backs to him. Position yourselves so that the broken horn isn't apparent. That's excellent. I think when you look at that photograph, William, that it will bring back a few memories.'

He seemed to have recovered himself and, in any case, we had to move, as I wanted to be back at the hunting car before dusk.

There was nothing to do about the buff as we didn't want him as a trophy and his meat was no good for eating.

We started back across the swamp, and it was very hard going. The mud just did not want to let go of our feet, so each step was an effort, "wait-a-bit" thorns kept getting hold of us and the strong smell of rotting vegetation was quite sickening.

Then through the scrub I saw ominous grey forms moving.

Damn me, it was the buffalo herd. What were they playing at? Were they actually following us to attack us? I had frequently seen them hassle a lion that had annoyed them, or even a pride of lions, but not a party of men.

I called out to Mkamba. 'What do you make of that?'

'I don't know but I don't like it.'

'Come on, William, we must make better time than this.'

'I'm sorry, Gavin, I just can't go any faster than this. But surely, we don't have to go at breakneck speed?'

He hadn't seen that we had company and, not understanding Swahili, he had not understood what the rest of us were saying. I certainly didn't want to panic him anymore than he already was.

'Don't worry, it's just that I want us out of this swamp well before dark. Come on, we will give you a hand.'

We shared out his rifle and kit between the rest of us so that he just had himself to carry.

The buff were now getting a bit more adventurous. One broke cover just behind our left flank and I ran back at him waving my rifle. Luckily, he decided discretion is the better part of valour and took off whence he had come.

At a word from Mkamba, Kidogo took William Evans's arm and helped him along.

Then what I feared might happen, happened.

A young but fully grown bull broke cover to our left and came straight for us.

I was carrying my .450 with my finger already on the trigger and the barrels resting on my right shoulder. I just swung the rifle forward and griped the stock with my left hand and it was already up in the aiming position. I had no alternative, it was the last thing I wanted to do, but there was only one way to stop him and that was to kill him.

God damn it! It was another frontal shot.

I dropped onto one knee, aimed up at the tip of his muzzle and squeezed off.

It knocked him back and he went down and didn't move. He was only some fifteen feet from me. I moved forward and made sure of him with a headshot.

'Let's move on as quickly as we can,' I said as calmly as I could.

William was now in a state of collapse.

This was an extraordinary situation; I had never had

anything like this happen before. It didn't help having a client who was next to useless.

Mkamba was now on the other side of William. He and Kidogo were supporting him, or very nearly carrying him.

Mkamba shouted and pointed to our left. There they were, they were still with us but being a bit more cautious.

As it seemed that the buff might now be thinking better of attacking us, I thought it time to take the initiative.

I shouted in Swahili that the three of them were not to take any notice of me but just to carry on.

Then I checked the Rigby, made sure there were plenty of loose cartridges in my left-hand safari jacket pocket, put two cartridges between the fingers of my left hand and strode towards the shadowy shapes among the scrub.

They stopped and stared at me.

I was now so close I could quite clearly make out their large ugly bodies. They clustered together and it was obvious that they were not sure what to do. It made me certain that the large broken-horned bull that I had had to shoot had been their leader.

'Go on, you shower of bastards, get out of it,' I shouted at the top of my voice and then I fired first one barrel and then the second just over their heads.

I broke the Rigby and reloaded.

But they had gone.

May the Lord be praised. It had worked, they had scarpered.

I turned and hurried back to catch up with the others.

They were struggling along; these were difficult conditions even for the fittest of people but in these circumstances, almost impossible.

'Kidogo, I'll take your place for a spell.'

William Evans was recovering to a certain extent and was making an effort to get his legs working, as legs should.

I thought that as soon as we were clear of the swamp, we would have a short rest and see what he could do under his own steam.

We struggled on for another ten or fifteen minutes when we at last left the swamp. What pure bliss to have one's feet on firm ground again, even if it was an area with a hard rocky surface where the stones were loose and first-class for turning an ankle.

'Okay. Well done, everyone. Let's have a short break. Have a drink of water, William. How do you feel after that terrible ordeal?'

'I'm sorry, Gavin, I didn't do very well, but it's just not like anything that has happened to me ever before.'

'No, don't you worry about it, I must admit it was all rather stressful and a very unusual situation. If you are tracking a wounded buff you have to be very careful that he doesn't turn the tables on you and end up tracking you, or lying in wait, for you. But this situation of a whole herd coming after a party of men is beyond my comprehension. In any case, William, think nothing of your behaviour, as most people would have reacted the same way as you.'

I spoke to the other two in Swahili, saying that I thought we could now move on as our client was well enough recovered.

'If you are ready, William, let's make a start and see how you get on under your own steam.'

We stumbled our way across the rough terrain and thankfully William was now able to keep up with a slow but steady pace.

At last, we left the area of rough stony ground and were back onto the short grass of the plains. This made the going much easier and we were able to increase the pace a bit without William being too distressed. But it was now getting close to darkness, and we were well behind schedule.

I was really pleased when we at last reached the hunting truck with Makanyanga, my driver, fast asleep on one of the back seats. Mkamba soon roused him with a few well-chosen words in Swahili.

Then out came the Primus stove for a well-deserved mug of tea, topped up with a drop of scotch.

While I gulped my tea, I puffed a Havana from the box that Evans had presented me with at the beginning of the safari and I felt really rather good. It had been a tough but fairly exhilarating sort of day.

My two gun bearers were not suffering any ill effects from the day's doings, but poor old William Evans looked as though he had been to hell and back.

It was already dusk by the time the hunting car was loaded and we were off on the journey back to camp which would, hopefully, only take us about an hour and a half.

As we bumped and crashed our way across the rough and pitted ground, William and I, who were sitting together in the rear compartment, talked generally about our future hunting plans and particularly about the next day.

'No hunting tomorrow, William, as I've got to collect those documents that are being dropped off by Philip at the airstrip. Actually, I rather think that you will be quite pleased to have a bit of a rest tomorrow after today's doings.'

'You're right, I don't think I'll be up to much for a day

or two. Don't forget to remind Philip that he's got to pick up Helen and me at the end of the safari.'

'That's already organised but I'll certainly remind him. The other ... what the hell's happened now?'

With an almighty crash, the safari car was suddenly stationary and at a distinct angle.

Getting out to look, we found that a rear wheel had dropped into an ant bear hole.

'Damn and blast. That's all we need. If you would all like to shove, I'll see if I can drive it out.'

But it was to no avail so after a few minutes out came the spades to ease the sides to make it possible to drive out. This all took time and sweat, and when we eventually had the car back on an even keel it was to find that we had a flat tyre. We changed the wheel and off we went again but not for long as damned if we didn't have another flat. That was okay as we had a second spare, but I just prayed we didn't have a third puncture as, if we did, we would have to take the tyre off and do an on-the-spot repair job.

Now we were well behind schedule, and it was going to be after nine before we reached camp.

'We're going to be much later than expected. I do hope Helen won't be too worried,' William commented.

'I'm sure she will have a pretty good idea of the sort

of thing that's happened. She may, however, think that you have got yourself a fantastic trophy and that we are delayed preparing it and celebrating.'

'That's a bit unkind. After all, it wasn't my fault that things went wrong, was it?'

'Come on, William, only pulling your leg old boy. Anyway, Helen was with us the day we had trouble with the half shaft, and we were certainly behind schedule that day, so she knows all about it.'

'Yes, I'd forgotten that. She thought that was quite fun.'

'And she's right, it is fun for everyone except the poor sod of a white hunter who has to sort it all out and get everyone home safe and sound.'

'But in your case, you love it, don't you? It's so obvious that you love every minute of it and everything that happens even if some of it doesn't appear to be so good.'

'Quite right, William. This is my country and my kind of life and there is nowhere else I'd rather be nor anything else I'd rather do.'

'You're a very lucky chap, there aren't many people that can say that.'

When we eventually arrived back at camp, the lovely Helen, although looking as gorgeous as ever, showed signs that she had been worrying about us. Quite understandable, as it was now some hours later than our proposed return time.

'Are you all right, William?' she asked, examining his gaunt, dishevelled appearance. 'Tell me exactly what happened.'

William slumped into a chair and then gave her an extraordinary account of the day's happening. Extraordinary because it was so concise and exact and was given in a clear monotone. There was so much about this man that did not seem to add up. I wished once again that I knew who he really was, what he had been doing and what he was going to do in the future. He was certainly a bit of a mystery as far as I was concerned.

When he had finished, Helen turned to me with a definite spark in her eye. 'Gavin, how could you have got him into such a position and risked his life like this?'

'I'm sorry, but if you don't want William taking any risks then you should not have come on a big game hunting safari. I can assure you that I put him in no additional risk to that which is always present when you take on large aggressive animals in their own backyard.'

'He's right, Helen, it all happened so suddenly there was nothing else he could have done. And, if I may say so, he was magnificent, a real man of action.'

'Well, thank you for that, William, but I assure you I did nothing out of the ordinary. Now, Helen, are you too cross with me for us to have a drink?'

'I'm sorry, Gavin. I overreacted but I was very worried about you both. Yes, I'm sure we could all do with a drink.'

We had a drink, and a quick clean up, followed by a bit of supper.

William wouldn't even stay for coffee; he was dead on his feet and just wanted to go to bed. Helen decided to skip coffee as well and as they said their goodnights, I reminded them that I would be off at the crack of dawn and would not see them until late afternoon.

CHAPTER 2

t was one of those perfect days when the sky was blue, the sun a burning orb directly overhead and there was a gentle hot breeze, carrying with it that elusive perfume of the African bush.

My hunting car was parked close under an umbrella tree to take advantage of what little shade there was. It was the middle of the day and it was hot—damn hot. Mkamba was dozing on one of the back seats and as I got out, he opened an eye and then closed it firmly again. I needed to stretch as my six foot two body was not too keen on being cramped inside a vehicle for too long at a time.

Leaning against the side of the wagon, I puffed another of those magnificent Havana cigars and looked across the plains towards the distant line of low hills. Nothing stirred; everything was like wise old Mkamba taking an afternoon snooze in any bit of shade it could find.

I laughed out loud; life was just so good. Mkamba's eyes twitched again—but only for a split second.

The previous ten years had been amazing, winning that medal had helped; some people, because of it, liked to have me as their "white hunter". If the rest of the 1950s carried on like this, I was going to have a ball.

My present client wasn't too good but there was only another week to go, and anyway, his wife made up for his deficiencies! How had they ever given a man like that a knighthood? It was obvious that whatever he'd done during the war had been for his own advantage and pocket. Sir William Evans—profiteer and double dealer if ever I saw one. Why he'd come on a hunting safari I just didn't know. He was scared stiff and as for his shooting, he couldn't hit the side of a barn at ten yards, and certainly not an enraged charging predator. So, it always tended to be me finishing the job for him. Not a happy situation.

Another question I asked myself and couldn't really answer was, why had Helen married him? It had to be money. But surely a good-looking woman like her— medium height with well-shaped full breasts, long attractive legs, a round nicely featured face topped by short curly blonde hair—could have found money with something a lot better than Sir William 'bloody' Evans wrapped round it. Still, even though she must be in her thirties, and, as he was old enough to be her father and slept, as I well knew, very soundly, perhaps she thought there was some merit in it.

That first night she came into my tent I knew I shouldn't have anything to do with her. One should never fornicate with a client's wife. However, she was so insistent, smelt so good and was so desirable, especially with my having been away from the flesh pots of Nairobi for several weeks, that I was forced to surrender my body.

Very nice too that first time was but it got better, and better. Evans made it easy by snoring away like a stuck warthog letting us, and, for that matter, the whole of Africa, know whether he was asleep or not.

Where was that plane? It should be here by now.

Why on earth did Evans want to have papers delivered to him out here in the bush? If his companies, or whatever he was involved in, couldn't survive without him for a few weeks there must be something wrong somewhere.

Mkamba got out of the safari wagon and pointed towards the horizon.

'Here it comes now,' he said in Swahili.

I couldn't see or hear anything but that didn't surprise me as, although Mkamba was a great age, no one knowing exactly how old, he could still see and hear things before most people. I'd known him all my life, as at the time I was born he was my father's tracker and gun bearer. He taught me all my bush craft when I was a small boy and he was with me when, aged twelve, my father sent me out to shoot my first Cape buffalo. He was the best hunting companion and most loyal friend one could ever hope to find.

At last, I could hear and see the little monoplane as it came towards us at treetop level. Mkamba and I had already checked the strip of bush that we used as a runway and knew that there were no pig holes or ant heaps or anything else to affect the plane's landing.

As it roared over our heads I could see Philip waving and was surprised that there was someone else in the plane with him.

He banked and, flying back, made a perfect landing on our makeshift strip. Philip was a first-class pilot who had started his flying career in Spitfires during the Battle of Britain. Being based in Nairobi he was one of my main companions when I was living it up between safaris. He always reckoned to wine and dine—and hinted at more—every new single female arrival in Nairobi, and that, before she'd been there a week. We, however, all maintained that he had to do it within a week otherwise she would have heard all about him from the locals and certainly would think twice before accepting an invitation from him. Still, he seemed to do all right, as it was an exception for him to sleep in the same bed, even his own, two nights running.

After the plane had come to a standstill, Mkamba and I walked across to it when the cockpit door was opened and out onto the wing stepped a girl, a girl who made my heart miss a beat.

I don't know why, I hadn't had a chance to assess her looks or body or anything else about her, but as soon as I set eyes on her, I got this tremendous surge of lust. It was something that hadn't happened to me since I was a teenager. I often fancied girls, but this was different. For a moment I felt weak at the knees and slightly sick.

'Hello,' she said, standing there looking down at me. 'I'm Carol Jefferson,' and then laughingly she continued, 'You must be the great warrior and white hunter Gavin McKenzie.'

I couldn't say anything, I just stood and gaped. For once I was speechless. She waited and at last, after a few seconds I managed to croak, 'Hello.'

'I've got to get out of the way for Philip. Can you catch me?'

Without waiting for an answer she took one or two steps down the walkway on the plane's wing and then literally launched herself off it straight at me.

I stretched out my arms and caught her but her weight and momentum made even my fourteen and a half stone of bone and muscle stagger back. I think I would have gone flat on my back if Mkamba hadn't moved behind me and supported me. I was about to ask her what the hell she thought she was doing when she started to laugh. It was a wonderful laugh, so warm and devil-may-care, it made me join in.

I stood there, with her still in my arms, while we both convulsed with laughter. As I laughed I was inhaling her fragrant smell. She was hot and sticky, and that odour, if you can call it that, was mixed with some expensive heady perfume. It was very musky and lust making. What with that and the feel of her soft luscious body pressed hard against me, I began to feel quite aroused. She must have got the general idea because after a couple more minutes, she said, 'Okay, Gavin, I think you had better put me down now.'

Philip, getting out of the plane, shouted down to us,

'What is up with you two? What's so funny? Did you introduce yourselves? Gavin McKenzie ... Carol Jefferson. Has she told you why she's here, Gavin?'

'No, I thought she was just along for the ride.'

'No, old boy, she wants to stay with you.'

'You've broken it to him too quickly, let me tell him. Gavin, I'm trying to catch up with Prince Gianne who is on safari with your great friend Harry. I understand that they intend to hunt the country to the south of you and are going to call at your camp on the way through. All I want is to wait in your camp until they arrive and then I'll join them. No problem is it?'

'Yes, it is a problem. It's not my camp, I'm only the hired help. We'd have to ask Sir William Evans whether or not he approves. Are you coming back to camp with us, Philip?'

'Not if you've brought the papers he wants me to take back.'

'Well, there you are, Carol. We're not going to have a chance to ask my lord and master whether he minds or not.'

'Surely you can take a chance on it. He's not going to mind little me being around for a couple of days.'

'He might do, he's a difficult sod.'

'I'm sure that's not going to worry you. It must be just

that you don't want me there yourself.'

'Not at all. In fact, I can't think of anything I'd enjoy more than your company, but I have to consider my client.'

'I don't believe you. Everybody I've met since I've been in East Africa keeps telling me how you're not frightened of anything or anybody.'

'You always want to take a pinch of salt with anything anyone in Africa tells you. But in any case, Carol, we don't have a spare tent.'

'I could always share with Sir William.'

'He's got his young, presumably, second wife with him.'

'What about your tent? I'm sure you've got room for poor little me in a corner or something?'

I laughed, and then I took my first real good look at her. Wow! What a figure. She was wearing KD slacks that showed off her bottom to perfection and a cream silk shirt with nothing but breasts and large prominent nipples under it. Her face was sublime: wide full lips high cheekbones, almond-shaped brown eyes and a golden complexion. This was set off by long luxuriant black hair. She was a real dish.

'Well ... perhaps if I take you back with me, Philip having gone, we shall be able to persuade Sir William to let you stay until Harry's safari arrives.'

'Oh, you are a darling. I just knew you'd help.'

Behind her back Philip was making faces at me. I got the distinct impression he thought I had some foul plan in mind.

While Philip and I exchanged packets of papers, Mkamba got out the Primus stove, kettle etc. so we could have a cup of tea before Philip took off and we set off for our camp. While we were drinking our tea I was updated with all the gossip and news from Nairobi and information concerning various friends and hunting rivals.

'Tell me, Carol, what are you doing in Kenya?'

'I came out as a model on a photographic expedition arranged to get photographs for an art calendar. That's when I met the Prince as his fashion house was supplying the clothes and accessories. Then we had to go up to Lake Nakuru, to get some photographs with flamingo in the background, leaving Gianne in Nairobi with the arrangement that I would be back in time to join him on his big game safari. My party got held up so by the time I arrived back in Nairobi the Prince had already gone, leaving a message telling me to join up with him when and where I could. That's why I'm here.'

'I'm surprised you didn't get Philip to fly you direct to your friend's camp.'

'I would have done that but Carol doesn't know exactly where they are,' interposed Philip.

'And you weren't going to find out as you didn't know whether anyone would pay you for flying her there.'

'Gavin, what a thing to say. You know me too well to think I'd have worried about being paid.'

'That's quite right, Gavin, after all, Philip has charged very little to bring me down here today.'

I just laughed. There wasn't really any answer to that.

'By the way, Philip, as I expect you've noticed, I've moved our camp. That's why I had to drive here and wait for you.'

'That's a pity, this is a nice site and very handy having the airstrip right by it.'

'Yep, but now we're about twenty or thirty miles southwest of here so we'd better think about starting back.'

'Gavin, will you tell your "boy" to get my bags out of the plane.'

'If by "boy" you mean Mkamba, perhaps I should explain that he is not some servant, he is one of the most experienced gun bearers and trackers in East Africa and has been a good friend of mine ever since I was a child.'

'Sorry, I didn't mean to be rude.'

'Don't worry, Memsaab, I'll get your cases for you,' Mkamba said in perfect English.

* * *

When Philip's plane took off it left a long trail of reddish dust, which floated across the surrounding countryside, and gave the sunlight a pink glow. It made the plains look even more romantic than usual. I was in my element what with the shimmering heat, dust, Mkamba sitting behind me in the hunting car with a full gun rack and a very beautiful, desirable girl sitting beside me. It was the personification of my beloved African life. I threw the hunting car into gear and headed for the track that would get us back to camp.

'How long will it take us to get to the camp?'

'An hour and a half to two hours.'

'What, to cover that short distance?'

'Not exactly tarmac roads you know. We follow game tracks most of the way. Just keep your fingers crossed we don't run into any trouble, like dropping a wheel into a hole, which could make the journey hours longer.'

'That sounds great, I'm already longing for a shower and change of clothes.'

'I can see you're hot, your shirt is really sticking to you.'

'I knew you'd noticed that but I think it would be better if you kept your eyes on the road, or lack of it.'

'You're right but that's not nearly as much fun.'

'Perhaps a silk shirt was not the best of things to wear in the circumstances.'

'I think it a very good choice, no complaints at all.'

She gave one of her infectious laughs.

'I was told in Nairobi that you're as randy as hell and an "old type" hunter. Pity I won't be with you long enough to find out how much of that is true.'

'Why not? You could stay on with me instead of joining your Prince.'

'I don't think so. I don't think you've got enough money to keep me in the manner to which I want to become accustomed.'

'You're not a gold digger?'

'I most certainly am.'

That stopped the conversation for a while. She was right about one thing: I certainly had a wild reputation and didn't want to settle down. After all, I wasn't even thirty yet. There were still a lot of exciting things to do before I became dull and respectable.

I decided that there was something about this girl that

really affected me. Forget her fantastic looks; it was to do with some sort of magnetism that I felt for her. She wasn't, I guessed, more than about twenty but I felt sure she'd already lived, as they say. She was boisterous and obviously fun-loving and although she was money orientated, and led the life of a model, she didn't appear to be one of those cold, hard, sophisticated types. A bit of a mixture, one way and another. All I knew was that every time I looked at her and saw her damp shirt stretched across her gorgeous breasts, with her nipples practically protruding through it, I got a most incredible ache in my groin. I couldn't recall exactly how many women I'd either slept with, or had an affair with, but I had certainly thought, for many years, that I was past the stage of ever meeting one again who made me feel quite breathless and, if I wasn't careful, uncontrollable in my actions—and then along comes Carol.

We bounced along in silence, cutting our way through the short brown grass, skirting scrub and bushes and then running alongside some forest. The line of low hills we were aiming for appeared almost blue in the shimmering heat.

'Guinea fowl,' shouted Mkamba pointing to a clump of scrub to the left of the track.

'Great, well done, that's just what we want. Carol,

you'll have to excuse us for a couple of minutes as there goes our supper.'

'I'm glad you stopped; I need to spend a penny. Will it be all right behind that tree?'

'Yes, but watch out for snakes and scorpions. Should I come with you?'

'I think I'd rather take a chance on the snakes, thank you.'

I laughed, and as Mkamba and I got out of the safari car he handed me a Purdey, a beautiful shotgun, one of a pair my father gave me to celebrate my getting the medal.

The guinea fowl had gone off in a line, squawking to each other. If only it had been dusk, they'd have gone up in the trees which would have made life easier. Mkamba was armed with my other gun and between us we shot the six birds that Juma, the cook, would need for our evening meal.

Back at the car, Carol was waiting for us with a grin on her face.

'I did it and didn't get my bottom bitten.'

'Good, it would have been an interesting but difficult job sucking the poison out of that. Come on, Mkamba, let's get the birds stowed and be on our way.'

Ten minutes later, Mkamba shouted again but this time it was just that magic Swahili word, '*Simba*'.

'There you are, Carol, have you seen lion before?'

'No, where are they?'

'See that outcrop of rocks, look at the bottom to the left by that stunted tree. They're just stretching themselves after their afternoon snooze.'

'I don't know how Mkamba ever spotted them, I can hardly see them and I know where to look.'

'I'll drive over so that you can see them properly.'

'Don't forget you haven't got any doors or anything on this lorry, or whatever you call it.'

'It's a hunting car designed to make life as easy as possible for our dearly beloved clients. Don't worry about the lions, they won't be interested in us.'

I drove slowly towards them. There was one rather fine black-maned male, two females and several youngsters of different sizes. As I got closer to them, so Carol gradually moved away from the open side of the car and nearer to me. When we were about twenty-five feet away from them the male rolled over and let out a half roar to tell one of the youngsters to stop fooling about. Carol gasped and by now was almost sitting on my lap. I took the chance to put my arm round her and to give her breast a small squeeze, just to reassure her, of course. She decided to take her chance with the lions and moved smartly away from me.

'Don't worry, they must have eaten well recently. They're quite docile and harmless.'

'That's more than can be said for some others.'

After a few more minutes watching them at play we moved off again.

At last, the camp came in sight. It was pitched on a hillock a short distance from a small river that hadn't as yet dried up. At the back and sides of the campsite there was a mixture of thorn and acacia trees that gradually became almost impenetrable. The accommodation comprised a mess tent, with open sides and a canopy at the front, where we ate, drank and socialised and could look out across the plain to the river. To one side of the mess tent was a big double-fly tent for Sir William and Lady Evans. On the opposite side was the tent for guns and hunting equipment, where Mkamba slept. Next to that was my single double-fly tent. On the other side of the clearing, at a distance of about fifty or sixty yards were the kitchen and servants' tents.

A short distance from the main camp, between two trees, we had rigged up a shower cubicle. This was simply a frame, which supported a water tank at a height of about seven feet from the ground and had canvas curtains that hung down from it. When filled, you stood under it, pulled a rope that released a valve, and got a fairly good deluge of rather dirty water that had been brought up from the river. Crude but effective, and after a hard day's hunt, almost luxurious.

Next to the shower was the lavatory tent, a small square tent containing a 'thunder box'.

This was always one of my favourite campsites and one that only my friend Harry and I seemed to know or use. At this time of the season, when a lot of water holes and rivers had already dried up, there was always some water left in this river, if only a trickle. This water was one of the main reasons for there always being a lot of game in the vicinity.

As we came to a grinding halt in front of the tents, I turned to Carol.

'Careful how you handle Evans, he may be a bit put out by your arrival.'

'I think he'll be all right,' Carol said with the confident smile of one who had become accustomed to men bending to her will.

CHAPTER 3

She had been right of course. Sir William 'bloody' Evans treated her as though she was an honoured, invited, guest. Strangely enough, Helen, whom I'd thought would be delighted by the arrival of Carol was a bit, to say the least, offhand. But then, in my experience, you can never tell how a woman is going to react.

The four of us sat down at the table under the canopy and tea was brought while we discussed what sleeping arrangements were to be made. I knew what the best arrangement would be but I didn't like to suggest it! After some discussion, interrupted while we watched a rhino enjoying himself rolling in the mud down by the river, I called for Mkamba and asked him in Swahili if he would mind moving out of the gun tent and sharing a tent with the second gun bearer, Kidogo. He, of course, agreed so I was able to suggest that I would give Carol my tent and move into the gun tent. Everybody seemed quite happy with these arrangements, except perhaps Helen.

'Could we dress up a bit for dinner tonight? We haven't once since we've been here and I'm getting fed up with being in trousers and a sweater every evening. Welcoming Carol to the camp is a good excuse. What do you think, Carol? Should we dress up even if these two stodgy men refuse to?'

'Fine by me, but I haven't got much with me and the facilities are a bit basic.'

'Come on, William, are you and Gavin going to make an effort? After all, you will have had two days in camp not hunting.'

'I didn't know you're not hunting tomorrow, William.'

'I'm sorry, Gavin, I was going to tell you if Carol had given me the chance. It's just that I must go through the papers you collected for me and I must admit I could do with another easy day. I should, however, be finished by lunchtime, so perhaps we could go after a few birds or something in this area in the late afternoon? Is that all right?'

'Yes, of course, whatever you want. In that case, as we now won't have to get up at the usual four-thirty tomorrow morning, I suggest we do what Helen wants and have a "gala" evening. I'll tell Juma to pull out all the stops and to give us a really good feed. William, shall we drink some of that special claret?'

'Seems like the ideal occasion.'

'What fun, I'm so glad you came, Carol, otherwise I would never have got these two to agree.'

I turned to Helen with what I hoped was a suitably apologetic expression. 'Helen, I'm afraid I don't have a dinner jacket or even a suit with me, so you'll have to put up with my usual bush jacket but, as it's a special evening, I'll make it a nice clean one.'

'That's fine, I'm sure that even in a dirty old loin cloth you'd still be your usual debonair self.'

'May I have that in writing?'

We all laughed.

'Can I have a hot bath instead of a shower, and probably, Carol, would like one as well?'

'No thanks, a shower will do me fine.'

'Okay,' I said. 'I'll fix that for you, Helen. Excuse me a minute, I'll get things organised.'

I went across to the kitchen tent and told Juma to pull out all the stops and to give us the best meal he could. We arranged to have game soup, followed by asparagus

(Philip had brought down in the plane two boxes of fresh vegetables and fruit), then roast guinea fowl with potatoes, tinned carrots and peas, and for dessert an enormous bowl of fruit salad—a mixture of fresh and tinned fruit. Juma was quite excited, he liked to show off his culinary abilities. I shouted for Opio and told him in Swahili—all conversations with the "staff", except Mkamba, had to be in Swahili as none of them spoke English to any extent—to have the folding canvas bath taken to the Evans's tent and to fill it with hot water, when the Memsaab shouted for it.

Going back to the mess tent I told everyone what arrangements had been made and then a general post took place. By the time it was all finished, and we'd had our showers etc. it was, time for a drink.

I was the first at the bar where I poured myself an enormous scotch. Well earned, I thought.

William and Helen arrived together.

Helen looked delectable in a full-length red silk dress which had a décolleté neckline showing the tops of her deliciously rounded breasts—yet again I wondered how such a miserable sod as William could have been so lucky.

'Helen, I must compliment you. You look ravishing,' I said as I took her hand and kissed it.

She gave me a sensuous smile. 'Thank you, Gavin.'

Sir William, as you'd expect, was wearing a rather crumpled lightweight grey suit with, would you believe, a shirt and tie.

I fixed them both a gin and tonic. They'd got used to drinking them lukewarm after three weeks in the bush.

Then Carol arrived—she looked stunning.

Her hair was piled on top of her head with long spirals hanging down each cheek, her eyes were made up and she was wearing pinkish lipstick, which accentuated her golden tan. How she had managed to create this impression, with so few facilities, I just didn't know.

From her ears hung long earrings formed by two rows of little golden coins.

And then the dress. Wow!

It was very simple but obviously a model and very expensive. Made of ink-blue silk with a tight bodice, it had a revealing halter neck and a slim calf-length skirt with slits either side that went almost to her hips. Round her waist was a belt that matched her earrings and on her feet she wore low-heeled ink-blue leather court shoes, her only concession to the fact that she was dining out in the African bush and not in some smart European restaurant. I didn't think she was wearing stockings, just her own brown legs. In fact I wondered if she was wearing anything under that dress, except perfume!

There was no denying Carol was one of the most sexually attractive women I'd ever met.

I mixed her vodka and tonic, and we all stood chatting, and sipping our drinks, until dinner was announced.

As we sat round the table on our canvas camp chairs, Opio, dressed in an immaculate white kanzu with a dark red cummerbund and matching fez, served us with our starter, the rich game soup. I saw to the wine myself. Everyone agreed to go straight onto the claret; an excellent wine, a Mouton-Rothschild, that didn't seem to have suffered too much by its ill treatment.

'I must compliment you on the wine, William. It's a real treat to have something like this on safari. It is, as you by now know, usually spirits or warm beer. In fact, the whole evening is rather unusual and fun.'

'Don't you do this sort of thing often?' asked Carol. 'I thought this is how you lived all the time on these things.'

'Good heavens no. Just occasionally I've had a party comprising of three or four rich American couples who had joined up together and wanted the works. It's doesn't happen very often and is not a very good proposition for me.'

'Why is that? You must be able to charge the earth.'

'Yes, but with a large number of people I have to hire extra equipment as I don't have enough of my own and another professional as well and lots of extra staff. You see, even with a safari of this size I've got two gun bearers and seven others.'

*   *   *

Earlier, the ever-amazing sight of the sun sinking below the horizon had been followed by the usual African night sky: incredible furry velvet-blue dusted with clear, bright stars. The air was comparatively cool after the scorching heat of the day and, as later it would get even cooler, Ngutu was building a fire twenty or thirty feet in front of the mess tent where we would be able to sit and enjoy our after-dinner coffee and brandy. There was another big fire over by the kitchen tent where Mkamba, Kidogo and the rest of the crew would eat.

While we had our soup the conversation continued in its general vein. Occasionally, however, my companions were silent to listen to the noises that came out of the night: a hyena giggled, baboons grunted in guttural tones and a leopard sawed in a nearby *dongo*. I hardly noticed most of these sounds as they were constantly with me, but there was one that I was listening to, a lion grunting. That same lion had been round our camp for two nights. I could tell he was alone and there was something else about him, but I didn't really know what and that made me curious and uneasy.

I got up and refilled the glasses, excused myself and, going out of the mess tent, walked a few yards in the direction where Mr Simba seemed to be. Mkamba and Kidogo were already standing at the camp's perimeter listening.

'What do you make of him?' I asked in Swahili.

'I don't know but I don't like it. He is showing too much interest in us.'

'We'd better have a look tomorrow and see what we can find out about him. Tell everyone to be alert and let's keep the fires burning brightly all night.'

When I sat down at the table the asparagus had arrived and the other three were busy eating it. I caught Carol's eye as she was sucking a particularly large buttery stick of asparagus and gave her a slow suggestive wink. She almost choked.

When we were ready for the main course Juma himself came over, with Opio, proudly carrying a great dish with the guinea fowl on it. And he was justly proud—it turned out to be delicious. During the serving there was a lot of laughter as the Africans chattered in Swahili and the three English people tried to understand and to answer. Juma and Opio loved it as, being very simple people, the smallest amusing incident or joke made them almost collapse with laughter. Dinners had not been so jocular on previous evenings, so I concluded it must be because of Carol who was obviously more relaxed than William and even Helen. Anyway, whatever it was, it was good to have them all so cheerful.

One had to be very careful on safari, as it was easy to fall out with clients or for them to have disagreements among themselves. I'd known occasions when by the time we got back to Nairobi no one was talking to anyone else. On this trip I knew I would have to be careful over my treatment of William Evans. There was just something about him that made my hackles rise. In fact, more than that, I actually disliked the man. I suppose I wouldn't have been knocking off Helen if I hadn't.

When at last we were stuck into the guinea fowl Carol raised the inevitable question. I had been surprised that neither William nor Helen had asked me before, all my clients did, most sooner, rather than later.

'What about your medal, Gavin, what did you get it for?'

In the early days that question had embarrassed, if not annoyed, me. But as time went by it became apparent to me that "the medal" was one of the reasons why I always had a long list of people waiting to go on safari with me. There were lots of guys who were just as good hunters, okay nearly as good, as me but they hadn't got a Victoria Cross. Once I'd realised that, I stopped minding talking about it and instead turned it into one of my self-marketing ploys. All my clients came through personal recommendations. I was an independent right from the beginning and not a member of a safari company or syndicate, so I had to find my own clients. From experience I soon found that people going after big game wanted two things: a first-class professional hunter, and that could be anyone who was a member of the association; and someone who would help to make the whole thing memorable and give them plenty to brag about to friends back home. So, in my case, when they were back in New York, or wherever, they could say: 'Blah, blah, blah and also he was a war hero and had been awarded the Victoria Cross.' And the women, if they were attractive, and very lucky, could say to each other: 'Blah, blah, blah and he screwed divinely.' So, then everyone wanted to come on safari with me.

I swallowed my last mouthful of guinea fowl.

'Carol, I'm sure you're not really interested and it would only bore Helen and William.'

'I'd love to know,' Helen said in a voice that I thought, in the present company, sounded a little bit too interested.

'So would I,' said Carol. 'Having only ever met one highly decorated man before.'

You little so-and-so I thought, I know your game, trying to take the mickey.

'How interesting, who was that?'

'Oh, some old boy who'd won a VC and masses of other gongs, in the First World War.'

This I felt sure was probably made up and was just a ploy by her to make me into an 'also ran'.

Clearing his throat and sounding more pompous than ever, Sir William 'bloody' Evans contributed his little titbit.

'I'd be very interested to hear that myself. It's always nice to hear of other people's achievements.'

What did he mean by that, other than achieving a fortune by profiteering? As I opened yet another bottle of claret—somebody was drinking an awful lot—my mind slid back to the war years.

* * *

I was lucky that my father had managed to get me back from Kenya to the UK to finish my schooling. So, in 1943, there I was, seventeen and rearing to go. I volunteered for the Black Watch, the regiment my family had always served in and was sent up to a training battalion in Inverness. When my training was finished, I was persuaded to take a commission, although I didn't want to. I thought it a waste of time. I just wanted to get in there to see some action. By the time all this was finished it was 1944 and I still hadn't fired a shot in anger. I went to one of our battalions and got a bit of experience and then volunteered to serve with a commando unit. I was accepted. This was great. I really started to have some fun as I was involved in a series of small, lightning raids in the company of a great bunch of guys.

I was good at that sort of soldiering. They couldn't understand how, even before I'd had much experience, I could be so good. But that was understandable as no one knew that from the age of eight I had had guns and rifles and hunted incessantly. I stalked and hunted everything, on my own except on occasions when I could prise Mkamba away from father. So, my fieldcraft, firearms proficiency and general awareness of dangerous situations was first class. To me this commando lark was just good fun. It was as though I had been reared from boyhood just to do what I was doing. Some people thought I was foolhardy, and others thought me brave, but it was neither. It was just that I was doing what I enjoyed.

It was on one of my early raids into France when two German machine guns placed at either side of a small wood tied us down. There were ten of us up front and another thirty waiting to come through behind us. It was important that we moved forward. It was dusk when we suddenly came under fire and three of my guys were instantly killed and a further two badly shot up. I surveyed the situation and knew I could get myself unseen through the wood. I told my corporal, my sergeant had been killed in the initial burst of fire, to hold everyone where they were and to give me as much covering fire as they could. Then I went off through the wood towards the machine gun that was the most difficult to tackle, so that if I was unable to get back at least my chaps would only have one left, the easier one, to worry about. I got to the first machine gun post, no trouble at all, popped a couple of grenades in among them, sprayed around a bit with the old Sten and that was that. Then I started to work my way through the woods towards the second post, but having seen their chums destroyed, the Huns in that one had decided it was time to leave, so I was saved a job. Everyone was then able to proceed and as we had with us not only my commanding officer but also a commando brigadier, I was awarded an immediate MC.

I didn't get any triumphant feelings from receiving that gong, I lost too many of my guys that day.

After that battle we went back to the UK to reform as we had taken a fair hammering and lost a lot of chaps. It was about three weeks before we were back in France going in behind the Germans to destroy their lines of supply and communications. I took ten chaps with me and by the time we were on our way back there were only two, beside myself, left.

When we reached one of our forward posts, I was told that someone, a general no less, wanted to see me back at Divisional HQ.

I left one of my boys behind at the forward dressing post, as he was quite badly wounded, and then we continued on our way. As we were now in an area only a mile or two behind the fighting that was considered to be enemy free, we were able to move in a relaxed manner. The HQ was in a large chateau in a small town and I was told how to get there by a military policeman. As we were going down a narrow street that led to the square, where the HQ was situated, three very attractive girls came out of one of the houses making a great fuss of us as "conquering heroes". They invited us into their family home to have a glass of wine. An invitation I was not going to miss, so in we went.

What a bit of luck that was. We'd only been in there for about twenty minutes when all hell was let loose with gunfire seeming to be all round us. I sent my sergeant out to see what was happening while I finished my wine. He came back very excited, hot-blooded young brigand he was, the Germans had counterattacked and taken everyone by surprise. They now had three Tiger tanks that had broken through and were covering Divisional HQ with virtually nothing to stop them from obliterating it and everyone in it. If we hadn't stopped for a social break we'd have been in there too. Sutherland, the sergeant with me, told me there was a company of British troops down the road, but they didn't know what to do. I went outside and just a matter of twenty or so yards down the road that led into the square was the back of a German tank. Round the corner I found the company of British troops behind a wall doing sweet fanny Adams. I had a word with the company commander who, although he was senior to me, was quite prepared to do whatever I said. So,

Sutherland and I were able to help ourselves to their arms and equipment including: a couple of anti-tank PIATs, grenades, and small arms. I told the major to get his men to create a rumpus behind the tank that was nearest to us so it would back down the street.

Then Sutherland and I slunk back and waited in a doorway with a loaded PIAT each. The PIAT, (projector, infantry, anti-tank), is a fearful weapon that just as often seems to kill the operator as it does the target. When the major and his men started their rumpus firing ineffectual shots at the tank it, as we'd thought it would, backed towards them. As it got level with our doorway we both fired an armour-piercing shell at it and, Bob's your uncle, it came to a grinding halt totally disabled. Sutherland was out like a shot, although I tried to stop him, up the side of the tank and dropped a grenade into an open hatch. Sad to say before it even went off he was dead as one of the other tanks, which I had seen out of the corner of my eye, had moved into our road and machine-gunned him. There was no need to check. I knew he was dead.

I reloaded the two PIATs and as soon as the second tank moved out into the square I followed and managed to destroy it with two armour-piercing shells. And that left one.

The remaining tank was bombarding the HQ with pretty devastating effect and something had to be done quickly before all the top brass were killed. Then I had a real lucky break when the commander from the tank I had just knocked out, together with another chap who had not been killed either, left their devastated and burning tank and ran towards the remaining one. I just ran like hell and, catching them up, followed them and in the heat of the action no one realised that I was not a German. I was not in a very strong position as I no longer had an anti-tank weapon and in fact only carried hand grenades and my automatic pistol. It was like a dream, they opened a hatch, I jumped forward with a grenade in each hand, which I tossed through the opening when I was rewarded by a loud explosion and a jet of flame coming out of it. One of the two Germans I'd run across with had a machine pistol and turning he mistook his companion for me and killed him. By that time I had my pistol out and that was the end of it.

A few minutes later, the major came up with his men and once I'd made arrangements about poor old Sutherland's body I was able to report to the HQ and the general.

Evidently they had been in a right tizz, thinking their number was up, and then had seen the whole of my action in the street, and in the square. It was quite unusual for a general to see an individual in action like that, so he thought it something out of the ordinary; hence the medal.

I put Sutherland up for a decoration and he was given a posthumous Military Medal, not that that was a lot of good to him.

I remembered the pain and anguish when I was wounded on a subsequent raid and being the only one left alive for three days had to hide during the day and to crawl and drag myself by night back to the British lines. Then it was to hospital in Blighty and the rest of my war was spent trying to entice attractive nurses to get into bed with me.

*   *   *

I went back to the table with the newly opened bottle of wine.

'All right,' I said. 'If you all insist, I'll tell you the story. However, there's not much to it and I may only bore you.'

'I don't think you'd ever be boring, but you have more experience of him than I do, Helen, what's your opinion?'

My God, had Carol already guessed that Helen had

been making nocturnal visits to my tent? I just hoped she was going to stop her game before she made it obvious to Sir William.

'I can only say that he's kept us very amused and happy. Hasn't he, William?'

'Yes, he certainly has my dear. Now, come along, Gavin, let's hear how you won that medal. I'm very interested in war stories. At the beginning of the war I tried very hard to get into the army myself but unfortunately I was classed medically unfit.'

Oh yea, I could just guess how hard he'd tried. I wondered how much he had to pay to get his unfitness certificate.

Now, which of my repertoire of stories should I tell them? I had found it too boring telling the real story time after time so I had made up a selection of bogus ones, which I used at my discretion. Which should I use tonight? The one about the General's wife. No, that might give William ideas. The one about the truck and the French girl. Yes, that's the one, after all, everyone was pretty drunk.

'Well, I must tell you right at the beginning that it was one of those occasions when I got it purely by mistake and not for anything courageous on my part. We were down in France at the end of '44 and life was pretty boring one way and another, so I decided I needed a little light relief. I had met a very charming French girl on the other side of the small, devastated town that we were now meant to be defending from a German counterattack. I had a great desire to see her again, so I told my CO that I'd just have a little scout around to see what was going on. Back down the road I found an abandoned truck which I promptly appropriated and drove to the girl's house which happened to be almost next door to the house commandeered by the general as his HQ. When I got out of the truck and ran to the girl's house the whole area was suddenly filled with Germans who obviously were after the HQ and its personnel. When I reached her door I found I hadn't got my haversack with me, very important as it contained a bottle of champagne and a packet of the "necessary", I just had to have it. I ran back to the truck and that's when HQ staff spotted me as I leant into the cab to find my haversack. This took me a few seconds, and then I grabbed it and ran back to Michelle's house. The Germans were just behind me pushing a small piece of artillery with which to blow the general and his merry men away. At that moment a shot must have hit the truck, which I hadn't realised was full of explosives, and there was an almighty bang and the gun and all the Germans disappeared in a puff of black smoke. To cut a long story short, the general thought I'd gone back to the truck, regardless of risk to life and limb, to detonate the explosives to save them all. Hence the medal.'

They were all sitting looking at me in a squiffy sort of way.

'Is that really true?' Helen asked incredulously.

'It seems a most extraordinary story,' William said accusingly.

'I believe it. It's just the sort of thing he'd do,' Carol said, followed by one of her laughs.

I was amused by their different reactions. It would give them something to think about when they sobered up.

'If you've all finished, shall we go and sit by the fire and have coffee and brandy?'

While we were sitting by the fire, I heard the lion grunting in the background.

'This must be your first night in a hunting camp, Carol,' I said. 'Don't you think it rather romantic with the full moon and everything?'

'Yes, I do; especially when it's accompanied by exciting stories from a war hero.'

What to make of that I just didn't know. Was she being nice to me, or just sarcastic?

Standing up, Carol stretched.

'If you'll excuse me, I think I'll hit the sack, it's been rather a long and exciting day.'

After we'd said our goodnights I remained standing and watched Carol as she went to her tent. Her back view, with sway to that fabulous bottom, was very, very sexy indeed.

It was not long before the remaining three of us decided to follow her example and to retire for the night— or what was left of it.

I went to the gun tent and collected my double-barrelled Rigby .450, and a torch, and then took a walk round the perimeter of the camp.

It was now some time since I'd heard any noises from the lion, so I hoped he'd moved off. I didn't know why I was unhappy about him, but I was.

There was a slight sound behind me, I spun round and shone my torch, and it was Mkamba.

'He's gone,' he said. 'I heard him move off about an hour ago.'

'Good, there's something I don't like about him. We'll have a look round in the morning.'

I went back to the gun tent where my bed had been made up and a pressure lamp was still burning. I put the torch on one of the cabinets but it rolled off and when I picked it up the bulb had gone. Damn, the spare bulbs were in my own tent so I would have to be torchless until tomorrow—unless I dared go in and disturb Carol—I decided against it!

CHAPTER 4

came out of a deep sleep; something had disturbed me.

In the pitch darkness I looked at the luminous dial of my watch. It was just after two.

There was something, or someone, in my tent. It was not an animal, my sense of smell was so good that not only did I know when one was around but also, I could even tell what sort it was.

That only left a human being.

A hand pulled my mosquito net aside and a pair of lips, together with a tongue, did sensuous and exciting things to my bare stomach and thigh.

Carol had succumbed! She hadn't been able to resist me after all. I felt a great swell, no actually two great swells, one of them of satisfaction. So, she wasn't so hard to get after all.

I stretched out my hand to run my fingers through her long and luxuriant hair.

It wasn't long and luxuriant.

It was short and curly.

It wasn't Carol.

It was Helen.

So much, I thought, *for this bloody Don Juan.* Still, Helen was delectable and she was obviously smitten by me.

'Do you think this is wise? I can hear William snoring but don't forget we've also got Carol to contend with now.'

She ignored my whispered wise words and instead took my aroused member into her mouth. No more arguments from me, just grunt and groan.

She stopped for a second, which must have been to remove her robe, and then her naked body slid onto the mattress beside me.

She was some woman this. I was lucky. I knew a lot of men would have found her even more attractive than Carol—but not me.

Her body was warm and firm but pliant and sweet smelling. As I caressed her breasts and rolled her nipples, she sighed and then lay flat on the bed beside me. My hand explored her thighs and I could feel the heat and moisture between them. She, like me, was on fire.

'Please take me. I want you inside me now, now, now.'

I rolled on top of her and penetrated her hot pulsating body. It was heaven.

She cried out uncontrollably, but by now I didn't care who heard, my passion had taken control, my mind was filled with salacious thoughts. I had to bring this physical embrace to a shuddering conclusion and nothing, no nothing, was going to stop me.

After what seemed like a volcanic explosion, we rolled onto our sides, still joined, and softly kissed and caressed each other.

'I wish I could stay like this until morning, but I think I'd better get back to my tent. William has stopped snoring.'

She got off the bed, put on her robe, leant forward and kissed me before she left.

God, that had been good. She sure knew how to make a chap flip his lid. I was already beginning to think an encore would have been a great idea.

I drifted off into a deep untroubled sleep.

* * *

For a second time I awoke with a start. What the hell was all that noise?

The first thing I made out was the snarling roar of a lion and then I realised that there was also a voice calling for help.

I staggered out of bed, put my feet into a pair of shoes, without even bothering to shake them in case of scorpions, grabbed my Rigby .450 and my torch and went outside my tent. I turned on the torch and threw it down in disgust; it still had the blown bulb. I just stood still for a second, listening. I had to admit my mind was a bit fuddled from too deep a sleep, caused no doubt, partly by Helen's administrations, and partly by having drunk too much at our "gala dinner". As my mind cleared, I realised what was happening, someone, probably Carol, was in the lavatory tent and a lion was under the trees near it making one hell of a din. Although it was bright moonlight I couldn't see him because he was in the shadow of the trees. It was Carol, I could now hear her voice above the roars as she shouted, 'Help, someone please do something.'

I moved across the moonlit clearing, paused beside the shower, and as the lion didn't come at me, moved to the doorway of the lavatory tent. I backed partially into the tent and felt Carol's hands clutch at my waist.

'Thank God, you've come, I didn't know what to do. I'm terrified.'

I still couldn't see the damn lion and by now he was making enough noise to make anyone feel nervous. There was no way I was going to risk a shot until I could see him more clearly. At present I wasn't even sure which was him and which was bushes. Wounding him would probably be the end of Carol and me, when I fired it must be a shot that killed him instantly. I just couldn't make out why, with all this display, he hadn't bounded on us already.

'Carol,' I said quietly over my shoulder. 'I've got to wait for the right shot. If he comes for us in the meantime wait until he and I are locked together and then run like hell until you get back to the others at the campfire.'

I was beginning to think that this was going to be one scrape when I didn't come out on top. Then, over to the right of the shower tent, I saw a flame approaching.

Good old Mkamba, you could always rely on him. Up he came with a great flaming branch, that he must have pulled out of one of the campfires, and went straight past us and at the lion that got out of his way. One thing even the bravest of lions has a great respect for is fire.

Unfortunately, I still couldn't risk a shot because of

Mkamba, so I had no alternative but to let Mr Simba depart.

As soon as he'd gone, and as far as I was concerned, the emergency was over. I became aware of something rather delightful pressing against my back. It was Carol's practically naked body as she hung onto me for dear life. I decided it was not the moment to move. I just stayed where I was and enjoyed the sensation.

After a minute, Mkamba, not being able to understand why I hadn't moved, came over and asked if everything was all right.

'Yes, *m'zuri sana* and thank you, Mkamba,' I said as I gratefully shook his hand in the African way.

Moving a couple of feet forward, I turned to face Carol. Then I realised she was in shock, and not surprising either.

She was trembling and hardly able to stand. I handed the Rigby to Mkamba and picked her up in my arms and carried her back to the fire where William, Helen and the boys were all gathered. It wasn't until I was putting her down into one of the chairs that it came to me what a sight we must look. Carol was in a transparent negligee which made my blood pump a bit—a bit too much in fact as I was only wearing a pair of shoes!

'Excuse me, I'll just put some clothes on while Opio

organises a good strong pot of tea for us.'

'Yes, good idea,' William said, actually laughing. 'Anyway, now we know why your nickname with the Africans is *Bwana Tembo*, don't we, Helen?'

I was quite upset that he should be so flippant when poor Carol was sitting there, wrapped in a blanket, still shivering with fright. Anyway Helen knew all about that, but not how I'd got my nickname.

'Actually, William, I got my nickname, Bwana Elephant, because everyone knows that I'm always prepared to go after a rogue elephant that's causing trouble.'

With that I walked as nonchalantly as I could to the gun tent. As I was putting on a bush shirt and KD trousers, I was listening to the outside noises. I didn't want that lion back among us again without any warning. I knew Mkamba was, like me, perplexed and a bit worried, that's why he'd hung onto the Rigby. As soon as I was dressed, I undid the padlock on the gun rack chain and took out my Jeffreys .475, loaded it and put it to safe. I left the chain unlocked, just in case I suddenly needed any other firearms.

When I got back to the fire a big pot of tea had arrived and cups were being poured with a dollop of scotch added to keep out the cold and to boost morale.

Carol, I could see was much more her old self but still, obviously, a little nervous. As I came up to the fire she got up and embraced me.

'Gavin, I don't know how to thank you. You saved me from a horrid end.'

I knew how she could thank me but this wasn't the time to mention it.

'You don't have to thank me, I did very little. It was Mkamba's quick thinking that saved the day.'

'Yes, Mkamba was fantastic but you risked your life when you came and stood between me and that raging lion and, from what you said, I knew that if it had become necessary you would have diverted the lion while I escaped.'

'Jolly well done,' William said, patting me on the shoulder. 'But there you are, once a hero always a hero.'

I was just about to answer with some fatuous comment when we heard, at some distance, that blasted lion again. This was getting beyond a joke: lions were usually pretty circumspect and respected humans unless they did something silly. This guy seemed to be roaming about in the moonlight looking for a meal wherever he could find it. This was just not on. I would have to teach Mr Simba a few lessons in manners and respect. The locals hadn't mentioned anything about a man-eater being in the district, but this most certainly must be one, so I could only assume that he had recently arrived.

Carol and Helen didn't seem too happy to know our friend was still around, but William seemed surprisingly calm. Maybe after the buffalo episode he considered himself an intrepid big game hunter.

'May I make a suggestion?' he said. 'Carol, why don't you sleep in my bed and I'll sleep in yours and then you'll have Helen for company?'

'That's very kind of you, William, but isn't it rather disturbing for you and Helen?'

'No, of course not,' Helen said. 'It's a very good idea of William's. I'm sure you'd rather have a bit of company for what's left of the night.'

'That sounds good to me,' I said thinking of another much better solution. 'But you don't have to worry, I'll fix up a roster so that someone is out here on watch all night. As soon as dawn breaks I shall take Mkamba with me and go and look for this gentleman. One of the team will be here by the fire keeping it stoked up and keeping watch. I'll leave Kidogo behind armed with a rifle—he's a very good shot—to take care of any emergencies. If you like, I could also leave a firearm with you, William.'

'I suppose that might be quite a good idea so that I can back up Kidogo if necessary.'

So, it was all arranged. Instead of sharing a bed with Carol, or having a visit from Helen, I was going to be crawling around looking for some lion that seemed to have turned man-eater. Still you can't win them all and anyway I wanted to thump this particular lion as he had, I must admit, scared the living daylights out of me, and annoyed me more than somewhat. With Carol out there in the moonlight there were much better things that I could have done rather than serenade an uninvited, unwanted predator.

I went back to the gun tent and got the Holland and Holland .375 magnum for William and a double-barrelled Holland and Holland .500, that had been given to me by a grateful American client and had a lot of punch, for Kidogo.

Going into my own tent I got a bulb for the broken torch together with a second torch. We shouldn't need them, but just after dawn it would still be dark under the trees and I didn't intend to get myself into the same predicament that I had earlier.

*   *   *

The first thing Mkamba and I did when the others had retired to their beds was to go back to the area round the shower and lavatory tent to examine the spoor of our lion. We immediately knew what this was all about; the lion was only functioning on three legs. Something had happened to his rear right leg as he was only putting it to the ground when he was standing still. We surmised that he had either injured it when he attacked other game, or else in a fight for supremacy with another male in a pride of lions. The second guess seemed the most likely, as he was now on his own.

Being alone and incapable meant he would not be able to hunt and kill his usual prey and would have to turn to the easy options: human beings and native cattle.

This being the situation meant that I now had an obligation to dispatch this beast as, if I didn't, he could create havoc with the local people and their cattle.

Anyway, now we knew why he'd been bothering us in the first place and also why he hadn't made mincemeat of me under the trees. I just hoped we could finish him during the day, as we certainly didn't want him around the camp again for another night.

When Mkamba and I left the camp just after dawn the area down to the river and beyond seemed alive with animals. There were great herds of zebra, impala, wildebeest and a small bunch of eland, to name but a few, and the air was filled with their combined grunts, hoots, snorts etc. As they were grazing or drinking in an undisturbed manner Mkamba and I took it that the lion couldn't be in that direction otherwise these animals would have been spooked.

We didn't pick up his spoor to start with, as the ground round the camp was crisscrossed by tyre marks and footprints of those in the camp. At last, on the edge of our hillock, we picked up his trail.

We found that when the cheeky devil had been frightened off by Mkamba, with his flaming branch, he'd not gone straight out into the bush but must have circled round the edge of the camp only yards from us all when we were gathered together. How long he'd watched us we didn't know, but eventually he'd left the environs of the camp on the opposite side to that of the lavatory tent.

A bit hair-raising to think of him sitting there weighing us up. He was dangerous. It was imperative to settle this fellow without delay.

From his pugmarks we could tell that he was big— probably weighing about four hundred pounds. I shuddered to think what would have happened to Carol if he hadn't been so lame. He would have jumped on her before any of the rest of us even knew what was happening. I laughed inwardly, I bet she wouldn't go to spend a penny during the night again without an escort.

Mkamba was signalling to me. I moved forward and looked to see what he'd found. Through dense "wait-a-bit" bushes there was a sort of tunnel that looked as though it had been made by a rhino, and this was where our lion had gone.

I didn't like it. I didn't like it at all. We were going to have to follow him, in single file, down this narrow path through impenetrable thorn bushes where he might be waiting for us.

Added to that was the thought that we might meet, instead of the lion, the rhino. This seemed unlikely as I felt sure this was where he went during the heat of the day for his afternoon nap. At this time of day he would be grazing out in the bush—please God.

I knew this rhino. He was the one we'd watched when he was down by the river the previous evening, and he'd lived in this area for ages. He was quite safe from hunters and native poachers as somehow or other his horn had been snapped off near its base, very unusual. I wouldn't have hunted him anyway as I always had a rule "no shooting, except in an emergency", in the vicinity of any of my camps. This poor old faro was pretty mild. He must have sensed that as he'd lost his horn no one wanted him as a trophy or for aphrodisiac reasons. That didn't mean, however, that we wouldn't be in desperate trouble if we met him head-on in the thorn tunnel where there wouldn't be any chance to avoid him.

Mkamba held up a handful of dust and let it trickle between his fingers to assess which way the breeze was blowing. Well, that was one thing that was in our favour, it was blowing down the "tunnel" towards us. I winked at him and started down the path, making as little noise as possible. My rifle was at the ready with shells in both barrels and the safety off. I could sense Mkamba right behind me with his rifle also at the ready, but if Mr Simba or Mr Faro arrived there wouldn't be much he could do until I was out of the way.

Even though it was only just after dawn and not very hot yet I could feel sweat on my brow and running down my cheeks.

Then suddenly I heard a noise in front, my rifle came up and my fingers started to squeeze the trigger, then I froze just in time. It was a bloody hyena. Hell! How I would have liked to shoot the damn thing. It had really made my heart jump. It turned and took off to whence it had come.

I turned and gave Mkamba a sickly smile. I could break silence now.

'The lion can't be here then. He must have gone on through.'

We came to a bit of a clearing where the "wait-a-bits" thinned, giving way to stunted trees. We could see that directly in front of us was an outcrop of rocks rising to some thirty or forty feet. This looked like a very likely place for our old friend to be lying up. Not too bad for us to meet him here either as he wouldn't, because of his injured leg, be able to jump down on us.

Then we heard the sound of a shot coming from the direction of the camp; a shot from a heavy rifle such as a .500.

We looked at each other. There was no need to say anything we just started back at full speed.

As we half ran, lugging our heavy rifles—they each weighed in excess of ten pounds—I wondered what we were going to find when we got back. I just prayed that our lion hadn't backtracked on us and managed to get into the camp. I reasoned that even if this happened, they should be okay; Kidogo was good, good enough to be my gun bearer when Mkamba finally gave up.

I came out of the end of the thorn tunnel and came face to face with my old friend, the hornless rhino. I stopped, so did he.

Mkamba came up beside me and also stopped.

What would he do? Rhinos were unpredictable at the best of times and this particular lad was also an oddball. He had a horn that had been broken or smashed in some way, very unusual, and he lived on his own, also unusual. During the time he'd lived here we had managed to avoid one another, but now we were practically eyeball to eyeball. One of us was going to have to give way. He was peering at us with his head on one side and his little piggy eyes trying to make out what these strange objects were.

Sometimes you can scare off a rhino quite easily, other times not at all. As there was no way we could get round him and I was not prepared to waste time, as I urgently wanted to get back to the camp, I decided it must go one way or the other without any further delay.

'Mkamba, I'm going to shoo him, if he doesn't move try firing a shot near him. If he charges I'll take care of him.'

I moved towards the rhino waving my arms and rifle at him and shouting: 'Get out of it, you bloody old fool. Go on, sod off.'

He gave an indignant snort and squared up to me.

Oh God, I thought, *I'm going to have to kill him and I don't want to.*

Then there was the crack from Mkamba's rifle and the bullet kicked up dust between the old chap's front feet.

He gave me a sort of hurt look, spun in his own length, and trotted off with his tail sticking straight up in the air as though he wanted me to know he wasn't really at all frightened.

I gave a sigh of relief, Mkamba and I grinned at each other and then we set off hotfoot for the camp.

The going was hard and it was only because we were both very physically fit that we were able to keep up the pace we did.

We were both used to following rogue elephants; on foot; mile after mile; up hill and down dale; in the heat of the day and the bitter cold of the night; carrying our rifles and other essential kit. Compared to that this was like taking a run through an English park, that is, as long as we didn't keep meeting headstrong rhino.

<h1 style="text-align:center">CHAPTER 5</h1>

Mkamba and I panted into the camp where Carol, Helen and William were sitting round the table being served breakfast.

'Hello,' they all shouted cheerfully.

'Come back for breakfast?' asked Helen.

'No,' I said coldly. 'We've come back to see why someone here fired a shot.'

'It was me,' said William. 'I was just looking at the .500 that you left with Kidogo as I thought I'd better familiarise myself with it. I loaded it with two cartridges, then to see how it felt, I sighted it at a tree and pulled the trigger. For some reason the safety catch hadn't gone on so when I squeezed the trigger it fired. It gave me an awful shock and a bruised shoulder. You'll need to get that safety catch repaired.'

'I don't think so. I don't think you put it on.'

'But surely you don't have to. I know I've only been using bolt-action rifles on this safari, but I am used to using a double-barrelled shotgun at home and safety goes on automatically when you close the barrels. Surely that is the same with these rifles?'

'No, it isn't. Even if they are supplied with an automatic safety, most other professionals, and I, have it altered to manual. The reason being that if, for instance, you are facing a charging buffalo and in the heat of the moment forget to push forward the slide to the firing position, by the time you've realised and done it you're probably dead.'

'Oh, Lord! I'm terribly sorry, I just didn't know and certainly didn't mean to fire it. It was just an accident. At least I didn't shoot anyone. So, no harm done.'

'I wouldn't say that. After sweating through the bush Mkamba and I found where the lion was lying up but before we could do anything about it, because of your "accident", we had to come back here.'

'Gavin,' Carol said. 'Why don't you go and have a shower, put on some fresh clothes, and come and have breakfast with us?'

She was right. There was no point in getting steamed

up, particularly as since the event of the lion William seemed to be getting a bit more human.

'Yes, good idea.'

When I got back to the table all squeaky-clean there was coffee and bacon and eggs waiting for me. I couldn't remain bad tempered, it was just too great sitting out there in my Africa eating a good breakfast with two very beautiful woman as companions—and of course William!

'What's the plan now, Gavin? I'm sure Helen, Carol and I will fall in with whatever you want to do.'

'There's no point in going out after him until mid-afternoon. You've got papers to read anyway, so the rest of us can just relax. I suggest we have a late lunch and then go and look for Mr Simba.'

'Are we all going with you?' Carol's voice sounded a little uncertain.

'Yes, as long as everyone wants to come. In any case I have to deal with this lion as he is a danger, not only to us, but also to everyone in the district. I'm hoping that William will shoot him for us and, if we took the truck, you two could come along to join in the fun.'

'You mean the big vehicle parked at the back of the camp instead of your hunting car?' There was relief in Carol's voice. I knew she didn't like the idea of the lack of doors on the hunting car and, in any case, she'd already been near enough to this particular lion.

'That's right, you'll be quite safe in that.'

I was lucky to have such a good truck as most of them didn't last long under the conditions that we used them. This one I'd bought from a very amusing, though somewhat suspect, Indian trader with whom I dealt quite a bit. When he first told me about it he said that it was a German Army vehicle that had transported Field Marshal Rommel's personal gear during the desert campaign and had then been "acquired" and hidden by Arabs. When years later Patel had heard about it, God knows how, he decided it would be just right for his white hunter sahib. When he told me about it, and assured me it had hardly been used at all, I said I'd have it. He'd never let me down over anything I'd bought from him so I was prepared to take his word. He also told me there were some spare parts to go with it. When it finally arrived, it was superb and the "few spare parts" he'd mentioned completely filled the rear of the truck and included rear axles. In fact, everything you could think of. When a few weeks later Mr Patel sent me a message to say that he was sending extra spares that they hadn't been able to put in the truck. I expected to receive a cardboard box of bits and pieces;

instead of which, it was two enormous wooden packing cases filled with every conceivable thing. He'd done me proud. It was a real bargain. The truck was mainly used to transport the goods and chattels from camp to camp, but very occasionally I used it for hunting. It would be good to have it out for a run and to give the driver, Makanyanga, something to do other than drive to and from the river with tanks of water.

We all agreed on a plan of campaign. We would have a large, late lunch to sustain us until whatever time we got back to camp. I suggested that we should set off at three o'clock and that we would all go in the truck together. Until lunch William said he would look at his papers, Carol wanted to catch up on some sleep, Helen would sit in the mess tent and read. And I would do a few jobs around camp.

This break suited me very well as normally all the extra jobs that needed doing had to be fitted in during the odd spare moments one had. The white hunter doesn't just guide his clients to the game that they want to shoot full stop. He is also responsible for a hundred and one other things. He must see that the camp is set up and then that it runs efficiently. This includes: seeing that supplies of food and other essentials don't run out, keeping the vehicles running and doing any mechanical repairs that are necessary. Seeing that all the firearms are in top order and are sighted correctly, which includes the client's own weapons, if he brings any, is quite a job in itself. Then there are the personnel matters: making sure there aren't any problems as far as the team is concerned, being charming, diplomatic and caring to his clients.

By the time I'd done my various jobs it was still only eleven, plenty of time left to shower and relax before lunch.

*   *   *

When I walked into the mess tent, I found Helen deep in some lurid novel.

'Am I disturbing you?'

'I always find you disturbing, that's part of your attraction. Are you going to come and talk to me or do you have more pressing matters to attend to?'

I pulled up a chair and sat down.

'No, I've done all my jobs but anyway you'd always be a top priority for my time.'

'What! Even if it clashed with doing something with Carol?'

How the hell had she worked that one out? Carol

hadn't even been with us for twenty-four hours yet, and didn't appear to be very enamoured with me, yet Helen had picked up my infatuation for her.

'Why do you say that?'

'Because it's true, isn't it?'

'I must admit, I do find her attractive.'

'Attractive!' She laughed. 'Every time you look at her you're obviously devouring her, or something, with your eyes.'

'Come off it, Helen, the girl doesn't even like me.'

'I'd say it rather differently to that.'

'How would you say it?'

'I'd say that she is very attracted by you, but she is determined not to fall for you or get involved with you. Carol is a very determined young lady and she knows what she wants and she's not going to let any feelings for you get in her way.'

'I think you're over-dramatising the position. I don't think she's even thought about me.' Which wasn't true, as I'd already decided the first night that she was determined not to be impressed by anything I'd done or to like me.

'Maybe, though I don't think so. But that still doesn't answer the question of how you feel about her. Admit it, it's more than just thinking her attractive.'

'It's not. It is just that I think her extremely attractive.' Lying hound, I thought her devastating. 'It's a great compliment to her as I have someone else in the camp that is so gorgeous that most other women would appear dull, or even ugly, in comparison.'

'Flatterer. I wish you meant it but I'm sure you don't. With me I feel it was just because I was available and not because you think me so gorgeous.'

'What are you doing, looking for more compliments? You know perfectly well without my telling you that you are an extremely attractive, desirable woman. You are the sort of woman that when you enter a restaurant all the men look at you with desire and all the women with dislike.'

'You do make me feel good. You say nice things to me during the day and do nice things to me when I visit your tent at night.'

We were both laughing when Opio arrived with coffee.

'Tell me something about yourself, Helen. I really don't know anything about your past.'

'Nothing as exciting as yours I'm afraid. I was brought up in a small Cornish manor on the cliffs above a secluded bay. My father's family had lived there for generations and because of it everyone thought us filthy rich but actually we were rather poor. I was sent to school at Cheltenham when I was ten as my parents thought I'd run wild for too long. I didn't like it, I missed my beloved Cornwell. After I'd finished at school I went to a rather snobby language and secretarial college in London where I shared a South Ken flat with a girlfriend from school. That was fun; lots of parties and my first experience of the opposite sex. After college, because I spoke French and Russian fluently, I got a job with the Foreign Office which was great; same flat, same parties and same friends. Then the war arrived. The War Office wouldn't release me at first so I was still in London during the Blitz, an amazing experience, then they released me and I was able to join the WRENS. At first I was down in Devon being trained, which was nice as I could get home occasionally, then I was back to London. The war was exciting and I met a lot of people and made a lot of friends.'

'Were you married before? I believe William was.'

'No, but I was engaged, funnily enough with someone who was with your lot. Perhaps you came across him, a chap called Cuthbert Fellowes.'

'Lord Fellowes, good heavens I know that name well enough; a real legend he was. I never actually met him he was killed before my time. So, what about William? I must admit I'm surprised that someone as young and beautiful as you should marry a man who is old enough to be your father.'

'William is the kindest, most generous man you could hope to meet. He is a very worldly, mature person and extremely intelligent. I know you don't like him, you've made that quite obvious, but he is actually very popular in London. Here, he is out of his element and although, for various reasons, he wanted to come he doesn't really like killing things.'

'What on earth were his reasons for coming on a hunting safari if he doesn't like shooting big game?'

'Maybe I'll tell you one day.'

'All very mysterious. When did you actually meet him?'

'In London. I was working for him when Cuthbert was killed and he was so kind to me that we gradually became good friends and eventually at the end of the war, married.'

'What were you doing working for him if you were in the WRENS? He wasn't in the services, was he?'

'No, he was ... He was to do with naval supplies.'

I got the distinct feeling that there was more to this than met the eye. Sounded a bit odd to me.

'So, what does he do now?'

'He runs an export-import agency.'

'Did he get his knighthood for naval supplies?'

'Yes.'

'He must have kept the Navy very happy.'

'Yes, he did. Here comes Carol.'

I got to my feet as that gorgeous, delectable creature entered the mess tent.

She was in her KD trousers, a semi-transparent lawn shirt with the top four buttons undone, and cowboy boots.

I got that awful ache in my groin again.

'Hello, I've had a nice snooze. Is it time for lunch?'

'Very nearly, in fact here comes Opio to lay the table. Who's for a drink?'

'I'll just go and tidy up and fetch William,' Helen said smiling at me.

'What about you Carol—vodka and tonic?'

'Sounds good unless there's some beer.'

'Yes, of course, I can offer you City Lager, but it will be pretty warm.'

'I'll chance it. I'll have the lager please.'

We were just starting our drinks and I hadn't had a chance to say anything much to Carol before William joined us saying that Helen would be with us in a few minutes.

When she arrived, we sat down with our drinks and lunch was served.

During lunch the conversation was of a general nature but there was a bit of an atmosphere, they were all feeling excited but also a bit nervous.

It was understandable as none of them had ever been after a man-eater before and they hadn't got the slightest idea what was likely to happen or how much they might become personally involved.

As soon as we'd finished lunch, we were ready to set off for the great "lion hunt".

*   *   *

By the time the truck, or as we always referred to it, Rommel, bounced away from the camp everyone, having had a few drinks and a good lunch, was in high spirits. Even William Evans was in a jocular mood, though I wasn't sure whether he was affected by the lunchtime ration of alcohol or whether his adrenaline was pumping at the thought of meeting Mr Simba.

Makanyanga was driving, an adventure in itself, with Helen and Carol in the cab with him. William and I were in the back with Mkamba, Kidogo, Boculy the skinner and one of the porters, Laboso. The truck had its canvas sides rolled up so one had a good view of the surrounding bush, in fact, being higher, a much better view than one got from the hunting car.

There were folding wooden bench seats along either side, but no one wanted to use them as the going was too rough for comfort and everyone was enjoying spotting game among the bushes and trees.

We even came across my old rhino friend who spotted us as we passed a tree he was grazing under. He gave a loud snort and came after us but when the truck went round some trees and turned off the trail we were on he lost sight of us and thundered on in a straight line. As we looked back we could see him stop, look around in surprise that we were no longer in front of him, shake his head in bewilderment, and start to graze again.

To get to the area where Mkamba and I thought the lion was we had to take quite a long drive round the thick scrub as it was not possible to get the truck along the "tunnel" we had used when on foot.

At last we reached the outcrop of rock that we had been heading for. It was an ideal place for a lion as it covered a fairly large area and had small caves and rocky ledges where he could lie in the heat of the day. There were patches of scrub, which made it difficult to assess whether he was up there or not. However, as it was the ideal place for a troop of baboons and there weren't any up there at the moment, we decided something must be among the rocks scaring them away.

I discussed the situation with Mkamba and we decided it was not an area we would want to take a client into, much too risky, so we would have to try to drive the lion out to him.

The eventual plan was for Mkamba to stay with me and Kidogo would take the three boys with him to the far end of the rocky hillock and attempt to drive the lion out to us.

I suggested to Carol and Helen that they should get into the back of the truck where they'd have a good view but would be perfectly safe.

'William,' I said. 'I'd like you to shoot him. It will be an extra lion for you. You are allowed another on your licence but this one won't count, as it is really game control work. So, you're getting something for nothing. Use the H&H .375, an ideal weapon for this job and you're used to it.

'Kidogo take this watch and I want you to start beating back in fifteen minutes. Also, take the 9.3-mm Mauser, but only use it in an extreme emergency. Do you understand … well, off you all go then.'

'Mkamba, Bwana Sir,' (that's what the Africans called William) 'will want the H.H.375. I'll use my Rigby .450 and I want you behind me with the Jeffreys just in case I need it.'

I was not taking any chances, I'd seen too many unexpected things happen to do that. It was always comforting to have a second rifle waiting if needed.

African gun bearers don't have the same reputation as their Indian counterparts. On many occasions a hunter has put out a hand for his second rifle only to find that all his entourage have panicked and departed. A very embarrassing situation! This was not something I had to fear with Mkamba. He was more dependable than the rock of Gibraltar. On one occasion when I was knocked down by a nearly dead buffalo, and a second one was coming in for the kill, Mkamba stepped over me and with a left and right blew the brains out of the one that was half on top of me and killed the second one as it closed in.

'Are you ladies comfortable? Good show. Now, William, we need to place ourselves over by those bushes. If Kidogo and the boys are able to drive him out he should come down that small gully, as it is the line of least resistance. With his bad leg he'll come slowly, or comparatively slowly, and should present you with a good target. I'll be right behind you so if there is any problem, I'll be able to deal with it. Now, if you're ready we'd better take up our positions. No talking in the truck please. We need silence until the job is done.'

Sir William Evans, Mkamba and I took up our positions and waited as the various flies made a meal of any bits of our flesh that they could get at.

I looked at my watch, Kidogo had been gone just on fifteen minutes, and they should be starting to walk back again any moment now. After a minute or two we heard them calling out and beating the bushes with their sticks, but they were still some distance away. Gradually their noises became louder as they approached.

Then it happened.

There was a frightening roar and a very large black-maned lion appeared on a ledge to our left front. It was not our Moonlight Predator. It was another gentleman who looked very fit and not in the least maimed. There was no way we were going to avoid clashing with him. He was glowering down at us emitting his blood-curdling roars. I touched William on the shoulder. 'Wallop him now.'

William didn't move. He seemed paralysed with fear,

but the lion didn't. With tail switching he was feeling with his feet for the best grip to launch himself at us.

There was no need for silence now. 'Wallop him, William, for God's sake wallop him.'

He seemed to come out of a dream, the rifle went up to his shoulder, and he aimed and squeezed off. The 270-grain Nitro-Express bullet was on its way.

Where had William aimed? Just where I'd warned him not to when we'd first hunted lions in the early days of his safari. Many people have been killed because of a similar shot. He tried a head shot and forgot about the size of the mane. A lion has very little forehead and an inexperienced hunter thinks there is a bigger target than there is. With this lion standing on higher ground than us, with his head slightly tilted as he looked down on us, William misjudged the placing of his shot and merely gave the old chap a parting.

William was trying to work another cartridge into the breach when the lion launched himself straight at us.

There was no time for niceties, I just shoved William to one side and walloped the lion when he was in mid-air and almost on us. The heavy bullet stopped him and dropped him.

William appeared beside me.

'Put one in his ear for good measure,' I said before he could speak.

As he walked forward, I saw a tawny flurry to my right and a lioness was going for William in great bounds.

I swung round and hammered her with a shot from my second barrel. Although she was dead, a good shoulder shot, her momentum carried her on until she finally stopped about four feet from William. A close shave.

'Bwana, look out, Simba,' Mkamba said as he held out the Jeffreys for me. I took it as he snatched the Rigby from me. There was another lioness cautiously coming down the rocks.

Oh my God, I thought, I hadn't wanted to kill either of those lions and I certainly didn't want to kill another.

She stopped at the base of the rocks as though she was trying to work out what had happened to the others, then she crouched down emitting a rumbling snarl and twitching her tail.

I wanted to scare her off and not to harm her. There must be cubs up in the rocks.

I walked towards her with the big rifle at the ready waving my free arm and yelling in a strident voice, 'Go on piss off. Get out of it.'

She seemed to sink back on her haunches and I thought

she was going to charge, and so did she for a split second, then she thought better of it and, turning, bounded back up the rocks.

I stood still and watched for a couple of minutes, just in case.

William had put one in the ear of both the lion and lioness, so they were now safe.

The male was a beauty and would make a good trophy, as William's second lion, but the lioness was not covered by his licence, so there would be a bit of explaining required by the Game Department and the skin would have to go to them.

'Gavin, I'm terribly sorry I muffed that shot but I was rather thrown when it was not the lame lion.'

'That's all right, old chap, a lot of people would have had the same reaction. Let's have a cup of tea, we've got all the kit in the truck.'

At that moment, Kidogo and the boys came in sight from round the side of the mound. He explained that they hadn't realised that they had a pride of lions in front of them until it was too late. They had themselves had a scary time as two half-grown males had approached them and aggressively demonstrated. I told them it was all right, I understood.

I asked Boculy to skin the lioness, which would be a comparatively easy job, as the skin was not wanted for a trophy. The male lion would be different we'd have to take him back to camp to be dealt with in the morning.

Carol and Helen had seen the whole action from the truck and were very excited and couldn't stop talking. I took my cup of tea, lit a cigar and wandered away from them. I wanted to be with Africa, and to think for a few minutes, and not with a lot of cackling women. I was upset at having had to kill the lioness and only hoped her cubs, if she had any small ones, would be all right.

And where, I asked myself, was our Moonlight Predator? This was probably the pride that he'd been the leader of and the male we had just shot must be the one that saw him off. Why he'd come back to his old haunts I couldn't imagine. He'd know the new dominant male would never allow him back.

We were back at square one. I hadn't the faintest idea where he was now.

The lioness was skinned in double-quick time with both Mkamba and Kidogo giving Boculy a hand. Even so, by the time we set off for base camp, there was only an hour left before dark.

We took the same positions in the truck as before;

Makanyanga driving with the two ladies beside him and the rest of us in the back, but this time, we also had the lion's carcass. I asked everyone to keep a good lookout just in case we were lucky enough to spot our old quarry.

As it was getting dark Makanyanga missed the track and drove into a dried-up donga where, in an instant, we came to a standstill up to the axles in soft sand.

I took over the controls myself and tried, without success, to rock the truck out.

'Okay, everyone out. Unload everything we can. William, if you and ladies would like to move out of the way, there's a nice log over there for you to sit on. We'll get this truck out,' I said sounding more cheerful than I felt.

'Let me help.'

'Yes, thank you, William, another pair of hands will help.'

We lugged everything out of the truck including the four hundred-pound carcass.

I always had shovels and strips of mesh stored in the truck as they were often required.

With a lot of digging, pushing and swearing we at last had the truck out of the *donga*. It was literally only a few yards we'd had to move it but it had taken us well over an hour and it was absolutely pitch dark.

When we put all the stuff back into the truck the carcass seemed, to us, to weigh twice as much as it had before.

I took over the driving as I didn't know why but I had a feeling of apprehension and wanted to get back to the camp as soon as possible.

CHAPTER 6

As I drove into the camp it was immediately obvious that something was wrong.

Both campfires were stacked with wood and burning brightly.

Opio, and the others, were grouped near the main fire. For a moment I couldn't think why, after all it wasn't that cold yet, then I was near enough to see their faces and realised they were contorted with fear.

Stopping the truck, I switched everything off and got out.

'*Jambo* Opio, what's wrong?'

'Bwana, the lion has taken Kieti.'

Kieti was the kitchen *mtoto*, aged about twelve, who assisted Juma.

'When did this happen?'

'Just after dark, Bwana.'

'Where are Kieti and the lion now?'

'Over there in the bushes,' he said pointing with his lips. 'But I think the lion went when he saw the truck lights.'

'Right. I want everyone to stay round the fire while Mkamba and I check out the situation. Mkamba, go and get the Browning Auto and load it with those three-inch magnum special load cartridges and bring two torches.'

I got my Rigby out of the truck and loaded it. I put extra cartridges into my pockets.

'William, will you get the .375 out of the truck and stay here with Kidogo to guard the rest? Mkamba and I shouldn't be long, if our friend has gone there's no way we can follow him until it's light.'

'Are you sure you wouldn't like me to come with you?'

'No, thank you, you'd be of more use here.'

'Are you ready, Mkamba, and is the Auto loaded with five? Good. Have you got plenty of spare cartridges? We're off then. Keep round the fire until we get back.'

As we went away from the camp into the darkness of the thick scrub I decided that this was really not the best way to spend an evening and I also had a feeling of guilt. I should have left Kidogo at the camp just in case something like this happened. It never even crossed my mind that we wouldn't dispose of our lion during the day, but that was no excuse, I should have thought of all possibilities. That was my job. I'd left these employees of mine, who relied on me for their wellbeing, without any protection. I was to blame for what had happened.

Mkamba and I had a torch each, mine was clipped onto the Rigby, which we used to illuminate our surroundings. We flushed out, first a little duiker and then two or three hyenas, but not our lion.

At last, we found Kieti, or what was left of him. The lion had made a good meal and I found it very sad to see the few bloodstained remains of what had been a faithful friend and servant.

'The lion must have gone, otherwise these bloody hyenas wouldn't be around the remains. I'm going to get rid of a couple of them. I'm not having them touch what's left of Kieti.'

I brought up the Rigby to my shoulder and, as the beam of the torch illuminated one of the hyenas, shot it dead and swinging round, shot another with my second barrel. Ejecting the empty cartridge cases I reloaded and felt a little better—at least I'd done something. I didn't usually shoot hyenas even though they were ugly in the extreme and classed as vermin, but when they got too cheeky and above themselves, as these were doing, one had to take some action.

'I'll stay here with Kieti while you go back and get something we can carry him in.'

As I stood waiting for Mkamba to come back I could hear the hyenas eating the ones that I had just killed. I felt very sad about Kieti. He was a nice cheerful lad and I'd known him since he was born as his parents worked on my father's farm. They would be very upset, but they would accept it as fate, or *shauri mungu*, when in fact it was my fault. I should not have left the camp unprotected.

* * *

We took Kieti back and buried him a short distance from the camp, putting plenty of rocks on top of his grave to stop anything from getting at the rest of him.

We were not a very happy party when we eventually sat down to dinner.

I arranged a roster so that one firearm-carrier—Mkamba, Kidogo or I—would be on guard all night. William, Helen and Carol were told that they were not to go to the loo tent, or for that matter to leave their tents, without an armed escort. Sleeping arrangements were to be the same as the previous night: Helen and Carol together and William in the single tent.

I arranged to take the first shift, eleven to one, Kidogo the second, one to three, and Mkamba the rest of the night.

I also arranged, with everyone's agreement, that Mkamba and I would see if we could spoor the lion as soon as it was light enough and then we would all go after him again.

In the morning Mkamba and I had a nasty shock when we picked up the lion's trail and found that after he'd left the remains of Kieti he'd circled the camp and then moved in behind the sleeping tents where he'd laid down. He was probably there, a few feet away from us, while we were having dinner.

Sometime during the night he had even clawed away a certain amount of earth at the bottom of the tent where Carol and Helen slept. We couldn't tell how long he'd remained there, but it was probably several hours before he moved off.

I decided that it was better not to tell the others what we'd found. It was too frightening to contemplate what could have happened if he hadn't already eaten his fill.

This was a very dangerous lion. He didn't seem to have any fear of humans at all. We must do something about him and quickly before there was another tragedy.

We followed his trail, which led us to the same thick scrub and the rhino tunnel we'd gone down the previous day.

'*Bwana*, we must have mistaken those tracks yesterday. We took it he had gone to the hillock as it was the ideal place for a lair but, at the time, we didn't know that his old pride was there. He must have either turned right or left along the side of the thorn bush area and be lying up there during the day.'

'I'm sure you're right but there are now so many tracks through old Mr Faro's path that it's hard to tell if he did go through here this morning or not. Let's cast around a bit first to make sure he hasn't gone off at this end rather than the other. I don't want to take any more chances with this one.'

We quartered the ground, each taking a different area. I found the tracks of another lion, also a very big one, but nothing belonging to ours.

Then Mkamba gave a delighted shout, '*Hapa, Bwana, hapa.*'

He'd found the tracks, not where we'd expected at all.

'*M'uzuri sana*, Mkamba. Well done.'

How lucky I was to have Mkamba on my safaris. A lot of white hunters take trainee hunters with them to whom they can delegate some of the day-to-day tasks and discuss with them tactics etc. Having Mkamba I didn't need anyone else. He was someone I could completely trust, a first-class second gun and an expert in every aspect of tracking and hunting. He was also my lifelong friend, someone, who if it came to it would lay down his life for me, as I would for him.

We followed the tracks as they ran alongside the thick scrub to our right. At last, we came to the end of the wait-a-bit bushes, which is where we had taken the truck the day before. He hadn't turned right towards the hillock where the pride lived but crossed the open plain towards a small forest some third of a mile away.

Mkamba touched my shoulder, we were now maintaining silence, and pointed off to the left. Fairly close to us was a herd of zebra, but Mkamba was drawing my attention to a herd of buffalo that were the other side of them towards the swamp that abutted the river that eventually ran past our camp. I couldn't see, at first, what he wanted me to look at—then I saw him. There was a magnificent old bull with a real head of horns on him.

I gave Mkamba the thumbs up. We had been looking for a good buff trophy for William and this would do very nicely. If only we could settle our account with the Moonlight Predator and get on with our hunting proper.

Our lion had kept moving at a surprising pace considering how lame he was. He had skirted the forest and branched left towards the swamp.

I broke silence.

'We'd better get back to camp. We've already been away two hours. They'll think we've been eaten or something.'

We laughed together, turned about, and started back.

*　　*　　*

When we panted back into the camp—we always seemed to be panting back into camp—William, Carol and Helen were sitting in the mess tent having coffee. They were slightly more serious looking than they had been when we'd arrived back the previous morning, but that was understandable.

I noticed that Kidogo was sitting watchfully, with the rifle I had left him across his knees, outside the gun tent. William had the .375 leaning against a chair beside him. Obviously, everyone was nervous and on the alert. That was not a bad thing, although our friend was by now quite a long way away.

'What happened? Did you find him?' they chorused.

I told them briefly what had happened.

'What's the form now then?' asked William.

'He's quite a way away and still going, so perhaps he wants to say goodbye to us. What I suggest is that we all go in the truck to where we left off this morning and see if we can either find him or find where he's gone. If we find him we'll deal with him, but if not we must warn some people. We'll have to go to the local game ranger and also into the village to let everyone know there's a man-killer loose. In any case we need to report about yesterday's lioness and we also need a few things from the village store so we will be killing several birds with one stone.'

They all agreed with the plan.

'I'll get Juma to make up a picnic lunch for us so that we can start without delay. Can you all be ready in twenty minutes? ... Good we'll leave then.'

I gave Juma his instructions concerning the picnic and then went to see how Boculy was getting on with the skinning of the fine male lion we'd shot the previous day. This was a different proposition to just whipping off the skin of the lioness, this one had to be done with great care and all Boculy's expertise as it was to be set up as a lasting trophy.

I would leave Boculy at the camp so that he could get on with his work. I would also leave Kidogo behind, no room for anymore miscalculations, to guard Boculy and the others that would be left in camp.

Going to the gun tent I found Mkamba and Kidogo cleaning and preparing the rifles we needed. I explained to Kidogo that I was leaving him to guard the camp and its personnel to which he just replied,

'*Ndio, Bwana.*'

A man of few words, but a good man to have with you in an emergency.

I filled my pipe with some good old strong Tanganyika tobacco and, puffing it, went out to see if everybody was getting ready.

I came face to face with Carol. It seemed an age since I'd brought her back from Philip's plane.

'How's it going? Ready for the next part of the adventure?'

'Gavin, I must tell you this isn't what I thought being on safari would be like. To be honest I'm frightened. I can't wait to get back to Nairobi.'

'There's no need to be frightened. I'll take care of you.'

'You mean like you took care of that poor little boy?'

'That's rather unfair, that was an unexpected accident.'

'There shouldn't be accidents.'

'Come on, be fair, accidents happen everywhere. If we'd been in Nairobi he might have been run over or something.'

I put my arm round her shoulders, just to comfort her, but she pushed me away.

'Please keep your hands to yourself. I must say, I didn't think all that much of you when we first met, you may be ruggedly good looking and physically attractive but you're obviously a letch and a conceited braggart and now it would appear, also an inefficient white hunter.'

With that she turned on her heel and went back to her tent, leaving me shattered.

The little bitch! How could she say such a thing to me after, out of the kindness of my heart, I'd brought her to the camp. Inefficient white hunter be blowed! I was, if not the best, one of the best. And as for being a braggart, I only told yarns of my exploits if people literally forced me to. What did she mean about being a letch? The only time I'd touched her was when I was saving her from our lion. As far as I was concerned the sooner her friend arrived to collect her the better ... though on the other hand I had to admit she was incredibly sexually attractive ... even more so when she was angry!

Mkamba was calling to me that the truck and boys were ready so I gave a shout to William, Helen and Carol that we were about to depart.

I put Makanyanga in the back and took the wheel myself, as I didn't want to waste any more time. I drove straight to the point where we'd discontinued our morning stalk. Then Mkamba and I got out and followed the lion's trail while Makanyanga took over the driving. We had no trouble following the trail until the lion went off into the swamp when I decided we had gone far enough. I discussed the situation with Mkamba and between us we decided our lion had moved on to "pastures new". I was pleased about that, but I was still worried about the local people, as he was almost certain to kill again. However, I was committed to my client and I could not, in fairness to him, take any more time looking for this killer. We would, in any case, be back at the swamp the next day to see if we could get that big buff for William, then we might even come across our lion again. William only had a few more days before Philip flew down to pick up him and Helen when, if necessary, I would take up the hunt again.

I took the wheel and drove towards the village where the game ranger was also to be found.

In the cab Helen was sitting squashed up against me and Carol was on the far side of the seat.

Helen was in good spirits and seemed to have recovered fully from all the trauma of the last few days. She chattered incessantly, but Carol hardly said a word and when I managed to glance at her she was sitting stonily looking to her front. Why, I wondered for the umpteenth time, was I so attracted to her? She wasn't half the woman Helen was or, for that matter, half a dozen of my girlfriends. But there was just something about her—damn her!

CHAPTER 7

The game ranger took a note of all we had to tell him about our Moonlight Predator and said he would go out the next day and see if he could find him. He accepted my story concerning the lioness and took charge of her skin.

When we arrived in the village the truck was surrounded by women and children. It wasn't very often they had visitors from the outside world, especially white women. Helen caused the biggest stir, her being so blonde. I left them all at the truck while I went to pay my respects to the village headman and also to inform him about our lion. He was very perturbed as they had very little protection of their own and relied on the Game Department and people like me. I assured him that I'd go after the man-eater, as soon as my clients departed, if he hadn't already been dealt with.

I collected the others from the truck and took them over to the village store which as usual was run by an Indian; a very cheerful, obliging man whom I'd known for many years. His little store was crammed with every conceivable thing. To have a visit from a safari party was, for him, a high day. Even though we didn't buy an enormous amount from him, one of our visits was worth more than a normal week's trading. I had a list from Juma and also a list of my own with the more important things on it like gin, scotch and tobacco. The two women purchased a few items for themselves so our friend, and his family, got happier and happier. But he wasn't so happy when I told him about our lion.

'Oh, *Sahib*, can you not kill him for us? These are not warrior people, they have no *Moran*, if he comes here, we will be defenceless.'

'But you've got the game ranger, he'll look after you.'

'He has other things to do and won't take especial care of us unless we pay him.'

'Well, that's not very good. As soon as I get the chance, I'll have a word with the game warden and see what can be done. In the meantime, I should be careful but not worry too much as Mkamba and I think the lion has moved off to another area. In any case, as soon as I'm free I'll deal with him if before then he hasn't become weak enough for the hyenas to take him.'

'Thank you, Sahib, I know we can, as we always have, rely on you to do whatever you can for us.'

As we left the village it was already getting dark; another day almost entirely lost because of that blasted lion.

I let Makanyanga drive us back to camp, as I preferred to be in the back rather than in the cab with Carol's stony silence and looks.

It did seem as if things were suddenly not going quite so well for me as they usually did. The worst of the lot was losing Kieti. I'd had boys killed on safari before but in the heat of the hunt and not in this unpleasant way and then being eaten. Ugh—very nasty.

Carol's attitude I also found somewhat baffling. Was I really what she said I was? I suppose I had become a bit self-centred and perhaps I was a little over-confident, but then I had to be in my job. As for being a letch I was no more that than any other red-blooded male in his twenties. Anyway, who'd jumped on whom when she'd first arrived; that was enough to give a chap the wrong idea. In my opinion, for the first thirty or so minutes of our meeting, Carol gave the impression that she both fancied me and was as randy as hell. Then she goes all coy and practically prudish followed by becoming downright insulting.

Why had I fallen for this cantankerous little bitch? For there was no denying I had. What was so special about her? So far as looks went, there was nothing much out of the ordinary there if you took away the fact that her bottom was rounded to perfection, her breasts were pert and delicious with nipples it was almost impossible to keep your fingers off, her long slender legs disappeared to God knows where, and her face looked as though it should have a halo. What was the matter with me, was I going soft in the head?

'Sorry, William, what did you say?'

'Will we look for the lion again tomorrow?'

'No, I've already taken up enough of your time and I think he is well out of this area by now. Tomorrow we are going to get you one hell of a buff. Mkamba spotted him down by the swamp and he's a terrific trophy. We'll leave camp about four thirty and sort him out.'

'What about Helen and Carol? Will they come with us?'

'No, I think they'd be better off in camp. It could be

a long, hard day.'

'Will they be all right there on their own?'

'We've left Helen on her own enough times.'

'That was before the event of Kieti. They might not like it now.'

'That old lion has gone. It would be much more comfortable for them to remain behind. I shall, in any case, leave Kidogo in camp as the rest of the team's morale is a bit low, so there is no fear there.'

'I think we should ask them and let them make up their own minds.'

'Yes, of course, William, if that's what you want to do.'

I hoped they would stay behind as it was going to make the hunting arrangements much more difficult if they were with us. William was right though, in the circumstances, it would be better for them to choose.

At last, the truck was bumping and grinding its way up the last slope to the camp, somehow it seemed to have been a long day.

When we had all disembarked it was already getting dark. I looked at my watch it was just after seven.

'Let's have a drink before we change and then we can decide who wants baths and who wants showers.'

Everyone agreed with alacrity.

William, in a good humour, started to fix drinks for everyone.

'Gavin, the gin's run out.'

'Opio,' I shouted. *'Lette gin-i.'*

I sank my teeth into a very large scotch. Umm, that was good.

'Now, hands up those who want a hot bath. William and Helen? What about you, Carol, are you for a shower?'

'That's what I'd like as long as someone stands nearby with a gun.'

'I'll do that with pleasure, though I don't think it's any longer necessary. We will keep the campfires burning well all night and I'll have one of the boys on duty just for reassurance purposes. What about tomorrow, will you girls stay in camp or come with us? Before you decide I should tell you that it will be a very hard day and mean you spending long hours sitting in the hunting car. I will, in any case, be leaving Kidogo in camp, so if you decide to stay here you will have ample protection. What do you think?'

'Well, I think, Helen, that he couldn't have made it plainer that he doesn't want us with him.'

'I think you're right, in which case, we will certainly be more comfortable here. Shall we stay? It would give us a chance to do our hair etc. without having endless interruptions.'

'Yes, let's stay and have a nice day together as long as everyone is sure that bloody lion won't come back.'

'No, he certainly will not be back, but anyway Kidogo is quite capable of taking care of him or anything else that turns up. That's fine then we can have a good long day's hunt if we need it.'

Opio arrived to say the baths were ready, so Helen and William went off to their tent.

'Give me a shout when you're ready, Carol, and I'll escort you to the shower tent.'

'I'll do that and, Gavin, I owe you an apology I shouldn't have said those things this morning. If it wasn't for you, I'd probably be dead or at any rate badly injured and obviously you can't be blamed for Kieti's death. I'm sorry I said all that it was just because I'm completely out of my element and, to say the least of it, scared stiff.'

'Thank you for saying that. I'm pleased because I wouldn't want you thinking hard things about me. I liked you, or to be honest fell for you, the moment we met. I'd like us to become really good friends.'

'That won't be possible. I don't intend to be around any longer than I have to.'

'Does that mean you still intend to go off with the prince?'

'I expect so as long as he arrives before the plane comes to collect the Evanses, in which case I'll beg a lift back to Nairobi with them.'

'I see. Is there no way I can persuade you to stay on here with me?'

'No, there isn't.'

'But I desperately want you to.'

'That's bad luck. I don't desperately want to stay with you. Even if I did, there's no way I'd want to be out here in this wild wilderness.'

'I think you'd soon get to know and love it.'

'No chance. I hate it a little more every minute. This won't get me cleaned up. I'll be ready in a couple of minutes for my escort.'

She went off into the tent leaving me feeling dispirited. I'd never felt like this about a girl before, the more offhand she was with me the more I wanted her—and not just physically either. I'd have to shake myself out of this or it was going to cause me heartache and perhaps even trouble. There was one thing that was certain: I wouldn't give up my life in the bush for anyone or anything.

She came out of the tent wearing that transparent

negligee again and turning towards me, she smiled.

'I'm ready for my shower.'

I couldn't help it, I let out a sort of strangled gasp.

'What's the matter, seen a ghost?'

'No, just you, and damn near all of you too.'

'I suppose this isn't the best thing for a safari camp, but it's all I've got with me.'

'It'll do.'

She handed me her towel, turned and walked towards the shower, her pert bottom swinging rhythmically as I followed her with the Rigby over my arm and the towel round my neck. She stopped at the canvas shower door and, facing me, took off her negligee and handed it to me.

'Hold that, there's a dear.'

I blinked and ran my eyes down her body, pausing at the entrancing tuft of black hairs sprouting from between her thighs. I stretched out my hand and she put the negligee into it.

'I won't be long,' she said, with one of those laughs of hers, as she entered the shower letting the canvas curtain close behind her.

I stood transfixed. I now knew why men committed rape. I was on the edge of reason. I had placed the rifle against the tree, put her negligee and towel over a branch and started to pull off my shirt when two of those damned hyenas came from among the bushes and stood looking at me. It brought me back to earth with a bang. *My God*, I thought, *if it hadn't been for those stinking, foul vermin what on earth would I have done?* It didn't bear contemplating. I shouted at them and ran towards them and they took off in their deformed, shambling way.

Carol put her head out of the shower.

'What's going on?' she asked with a touch of fear in her voice.

'Nothing to worry about, just shouting for joy.'

'That sounds like you. May I have my towel?'

As I handed it to her our fingers touched; it was like touching a piece of white-hot metal—the shock went right through my body.

When she appeared a few minutes later the towel was wrapped round her head and her hand was stretched out for her negligee. I held it just out of her reach for a minute so that I could study her body again.

'Come on, don't fool around, I'm feeling chilly.'

I gave the negligee to her and she shrugged into it what there was of it.

'I thought you'd ask me to come in and scrub your back.'

'I thought you'd come in anyway whether I asked you or not.'

'You mean, you wouldn't have minded?'

'Of course not, why did you think I was displaying my body or do you think I'm a prick teaser or something?'

'God! Let's go back again, I didn't know.'

'Too late now, you've lost the chance.'

'What about tonight?'

'Depends on where we all sleep. If I'm on my own you can come and see how I'm feeling, if you really want to.'

'Really want to! What do you think?'

'We'll see then,' she said as she disappeared into the tent.

*   *   *

We had a good dinner with us all in better spirits and no grunting predator in the background. I had difficulty in keeping my eyes and thoughts off Carol and in not imagining what might happen later.

We discussed the plans for the next day in more detail and I arranged for the girls to have a nice lunch in camp while William and I would do with sandwiches and flasks of coffee.

I said the two of us should be on our way by five at the latest, which would mean breakfast at four-thirty.

'Carol and I don't have to be up at that time if we're not coming with you, so we could have our breakfast at a civilised time, couldn't we?'

'Of course, what time would you like it?'

'What do you say, Carol, eight-thirty?'

'That sounds fine.'

'No problem, I'll give the necessary instructions.'

'In that case,' William said, 'I think it's better that Helen and Carol share a tent again tonight so that I won't disturb Helen in the morning.'

'That's a very good idea,' Helen said giving me a surprisingly knowing, amused look. 'What do you say Carol?'

'Suits me.'

I felt my stomach muscles clench and I opened my mouth to shout my disapproval but, seeing the three of them looking at me expectantly, I shut it again.

William and I had had our breakfast by five the next morning and were on our way out of the camp by five-thirty. We had Mkamba, Makanyanga and Ngutu with us; Ngutu had to stand in as an extra gun bearer as we had had to leave Kidogo at the camp.

The sun was now well up and the plains around our camp were alive with game. It was just too damned good to be alive even if I'd had to leave Carol and her wonderful body behind.

'William, we're going to make straight for the swamp area where we were yesterday and see if we can pick up the trail of that big bull buffalo. He will make a fine trophy for you. I think his spread will be well over forty-five inches. Anyway, let's see what happens. He may be miles away by now. On the hunt I'll get Mkamba to look after you and Ngutu can carry a spare rifle for me. I'm afraid Ngutu hasn't had much experience as a gun bearer but he's willing.'

William seemed pretty quiet. I came to the conclusion he was in his usual funk about the coming adventure. Why he'd bothered to come I just didn't know.

We were driving down the edge of a small forest when Ngutu called out to catch our attention. He had spotted in among the thorn bushes a leopard's tail and hindquarters, the rest of him being obscured from view. I swung the car round so that we would have a better view of him. He was lying half across a baboon that he must have just killed and now was chewing on. It was a big male leopard and one well worth having.

I drove on a hundred yards or so and stopped the hunting car.

'That's an incredible bit of luck, something that doesn't happen very often, to come across a leopard, out in the open, in broad daylight. There's a damned good trophy for the asking, William. Mkamba, I want the .375 for Bwana Sir and the 9.3 for me. Slip out on your side, William, and I'll follow you. Makanyanga, I want you to climb over to the driving seat and to move the car over to those trees when I give the word.'

William was now crouching beside the car on the side away from the leopard. Mkamba handed him the H and H and when I was also out of the car, he handed me the Mannlicher.

'Get down,' I said to William. 'When the car's gone we'll crawl over to that small bush. I think we'll have a good position for a shot from there. Make as little noise as possible and go for a shoulder shot when you're quite ready. Don't rush it, rest by the bush until you've got your breath back. He won't want to give up his meal so if we disturb him he may come for us in which case aim at his nose and let him have it.'

We crawled across the open ground until we were beside the bush.

I'd been right. We now had a perfect view of the leopard as he munched away at his breakfast and, even if I'd placed him myself, it couldn't have been more perfect for a shoulder shot.

I touched William gently on the upper arm and whispered, 'Wallop him when you're good and ready.'

The leopard had heard us and turning in our direction let out a sawing, rasping growl.

The .375 jumped in William's hands. There was a puff

of dust from the leopard's shoulder. For a split second he looked straight at us and then rolled over stone dead.

I slapped William on the back.

'Great stuff, well done, old boy. What a bit of luck to come across him like that; a chance in a thousand to find one in daylight, out in the open. You've got yourself a real beauty, he must measure over eight feet.'

The car drove up and the other three got out whooping and hopping about patting William on the back and shouting, '*Chui kufa. Piga m'zuri; m'zuri sana Bwana.*'

I really felt pleased with the whole business, a perfect bit of hunting. When we examined the leopard, he was a beauty and William's shot had been exactly right. It had drilled him right through the shoulder without doing any damage to his coat.

I got out the camera and took a photograph of William squatting beside his kill. Looking through the aperture of the camera I wasn't sure which, out of the two of them, looked the most dead, William or the leopard!

We loaded the carcass into the back section of the car—he was heavy, must have weighed well over one hundred pounds—and were ready to move on to the swamp area.

As we crossed the savannah, approaching the swamp, we came to another area of forest. I was driving again and pushing along as fast as I could when Mkamba shouted, '*Tembo.*'

I slurred the car to a halt and looked where he was pointing and at once I could see the bodies of several elephants as they tore at the branches of the trees.

'This is great. William, you must have been born under a lucky star: first the leopard and now elephants in this area which I wouldn't have expected at this time of year. This is an opportunity not to miss. Mkamba, I'm going to drive as near as I can and then drop you off. I want you to have a look to see if there's anything there worth having.'

I drove over to the edge of the trees and Mkamba slipped out and disappeared into the forest. Then I parked and waited.

'Will he be all right in there with that lot?'

'He should be. He won't get too close. He'll just have a look around to see what's there.'

We sat and waited for about ten or fifteen minutes and then Mkamba suddenly materialised beside the truck.

His face was one big smile as he gabbled away to me in Swahili.

'William, the Lord is really smiling on you. Mkamba says there is a bull in there carrying tusks that must be the best part of a hundred and eighty pounds of ivory. I can tell you that, for these days, that's real good. Let's go and get him. The buff can wait for another time.'

'Do you think I'm up to elephant?'

'After the professional way you shot that leopard, yes.'

What a lying bastard I was, but I wasn't going to pass up the chance of an elephant with tusks like this one.

'Right, Mkamba, I want the .375 H and H for Bwana Sir, the Rigby for me and you take the Jeffreys. Ngutu can carry the .500 in case I need a second rifle.

'Now, William, we are going in among this lot and going to try to get near enough to the old bull for you to take a shot. What we want is a shoulder shot. If he should come for us head on you must just get out of the way so that I can deal with him as your rifle is too light to stop him in that situation. Is that all clear? ... Good. To start with, Mkamba will lead, as he knows where we are going, but once we make contact with the bull I'll move into the lead with you behind me and Mkamba behind you and Ngutu bringing up the rear. We'll leave Makanyanga with the car so that he can move it if required. All clear to everyone? ... Right, let's go.'

We left the safety of the hunting car and moved into the cool, dark forest. Some of the trees were very tall, but there were also a lot of smallish stunted ones and at ground level there was a mass of thick scrub and thorn bushes. Good for us in one way that it gave us cover but not so good having to push a way through it. In the distance, above the noise the monkeys and various other small animals and birds were making, we could hear the elephants tearing away at branches and occasionally the crash of a tree coming down when they found they could not reach the bits they wanted. There was also the noise of their grunts and tummy rumblings. We actually passed a few feet behind one of the cows without disturbing her and as it was perfectly still in among the trees she fortunately didn't pick up our scent. Then there was another cow, right in our path, which meant we had to go to the right to avoid her and, because of this, through some nettles. The sting of an African nettle is very painful, and very poisonous, but luckily none of us appeared to be stung too badly.

Mkamba moved to one side and beckoned me on. As I got level with him he pointed to a large blackish object twenty or thirty yards in front of us. It was our bull and he was big, but for the moment I couldn't see his tusks. I stood and waited. Then his head appeared as he stretched up to pull down a branch of foliage. Mkamba was right, his tusks were big, very big.

I moved a few yards nearer and then stood still and beckoned to William to come up beside me and to take aim at the old chap's shoulder.

There was a sudden flurry and scream of surprise and rage as a cow that we hadn't noticed in the foliage, to our left, picked up our scent.

The bull swung round just as William fired and although the shot hit him it was not instantly fatal. He tucked his trunk to one side, put his ears back and came straight for William.

I brought up my rifle, but William moved to the right hoping to get out of the enraged bull's way, but in doing so he collided with my barrels and pushed them off target. I was unable to fire a shot.

My God, I thought, *that's the end of William*. But at that moment Ngutu, terrified, decided to take to his heels. The bull seeing a moving object switched his attention to this new menace. As he raced breakneck speed after Ngutu he actually bumped William who was cannoned out of the way. As the bull caught up with the fleeing Ngutu he stretched out his trunk and took hold of him round the chest then he pulled him back so that a tusk penetrated Ngutu's body. By this time the poor boy was screaming and his blood was pumping out of the gaping wound. I swung round and pumped a shot into the joint of the elephant's rear leg to slow him down. He swung round and came for me with Ngutu still hanging, screaming, on his tusk. I jumped to one side, went down on a knee and took a shot at the elephant's chest, a difficult shot because of Ngutu. The force of the heavy bullet stopped the charge and put him back on his haunches. As I was frantically pushing two more cartridges into the breach there was an explosion and the elephant keeled over. Mkamba had run round to the side of the old bull and put a bullet into his shoulder. I moved forward and put another through the back of his head.

As I stepped away from him one of his cows came out of the trees straight for me. I gave her a frontal shot and she dropped in her tracks when Mkamba ran up and dispatched her with a shot to the back of her head. I reloaded as quickly as I could and saw Mkamba doing the same, we both expected more trouble but suddenly all was quiet, except for the decreasing cries of agony from Ngutu.

Where the hell was William?

Then I saw him; he was in a crumpled heap among some bushes. I only hoped he wasn't dead. As I went over to him he groaned and tried to sit up.

'Stay still for a moment,' I said as I went over to the bull elephant to look at Ngutu.

Mkamba was already bending over him.

'*Kufu*,' he said.

I didn't expect anything else, with a wound like that no one could live.

What was happening? I'd lost as many boys in a couple of days as I had in the rest of my hunting career and, I'd nearly lost my client as well.

I went to William and checked him over. He was lucky, he was just shaken and bruised, and that, after colliding with an enraged bull elephant!

'Just stay there and rest for a few minutes, William. Mkamba, stay here and keep an eye on everything while I go back and see how near I can get the car before we start doing what we have to do.'

Makanyanga saw me come out of the forest and drove to meet me. I told him what had happened to Ngutu and he was shocked but not over surprised as one learns to expect the occasional accident when the hunting of dangerous animals is undertaken.

I took the wheel of the hunting car and drove it alongside the edge of the forest looking for some sort of path we could follow to get us deeper into the forest. We found a bit of a game trail that seemed to go in the direction we wanted, but it soon petered out.

Nothing for it, we'd have to leave the car and walk, and then carry everything back to it.

Then I heard a shot followed in quick succession by another.

'What the hell? Come on, Makanyanga, let's go.'

We ran as fast as we could force our way through the thick undergrowth. Then there was a third shot.

When we had almost reached the place where I'd left the others the undergrowth in front of us suddenly parted and an enraged cow elephant came charging out ears back and trunk already extended to take hold of me. She was only fifteen or sixteen feet away from me. No time to bring my rifle up to my shoulder I just had to fire from the hip. With her trunk being extended and her mouth open to emit her murderous scream I was able to put a bullet straight through the back of her throat. The heavy calibre bullet halted her charge and killed her outright. She dropped dead literally at my feet. As I climbed round her I saw she had already been shot behind the shoulder and would probably have been dead in ten or fifteen minutes without any assistance from me.

At last, I could see the other two standing by the dead bull.

'What the devil's been going on? What were those shots?'

'Better ask Mkamba. I'm just in a daze. There seemed to be elephants everywhere.'

'Bwana, two cows came back looking for their bull. I fired a shot to frighten them off but one kept on coming, so I had to shoot at her but didn't kill her. Then, just as I'd picked up the .500 that Ngutu had been carrying, the other one circled round and came in again. I got in a good shoulder shot, which I think will have killed her by now.'

'It won't because I just have. What about the first one? What's happened to that?'

'It was a frontal shot, but I don't think it will kill her for some time, if at all.'

'Right, we'll deal with that later. First of all, we must get poor old Ngutu off that tusk. What do you think we should do, Mkamba, should we take his remains back and bury them at the camp, or should we bury him here?'

'Bwana, there is not much point in taking him back, I think we should bury him here.'

'I agree, that means we'll need the shovel from the car and some rocks or large stones, if we can find any. I don't want any bloody hyenas digging him up and eating him.'

The two Africans couldn't really understand this

sentiment as it was accepted that hyenas would eat most of them when they died, or, if they were unlucky, when they were ill or old.

'Do you think any more will come back?' William asked in a dazed voice. 'Why did they come anyway?'

'Elephants do that, they look after each other. I've often seen a wounded one being supported on either side by members of its family. I don't think any more will come back now but we must be vigilant, just in case. Mkamba, go back to the car and get the spade while I look after things here.'

*   *   *

It took us quite a long time to bury Ngutu and then to get the tusks out of the old bull and the cow. After that we had to make two trips to carry everything back to the car. Once it was all loaded, I drove it out of the forest and parked it under a couple of trees a few hundred yards out on the savannah.

Makanyanga made tea and I lit another of those super cigars.

'I'm going to leave you and Makanyanga here while Mkamba and I go and see if we can find that wounded cow.'

'Good God, haven't you had enough for today?'

'Yes, but I can't leave a wounded beast. That's the unwritten law, particularly if it might be dangerous.'

'Should I come with you?'

'There's no obligation, but if you really wanted to, of course, you could. I would say, however, that we will probably be quicker and safer if you stay here.'

'There seems no option then. I'll stay.'

'Fine. There is food in the tucker box and everything you may need, including scotch. I shall give instructions to Makanyanga that if we're not back by four he's to drive you to camp and then to come back here and wait until we turn up.'

'We can just wait until you turn up. There's no need to go to the trouble of a double journey for him.'

'That's even better. We'll be back by dark, whatever happens.'

*   *   *

When we got back to the remains of the bull elephant, to start our tracking, we found the corpse alive with hyenas. We sorted around for some time before we were sure which set of prints were the ones to follow. As we progressed there was more blood on the trail and we could tell, from its colour, that the beast was heavily wounded and that her lungs were affected. It's always a fairly tense business following elephant and even more so when it's a wounded one. Mkamba and I were both moving very carefully with a watchful eye on all the possible hiding places from which she could suddenly erupt in full charge.

We both saw it at the same moment: a large blackish object lying down among some bushes.

I signalled to Mkamba to stay where he was and I slowly moved forward, my rifle at the ready, waiting for her to get up and get on with it.

She didn't.

When I reached her and pushed the bushes back to get a good look, I found she was already dead.

I breathed a sigh, not really sure whether it was of relief or of disappointment that the hunt had ended that way.

It didn't take us long to get her small tusks out, these were the property of the Game Department, as were those of the other cow, as William's licence only covered the bull.

To get back to the car we decided it was better to return the way we had come, via the bull's carcass. We staggered along carrying our heavy rifles and a twenty-pound tusk each. As we came into what was now almost a clearing, where the remains of the bull were, I realised that the hyenas were not eating but were grouped in a circle some distance from their evening meal. Then I saw the reason why—there was a lion having a feed. I took no notice as I wasn't really interested, but then he got up to go into the bushes as we got what he thought too close.

'My God,' I shouted. 'It's him.'

For as he moved away I could see he was lame on one rear leg. It was our Moonlight Predator! I tried to get my rifle up but, what with the tusk and everything, by the time I had he'd disappeared into some thick wait-a-bit thorns. Mkamba hadn't been able to do anything as I'd blocked his view and he hadn't even realised it was *the* lion until I shouted. I tried to get myself sorted out, put the tusk down and went across to the thorn bushes. There was no way I was going to get through unless I went on hands and knees, and I wasn't prepared to do that with the predator waiting for me.

'Damn, damn, damn. We had him for a moment then. We just seem to have a jinx on us where he's concerned. Nothing we can do now, we'll just have to let him go. We must get back to the others.'

Mkamba agreed there was nothing to be done, so we

picked up our tusks and started on our way again.

Once back at the car I took a long pull at the bottle of scotch and had a smoke of the old pipe. After that I felt considerably better and ready for the drive back to camp.

William also had a scotch as he was now feeling a bit the worse for wear and stiff from his contact with the elephant. I had a look at his shoulder and side, which were turning a nasty shade of blue-black, and was sure that there were no bones broken. He'd had a very lucky day, one way and another.

*   *   *

By the time we got back to camp it was already dark and I must admit it was good to see the campfires burning and two lovely ladies waiting to receive us. They were very shocked when we told them about Ngutu, but as they hadn't actually been there, they were slightly removed from the horror of it and seemed more concerned about William's injuries, even though, in comparison, they were very minor. They were, also, very impressed by William's two trophies, particularly by the leopard, not realising how lucky he'd been to get such big elephant tusks.

Nothing was said about our lion as I'd told Mkamba

not to mention it to anybody, so we were the only two that knew he was once again not too far away. I wasn't too worried about him for the time being as we had left enough dead elephants around to feed him, even with the hyenas and other scavengers, for at least a couple of days.

William went off for a bath and I went for a shower, but not before we'd had a large drink each. When he'd finished his bath, I went to his tent to check his injuries. He was beginning to stiffen up as the bruises came out. I re-checked to make sure no bones were broken while Helen clucked in the background. I hadn't really seen William stripped to the waist before and I was surprised at his build. He was muscular and in good trim.

'Nothing to worry about there,' I said. 'A few days and you won't even remember it happened.'

When we were having dinner, after a few more drinks, we discussed the next day's arrangements.

'I'll have to go and see the game ranger to report the killing of the two elephant cows and to hand in their tusks and I also ought to go and report to the local District Commissioner. That's going to take more or less the whole day, but I don't think you'd want to hunt tomorrow, William, would you?'

'No, I think a day's rest would be in order.'

'Would you like to come with me for the ride and to call in at the store?'

'No, I think I'd be more comfortable if I just have a quiet day here then I should be all right again by the next day. But why don't you take Helen and Carol?'

'No, I want to stay here to look after you. Carol, you could go if you want to.'

'Yes, I'd like to do that. It would make a change. Will that be okay with you, Gavin?'

'Great by me.'

So, that was that, I'd have Carol to myself for the whole day.

After dinner, when we were all saying good night, I said to Carol, 'See you in the morning.'

To which she replied in an undertone, 'If not before.'

I took it that this comment was meant as an invitation to visit her tent during the night.

When I'd undressed I turned off my light and got into bed, intending to wait for the camp to settle down before going to her.

After I'd been there for half an hour or so Helen arrived and climbed into my bed. She made love to me and then I made love to her, after which she departed.

I thought I'd give her a few minutes to get back to

her tent, and to go to sleep, so that she wouldn't hear me going to Carol.

I lay back and relaxed. It had been a long and arduous day and to my shame I fell sound asleep and didn't wake until after dawn.

I felt really embarrassed when I met Carol at breakfast but she made no sign that I had disappointed her. Perhaps, I thought, I'd misunderstood what she'd said to me the previous night, and I hoped that was the answer, as I'd hate to have disappointed someone as lovely and sexy as her.

CHAPTER 9

As I drove the hunting car away from the camp, I was excited. A day with Carol all to myself!

I'd managed to get away with taking just Makanyanga, who was now sitting on the seat behind us. Mkamba had known what I was up to and he'd given me the sort of look he used to when I was a boy about to do something he knew my parents wouldn't like. It was very unusual for me to go anywhere on safari without him, but I'd made up a good story why he shouldn't accompany us. Everyone else believed me, but not Mkamba. He didn't believe a word of it. He knew I wanted to have someone with Carol and me who didn't understand English and was, basically, a servant who would mind his own business and just do what he was told.

It was another gorgeous morning, unbelievably blue skies, the sun a hanging ball of fire, and clear invigorating air.

I turned and looked at Carol; she was more delicious than ever. Her few days on safari had deepened her tan and made her eyes crystal clear. She was absolutely radiant. She made my stomach contort with desire.

I cleared my throat. I had to.

'I thought we'd go to see the game warden first and then into the village to pick up some needed supplies. Then we can find a place for a picnic in the direction of the District Commissioner. How does that sound?'

'Sounds fine to me. The only thing I would add, if I didn't already know it's not possible, is a swim.'

'Who said that's not possible? If that is what you want, I know the perfect spot.'

'But I haven't got a swimsuit with me.'

'That doesn't matter, there won't be anybody else there. I'll park Makanyanga well away from the river where he won't be able to see you.'

'What about you? Are you going to stay with me?'

'Most certainly I'm going to stay with you to look after you. You can always leave your undies on if you're shy.'

'I'm not wearing any.'

'Oh, you won't be able to then, will you?' I laughed.

'No, but I'm sure you're such a gentleman that you'll look the other way.'

'Come on. I may be a gentleman, but I wouldn't be fool enough to miss a sight like that.'

'How do you know? I might look an awful lump without my clothes on.'

'You're forgetting I've already had the pleasure of seeing your fantastic body on two occasions.'

'Two occasions!'

'One when the lion was serenading you and secondly when I kept you company at the shower.'

'When the lion was there that was rather different and anyway, I was wearing my negligee. On the second occasion I didn't think you'd noticed, or that you'd found me unattractive, as you were so cold and calm about the whole thing.'

'Calm! My hair was nearly standing on end.'

'If it was only your hair then you must think me unattractive.'

'It wasn't just my hair, it was everything. I felt quite ill and weak with desire for you.'

'You have a funny way of showing it. I thought that after what I said to you, you'd come to my tent last night.'

'I longed to, but I wasn't absolutely sure that that was what you wanted. Also, I had a lot of jobs to attend to, and by the time I'd finished it was too late.'

'Poor Helen. I'm sure she wouldn't be very flattered if she knew that you considered screwing her as "one of the jobs you have to do". Not very gallant.'

'You are a little so-and-so. What makes you think I was with Helen?'

'Because, my dear Gavin, I came into your tent to find out what had happened to you, and you were bouncing up and down on top of her as if your very life depended on it.'

What did I say to that? I decided I was in a bit of a fix to say the least of it.

'It's all a matter of looking after the client's needs, one has to do these sort of things to keep everyone happy.'

'I thought Sir William was the client. I suppose he asked you to screw his wife whenever possible?'

'Well, no, not exactly.'

'Not at all you mean. I'm sure William hasn't asked you to do it or even knows you are.'

'Perhaps not, but it's a matter of knowing when you should and when you shouldn't.'

'You are a lying sod, there's only one reason you're carrying on with Helen and that's because you want to.

It's just as they told me in Nairobi. You can't get enough of it and what better proof than this: not only are you screwing the client's wife but you're also trying to have your way with me.'

'It's different with you, Carol, I've really fallen for you. I haven't been so attracted to anyone for a very long time.'

'What, you mean since last night?'

'No, you know that that's different.'

'I don't know anything of the sort. You are, as I've just said, nothing but a randy sod.'

'I'm sorry you feel like that about me as I'd hoped we might have had a good thing going for us. I really mean it when I say I think you're devastating, and I want you more than I would have thought possible.'

'You just don't give up, do you? I would have thought one woman on this safari would have been enough to satisfy you and here you are sniffing after another one. It's not as though Helen isn't attractive. She's beautiful and obviously very sexy judging by the performance last night. I mean not just once but twice.'

'How do you know it was twice? You stayed and watched!'

'Umm ... yes ... I did actually. I just sat quietly and watched, well listened really, it was too dark to see in detail ... It was rather arousing.'

'Well, you're a fine one to talk, even I'm not a voyeur.'

'Do you mean to say that if you got the chance of seeing me screw someone you wouldn't look?'

'I most certainly wouldn't. It would upset me too much.'

Carol's wonderful laugh rang out.

'I give up! You're incorrigible.'

I laughed too, our little talk seemed to have cleared the air, maybe things between us would progress now. I certainly would give up Helen if it would help my chances with Carol. In fact, I'd be willing to give up more or less anything that did that.

*   *   *

When we arrived at the game ranger's compound, I handed over the tusks from the elephant cows. He did not seem too pleased, and I had to go over the story two or three times and then fill in a form. He said he would be reporting the incident to the game warden, as I seemed to be shooting a lot of extra animals. I got a bit huffy in the end as I wasn't used to being questioned in this way and we didn't part on very friendly terms. I didn't get a chance to tell him we'd seen the lion again, as I didn't want Carol to hear.

We left the compound to go to the village.

'Gavin, I don't think you're that man's favourite hunter. From what I could understand he seemed distinctly unfriendly.'

'He's a silly fool. I've been hunting long enough for everyone to know I don't shoot anything unless I have to. If we hadn't shot those two cows we wouldn't be alive now. It's as simple as that and he knows it but he was just trying to show off in front of you.'

When we arrived in the village we went to the store and bought some supplies we needed for the camp and Carol bought one or two personal things for herself.

Mr Patel asked if I had killed *that* lion yet and I had to tell him that I hadn't and that, in fact, it was still very much alive and not far away. That upset him and he seemed surprised that I hadn't dealt with the situation. Everyone suddenly seemed to be blaming me for everything when I was doing my best for all concerned.

'Come on, Carol, time to go. I'm going to take you to a super place to swim and to have our picnic. Afterwards we'll go to see the DC on the way back to camp.'

*   *   *

When we arrived at our picnic spot, Carol was impressed.

The river was quite wide at this spot, where it passed through a small group of acacia trees. The ground was mainly covered by short grass but there was a twenty-five-foot long section of flat rock that formed a ten-foot wide platform, five or six feet above the level of the water. One end of this rock platform protruded out into the river and this formed a fairly deep pool of clear water, enclosed on two sides. The air was heavy with the perfumes of Africa and filled with the songs of birds.

Once we'd unloaded the picnic kit, I moved the hunting car down river a bit where I parked it, out of sight of us, under the trees. Makanyanga had his own food so he would be quite happy eating and sleeping there until we were ready to go.

When I got back Carol was sitting on the edge of the platform looking at the river.

'What a perfect spot. It could almost be in the wilder parts of England, that is apart from the heat.'

'Great, isn't it?' My voice sounded a bit strange, I hoped Carol didn't notice but I was excited, and sexually aroused, to be here alone with her. I wasn't sure how to play it although, from what she'd said earlier, I felt sure she was ready for some fun and games herself.

'Do you want to swim or eat first?'

'I can't wait to get into that deep cool water, shall we go in straight away?'

'I can't come in with you as there are crocodiles in the river so I shall stand guard while you swim.'

'Crocs! My God, you won't get me in there.'

I stood and laughed at the expression on her face.

'Don't worry, we often come here and it's quite safe. I shall stand on the platform where I have a view of all the surrounding water and tell you if one appears when you will have plenty of time to get out before there is any danger. I'll also have my rifle with me but that won't really be necessary. We sometimes all go in together but that is a bit silly as being on the same level it's difficult to see one coming until he's quite close.'

'Are you absolutely sure it's safe? I don't want to take any risks with those vile things.'

'You know I wouldn't even let you put a toe in if I wasn't one hundred per cent sure.'

'Okay, I'll take your word for it and have a quick, very quick, dip.'

With that she turned her back on me and languidly peeled off her shirt, then she stood for a second before she stepped out of her KD trousers.

What a back view! What a bottom. I'd never seen anything so rounded and pert in all my life. I just wanted to cup it in my hands. I forced myself to stand still as she moved towards the end of the stone platform where it was possible to get down into the river as the rocks actually formed several descending steps. This was another great advantage of this particular spot as there was no way that the crocs could get out onto the bank in this area and a crocodile, although not quite as dangerous on land as he is in the water, is still very deadly.

As Carol turned sideways to descend, I could see her breasts with their long, protruding nipples. I had to swallow and gasp, I could feel my temperature going up in leaps and bounds, she was the sexiest thing I'd ever clapped eyes on. She was unusual, her body looked even better without anything on than it did when it was scantily clothed. I was fully aroused. I just wanted to throw off my clothes and follow her into the water, but I couldn't do that.

I spotted a crocodile sliding off the bank and into the water but he was several hundred yards up river and no danger yet but he must be watched.

Carol was submerged up to her neck and laughing she called out, 'Gavin, you don't know what you're missing. It's great.'

'I know exactly what I'm missing and it's more than great.'

'I didn't know you were so keen on swimming.'

'Who's talking about swimming?'

'There you go again—"old one-track mind"—still, I know what you mean.'

Wow! Did that sound like agreement to better things.

'Don't go beyond the enclosed pool, I don't want you taking any risks.'

'I've got a feeling that the biggest risk is on the bank and not in the river,' she shouted back, laughing.

As she swam back towards the bank her luxuriant black hair was flowing behind her.

I could see another had joined the old croc and they were both heading downstream towards the pool.

'Right! Time to get out, Carol.'

'Can't I stay in a bit longer?'

'No, better not, you've got two friends coming down to have a look at you.'

'Oh my God,' she gasped and started an Olympic stroke towards the bank.

The crocs were still a good way off, but better safe than sorry, and anyway this "old croc" on the bank was waiting to sink his teeth into this delectable piece of womanhood.

I laid my Rigby down by the picnic baskets and went down to give her a hand out.

She tried to get up the rock without my help and ignored my hand but when I said, 'Plenty of time they're still quite a way behind you', she changed her mind and grabbed it.

I heaved her out of the water and, when she was standing on the bank, I stepped back and just stood and looked at her. The sight was mind blowing.

CHAPTER 10

As Carol stood before me on the riverbank, with trickles of water running down her, I had to swallow hard or I would have choked with desire.

I just stood, stared and took in the full beauty of her.

She wasn't embarrassed or shy, she looked straight back at me with her almond-shaped eyes wide and a half smile on her lips.

The sensual beauty of her body made my stomach contort and I found it difficult to breathe. As my eyes travelled down her body, I saw that the black triangle of hairs that had protruded between her thighs, when I'd seen her naked outside the shower tent, had gone. It was now smooth and clear. Had she done this for me so that the centre of my desire was no longer obscured?

I stretched out my hands and placed them gently on her shoulders looking into her clear eyes. She smiled back into mine. I let my hands slide off her shoulders and down her body until they were resting on either side of her delicious bottom. She didn't move, she just stood still, smiling.

I pulled her body to mine and, looking down at her, my lips sought hers.

She leant her head back and partially opened her mouth to receive my inpatient lips.

When our lips met it was pure heaven and, as our tongues caressed, my mind began to spin.

I picked her up and carried her across the rocks to our picnic spot. Putting her down on the rug I'd spread out for us, I took a towel and gently wiped the water off her body. She felt cool and smooth to my touch. Neither of us said anything, she just moaned slightly when I was drying her thighs.

Then she said in a husky voice, 'Why have you got all your clothes on, are you shy?'

I stood up and literally tore my clothes off and then stood looking down at her.

'*Bwana Tembo,*' she laughed as she half sat up and took hold of me by a convenient handle! 'I don't think I can wait much longer.'

Letting go, she lay back and opened her thighs where I could see that her incomparable jewel was swollen in anticipation of receiving me. Dropping on all fours between her legs, I kissed it and then caressed it with my tongue. I could hear her moaning and then saying or almost shouting, 'Now, *Bwana Tembo*, now.'

I slid up her body until I was able to kiss one of her nipples. It was magnificent: large and rock hard. I took it between my teeth and bit it gently.

Her body was beginning to thrash about under me and she was panting and gasping.

'For Christ's sake, you randy sod, get on with it. Screw me, God damn you, screw me.'

My lips were on hers as I drove into her. Her body bucked to meet mine then her legs were clasped behind my back as she climaxed. After she'd climaxed a second time I came in great gushes. I felt as if I was shooting out my entire innards. I had never encountered anything like it before. My head was spinning but my desire was not diminished, being inside her was so tremendously exciting that I didn't even soften to any extent, I just went on pumping away. Then she pushed me so that we rolled over and she was on top. Somehow she got her legs up, without ever letting me slip out of her, so that she was squatting on me. Leaning back against my raised knees she started to gyrate, it was fantastic—mind blowing. I had another tremendous ejaculation and even after that her soft, sensuous, creamy interior kept me hard until I actually came again for the third time.

After that I softened and slipped out of this magnificent woman. We rolled over and lay side by side in a trance.

When I came to Carol was curled up sleeping. I got up, had a look at the river to see where the crocs were and as there were none around the pool I went in for quick freshen up.

As I came back to our picnic site Carol stirred, opened her eyes and smiled at me.

'You were fantastic. That was terrific. Just what I needed and what I'd hoped for last night.'

Then she laughed that wonderful laugh of hers and held out her hand to me. I took it and sank down beside her and kissed her.

'You're mind boggling, Carol. Just out of this world.'

'Does that mean you enjoyed making love to poor little me?'

'Enjoyed it! It was indescribable. I've never experienced anything like it.'

'Not even with your French girlfriend.'

'Which French girlfriend?'

'The one whom you got the medal for screwing.'

We both laughed. Then I kissed her again.

'Don't get me all worked up again, Gavin. I'm hungry, can we eat?'

'Of course. Do you want to go in the pool before I get the food ready?'

'No, I'll go in afterwards before we leave, I just want to keep the feel of you inside me for a little longer. Oh dear, what did I say? That's made you go hard again.'

And it had.

To hell with food! Before I knew what had happened, I was inside her again to the sound of her laughter which soon turned to gasps.

Afterwards we took it in turns to have a quick dip in the pool and then we put on a few clothes and settled down to lunch.

'Juma certainly did us proud. That was delicious. He's a very good cook, you're lucky to have him.'

'Yes, I am. He's been with me ever since I started doing safaris. More coffee, and what about a cigarette? No. Do you mind if I puff my pipe?'

'No, not at all. Anyway, it suits you, a pipe goes well with the image of a white hunter.'

'I wouldn't know about that, but I can assure you I don't smoke it for that reason.'

'I didn't think for a minute that you did. I wouldn't expect you to do anything for show only because you want to.'

'Is that a compliment or a criticism?'

'Certainly not a criticism. I admire anybody who can be his or her own "man". I wish I could.'

'But surely you are. I don't think you would ever do anything that you really didn't want to.'

'I'm afraid I would and do, I have to.'

'Why do you have to?'

'Because I'm not as lucky as you, I can't be totally independent.'

'How come? I'd have thought you had everything going for you.'

'I come from a different background to you and that makes a lot of difference. That's why I didn't like you when we first met, well, not right at the beginning. When I saw you waiting for the plane I thought: Wow! That is some man, I'm going to seduce him for sure. Then after a short time I decided I didn't like you. You were too confident, sure that everything you did was right, obviously successful at everything you did, well-educated and from the right background. You made me feel like a second-class citizen.'

I couldn't believe it. I leant forward and, putting my hand under her hair, pulled her head towards me and kissed her.

'I'm sorry, I didn't feel any of those things. I don't know how I could have given you that impression. I'll admit to you that I was almost struck dumb when you arrived. I didn't think I'd ever seen a more superb girl and now I know that I was right.'

It was her turn to lean forward and to kiss me.

'That's kind of you, but I'm sure you're only saying it because we've just made love.'

'No, Carol, I mean it and I don't know how you can think those things about yourself. What on earth gives you such strange ideas?'

'Surely you can tell I didn't have the same sort of up-bringing as you?'

'Hadn't thought about it. In what way was it different?'

'I've had to fight for everything I've got, however little it may seem.'

'In what way have you had to fight? Tell me about it.'

'If I tell, promise you won't laugh at me or not want to have anything more to do with me?'

'Of course not. The only trouble you're going to have with me is getting rid of me when you've got fed up with me.'

'I don't think I'll do that. I'll only go when I have to.'

'It won't be a case of your having to, will it?'

'Yes, it will, when the prince arrives.'

I felt my heart sink.

'But you don't have to go with him, do you?'

'He can offer me everything I need for my future.'

'We'll see about that at the time. Anyway, there's someone who accepts this funny background of yours that you keep on about.'

'He doesn't. He just thinks of me as a hot little whore who would be fun for a time as his third wife. When he's had his fill of me, he'll pay me off with what, to him, is a paltry sum but to me will be enough to secure my future.'

'Come on, Carol, I think you're having me on. I'm sure you wouldn't compromise yourself like that.'

'I've no alternative.'

'Of course you have. Apart from anything else you're already a top model.'

'You just don't know what life is like, do you? If I don't do what the prince wants me to I'll never work for one of the big fashion houses again. He'll make sure of that.'

'I don't know how your parents ever let you get into a situation like this.'

'That is what I've been trying to explain to you. I don't have that sort of thing behind me.'

'Tell me about it so that I can understand.'

'All right but I hope it won't turn you off being my friend. I never knew my father. My mother, who was a complete slut, was never quite sure which man-friend was responsible for me. She worked in a factory and, when she was short of money, as a part time "hostess" working for a local nightclub. I had two younger brothers who, from the time I was about eight, I looked after. I got to school when I could and was always in trouble there for having been absent or for being behind with my work. We staggered on from disaster to disaster until I was thirteen and then the worst possible thing happened. My mother married. She married the foreman from her factory, a brute of a man. We lived in this little council house which had two bedrooms, one of which I shared with my mother until she married, then I had to share the other one with my two brothers. I had no privacy and had to put up with my brothers' comments about my boobs and when I started having the curse it was even worse. Jim, as my "stepfather" was called, always got drunk on Friday and Saturday nights when he used to do awful things to my mum, things that we could hear quite clearly through the paper-thin walls. After they'd been married for a couple of years my mum was knocked down by a car and went into hospital. The following Friday when Jim got home drunk, he came into our bedroom and shouted. "Carol, you come into my room, you can share my bed while your mum's in hospital". I nearly had a heart attack at the thought of it and refused. He grabbed me by the hair and tried to drag me out of my bed. I fought him and my two brothers came to my assistance. We were all knocked about and the noise was so terrific that our neighbours called the police. To cut a long story short, my brothers and I were taken into care and after a while I was fostered. That was the best thing that had ever happened to me, I ended up with a nice middle-class childless couple who couldn't have been kinder to me. My foster father worked as a cutter for a fashion house and through that I got into the fashion business; starting in the workrooms and because of my looks and figure being used sometimes to model a dress so that the designers could see what it looked like. I was eventually given a shot at modelling proper, which I was good at and which I enjoyed, so it became my life.'

'My dear Carol, what a life. I really wouldn't have known. I thought you were the spoilt daughter of well-to-do people. I would just never have guessed that you'd been through all that. What about your real mum, did you never go back to her?'

'I went to see her once but that was enough, never again.'

'Do you still live with your foster parents when you're in England?'

'Good heavens no. I've had my own little flat in London for years.'

'How did you meet the prince? Through your work I suppose?'

'Yes, at the Paris fashion shows.'

I wanted to ask her a question but I didn't know how to, I'd just have to go round it in a few circles!

'Have you been with him long?'

'I haven't been with him, as you call it, at all. I've been playing hard to get. I don't want anything to do with him unless he marries me. As I've already told you I'm only interested in him as an insurance for my future.'

'So you haven't been living with him?'

'No, I most certainly have not.'

How could I ask her? I just had to know whether she'd been sleeping around with a succession of men and whether I was just another passing ship.

'Were you living with anyone when you first met the prince?'

'I know exactly what you're getting at. You think I'm some sort of tart like my mother. Well, I can tell you categorically that I was a virgin until I was twenty-one when I was seduced by a very sophisticated French fashion designer, who you may have heard of, Charles Lamont. I lived with him in his beautiful home in Paris and he did a "Pygmalion" job on me. He taught me everything, including the art of physical lovemaking. He was tremendous and at one time I was convinced that I was deeply in love with him. Then six months ago he tried to make me have sex with various friends of his, so that he could watch, and at that time I also caught him in bed with a friend of mine. So, that was the end of that. I moved out of his house and his life. He is the only man, up until now, I've ever made love with in my life, but he did give me an appetite for it as you must have realised.'

'I'm so glad you've told me all this. I've really fallen for you in a big way. Do you think you could like me just a little bit?'

She laughed that wonderful laugh of hers. 'I would have thought the last hour or two would have shown you whether I liked you or not.'

'But I'm not some terrific lover like your Charles Lamont.'

'Darling, you are sensational. *Bwana Tembo* is certainly the right description for you. What stamina! Leaves poor old Charles as a non-starter.'

'Are you going to stay on with me then?'

'I must join the prince when he arrives. There's too much at stake.'

'But think of the fun we could have together when we've got rid of William and Helen.'

'That sounds great but when you've had enough and go off after another lion, or woman, where does that leave me? No, Gavin, I think we must just consider this as a very pleasant interlude.'

'I think Carol ... who is that calling? It's Makanyanga.'

I got up and walked through the trees and met Makanyanga. He had been coming to remind me that it will be dusk in about an hour. Where had the time gone? I told him to bring the car so that we could load it.

I went back to Carol, laughing that if it hadn't been for this interruption I might have asked her to stay with me forever, perhaps even as my wife. Phew, that had been a near thing.

'I just don't know where the day's gone. We shall have

to go straight back to camp there's no time to go and see the DC now. I'll do it when my clients have gone.'

'Won't you go back to Nairobi with them?'

'I've got that lion to look after. I must make sure he's out of the way. I don't want any of my friends in the village getting into trouble.'

'You do feel responsible for these people, don't you?'

'Yes, I do. One has to do whatever one can for them.'

'I think I could become very fond of you, Gavin.'

'You mean you're not already. You just wanted my body?'

'All right, if you must know, I'm already very fond of you.'

CHAPTER 11

t was dark by the time we arrived back at camp, as I had told Makanyanga to drive so that I could sit on the back seat with Carol. Actually, the journey was not long enough for me and I was quite sorry when I saw the campfires.

Helen and William told us that they'd had a quiet day and that William, although still a bit stiff, was almost recovered from the events of the previous day. They asked what the DC had said, which was a bit awkward, to which I simply answered that he'd been away from his boma.

I noticed Helen first looking at Carol and then at me, with a quizzical smile. 'Anyway, the pair of you seem to have had a nice day together.'

She was a very smart lady, Helen. You couldn't fool

her easily. I'd come to the conclusion, right from the start, that there was more to her than met the eye. She wasn't just a very attractive blonde; she also had an astute mind. I had a sneaking feeling that she was much harder and more calculating than she appeared. It was the same with William, although with him it hadn't struck me at first. He wasn't the soft inept chap he appeared. He might be scared of hunting big game, but he could take whatever you threw at him as he'd proved the previous day. It had also been a surprise to me that he was so muscular and generally fit. It seemed somehow out of character with what one would expect of him.

Why should I be worrying about them? As long as they coughed up what they owed me that was all that mattered. Or was it? I didn't know what it was but there was a little niggle at the back of my mind that I couldn't get rid of. Basically, it all came back to the question: what were Sir William and Lady Evans doing on a big game safari? That was the crucial question and the one I couldn't answer. Anyway, not to worry, only one more hunting day and then they'd be off.

God, how I hoped Carol would stay with me. She hadn't realised that because I'd moved camp Harry and the prince wouldn't pass us and, unless they actually decided to look for us, we certainly wouldn't see them. Poor girl, I suppose I should have told her at the beginning then she could have gone back to Nairobi with Philip. Then I'd have missed getting to know her and, I had to admit, falling for her.

Now, at this stage, believing that all's fair in love and war I'd do whatever I had to to keep her with me and sod the rest.

Over dinner we discussed what William would like to do on his last day on safari.

'William,' I said, 'there is a small herd of *tendalla*, kudu, that's been spotted in the low hills past the swamp where we hunted the buff. I'm told there is an old boy with them who has a magnificent head. Kudu is something special. You always think you've got him and then he's gone and you have to start again. He's a grey blur, swift to vanish. But what a trophy if you nail one. On your wall those heavy-ridged, mahogany-coloured, double-curling horns with their tremendous sweep will be the envy of any hunter that sees them.'

'You make that sound very enticing, Gavin. Let's try for one tomorrow.'

'Good. That will make a super final day. We will need to be up early and I suggest that the ladies accompany us.'

'You try and stop us, eh Carol?'

'Agreed, I don't want to miss this one.'

'Good, that's fixed then. We'll breakfast at four-thirty and leave camp at five.'

During that night, when Carol was sleeping beside me, I heard someone come into my tent and knew it must be Helen. She came over to the bed and was about to lift the mosquito net when she must have realised that I was not alone. She crept out without saying, or doing, anything. Carol, luckily, didn't wake so she never knew that we'd had a visitor.

I felt sorry that it had happened, but was surprised that Helen had come to me as she had obviously worked out what had happened between Carol and me during the day. Yet another thing I couldn't understand: why was she so hot for me, hot enough to take such risks?

CHAPTER 12

We managed to make our early start and by half-past seven, on a beautiful African morning, we were well on our way to our proposed hunting ground.

I used the safari car, which I drove, with Carol and Helen beside me in the front, William with Mkamba behind us and, on the back seat, Kidogo and Makanyanga.

After an hour or so we came across a small group of herdsmen with their scraggy cattle and I stopped to have a word with them.

Yes, they had seen the herd of *tendalla* shortly before we had arrived and they were heading towards the hills and, yes, the bull was "*m'uzuri sana*".

I turned to speak to William. 'It seems that the big bull

we'd heard about is a few miles in front of us. It looks as if you're going to have your usual luck.'

But it wasn't quite as easy as that.

When we were fairly close to where the kudu should have been we left the two girls and Makanyanga with the car and William, Mkamba, Kidogo and I set off on foot.

We then had a frustrating few hours as we tracked and followed the herd, continually getting within sight and range, only for them to suddenly pick up some hint of danger, which made them take off. Then they'd stop and start grazing again and we would work our way laboriously towards them only to have a repeat performance.

When we'd started our stalk the grass had still been dew-wet and the sun only just warm enough but by now everything was tinder dry and the sun, through the stunted trees, blazing hot.

Then there he was again, this magnificent bull kudu, in a good position for a shot.

I whispered to William, 'Take it steady and when you're ready, wallop him in the shoulder.'

William took careful aim and squeezed off a shot.

Thump.

The kudu jumped high in the air and then collapsed

where he landed.

We all shouted in glee and Mkamba, Kidogo and I thumped William and congratulated him on shooting such a trophy.

I sent Kidogo off to tell Makanyanga to get the car as near to us as he could.

I then relaxed and lit my pipe. It tasted good, and I felt good. That was the last hunt with William and I was not sorry. There was still something about this man that I didn't like and something else that I felt but couldn't put my finger on. I would be glad to see the back of him and, strangely enough, of Helen as well.

Makanyanga was able to get the car fairly close to where we were and then it was just a matter of heaving the poor old kudu the rest of the way.

When we reached the car Carol and Helen were very impressed with William's beautiful prize and exclaimed over it and him.

'Just nice time for lunch,' I broke in when I thought he'd had enough adoration. 'If we drive a short distance we can park by the river where you may see some game while we're eating.'

After lunch Carol and William walked off along the bank to look at the bird life. I sent Kidogo, armed with the .475, to look after them while I stayed and chatted to Helen.

'So, Helen, this is your last day on safari. Have you enjoyed the experience?'

'Very much indeed.'

'I'm sorry about last night but I didn't think you'd come to my tent.'

'It was silly of me, I should have realised Carol would be there.'

'As you're going tomorrow tell me why you've been coming to see me. It's obvious that you are very much in love with your husband. Why have you been cheating on him, particularly, in such risky circumstances?'

'I haven't been cheating on him.'

'I don't know how you can possible say that.'

'Because he knew.'

'He knew!'

'Yes, he knew and approved.'

'I just don't understand. How could he approve?'

'You think him some sort of cowardly fool, don't you? Well, he's not. He's no fool and he knows what he wants and is prepared to go after it. As we are about to change our lifestyle we decided this was the opportunity to have the child we've wanted. For reasons I'll not go into, it's not possible for William to father one, so, we decided jointly to select someone that could sire one for us.'

'Good God! That's weird, completely bizarre. I can't believe it. Anyway, why choose me? You didn't know me. You hadn't even met me.'

'We checked the records of hundreds of war heroes and found yours and, with your various attributes, you fitted the bill admirably. Just the sort of intelligent, daredevil father we wanted for our son.'

'You say for your son, but you can't be sure what sex it will be and my attributes, whether good or bad, probably would not suit a girl. So, in fact, you knew all about how I won my medals etc. and were just playing me along at dinner that night?'

'Yes.'

'And you didn't enjoy our lovemaking at all, you were just doing it clinically in the line of duty?'

'I wouldn't say that. You're very good at it, there's no denying.'

'Well, thank you for something, even though I must say I think you have both been pretty underhanded and devious, and you have left me with a distinctly unpleasant feeling about the whole thing. I still can't think why you came all this way and chose me when you could have found someone nearer home. What an enormous risk you took. After all, in person I might have been completely different to me on paper.'

'We had a personal report on what you were like in person from some friends who came on safari with you.'

'Who on earth was that? No one has ever mentioned you to me.'

'No, they wouldn't have done. They were asked not to. It was the Ulianoffs.'

The Ulianoffs! I certainly remembered them. They had come out a couple of years before the Evans on a two-week safari arranged on their behalf by the Russian Embassy in London. They were what can only be described as dreadful. She spoke no English at all and was awful to look at and smelt of cheap soap. He did speak English quite well being a Russian diplomat of some description. He had no sense of humour and no conversation except world politics. Neither of them was interested in the animals and he didn't even touch a firearm during their stay. Neither was he interested in big game trophies to take home, so at least I didn't have to go out gathering them for him. They were, however, surprisingly interested in where various places were and wanted to travel round a bit. They didn't say why or what they were looking for but sat together in the back of the hunting car poring over maps. As far as I was concerned the whole thing was just one big bore and I couldn't wait to get rid of them. The only relaxation was when Mkamba and I went off to shoot for the larder. We also had to visit my old friend Patel in order to replenish the supply of vodka. They drank it as if life depended on it ... and I think it probably did! I was so pleased to see the back of them when, after what seemed like an eternity, they finally left and I had not thought of them since until this extraordinary revelation by Helen.

'So, they must have given me a good report even though I wouldn't have thought that we got on at all well, not really my type nor I would have thought yours. I'm surprised that on their say so you decided to progress the project. What did you call it: "project milking sperm from Gavin McKenzie"?'

'Don't be like that, Gavin. I wish I hadn't told you if you're going to be all stroppy about it. Anyway, we decided you were definitely the perfect person, as long as I could seduce you, added to which we had to come out to East Africa and we also wanted someone that we'd never see again.'

'How do you know you'll never see me again? I often visit England.'

There was rather a long pause for someone as glib as Helen.

'Well, it's all to do with law of averages etc.,' she said in a not very convincing manner.

'On the other hand just supposing I'd fallen madly in love with you and hadn't wanted to let you go?'

'We knew that couldn't happen.'

I didn't know what to make of all this. Particularly what she meant by they were going to change their lifestyle, they would never see me again, and it wouldn't have mattered if I'd fallen madly in love with her. They certainly were a very strange couple. What the hell was going on and what was my next move? Nothing, I decided, nothing. There was no point in having a monumental bust-up because, at this late stage, it would not do any good. I had been used but on the other hand I had had some terrific sex without any commitment of any kind. So be it, they were off tomorrow so I would just let it go. My main concern was retaining Carol. I realised Helen was saying something.

'I beg your pardon, what did you say?'

'What about Carol, is her prince likely to arrive with your friend?'

'No, I haven't told Carol but as we've moved camp they

won't know where we are. They would only have come at the latest yesterday if they'd made a big effort to find out where we were.'

'I see,' she said looking strangely pleased. 'So, they won't be visiting, in any case, for a week or so?'

'That's right and we won't be here after tomorrow.'

Why was she now interested whether my affair with Carol would be interrupted by the arrival of Harry and the prince?

I felt the back hairs on my neck prickling. There was something in all this I still didn't understand, but what could it be? It must just be my imagination getting the better of me, but I did have the distinct feeling that all was not as it should be.

*   *   *

That evening we had a farewell supper, which was quite merry and full of fun.

Nothing further was said about Helen's disclosures and I had the impression that she hadn't mentioned to William that she'd told me anything.

'Can I come with you in the plane tomorrow?' Carol asked William.

My heart gave a lurch and then sank.

'Aren't you going to stay and travel back to Nairobi with me?'

'No, Gavin, I think it's better for me to get back.'

'But there's no rush is there? The prince won't be back for several weeks yet.'

'If I find out where he is I can get Philip to fly me to his camp.'

'Doing that a few days later rather than tomorrow can't hurt, can it?'

'I think the sooner I do it the better.'

I looked at Carol, her face looked strained and her eyes had lost their glitter. She didn't want to go.

'Stay and go back with me.'

'No, I can't.'

William and Helen were looking at us. I decided to stop the argument and to try to persuade Carol later.

Then I heard it—a grunting roar—our Moonlight Predator was back.

That roar broke up the party.

Mkamba and I armed ourselves and went to have a look, leaving Kidogo and William behind to look after the camp.

I was cursing myself, thinking about how I'd had an

opportunity to finish this chap but had muffed it.

We didn't find him, or even hear him again.

We spent an uncomfortable couple of hours among the thorn bushes all to no avail.

When we got back to the camp William and Kidogo were sitting by the blazing campfire and the others had gone to bed.

'Did you find any signs?' asked William. 'No ... I did think you would. The girls have gone to bed; Helen insisted that we revert to the old style, so she and Carol are sharing my tent.'

God damn it! Helen had done this on purpose—just to spite me. Now the chance was gone to talk Carol into staying with me or even, at worst, to have had one last night in each other's arms.

CHAPTER 13

The next morning I didn't have much of a chance to talk to Carol, as the departure preparations had to be made.

William had said—why, I couldn't really understand—that they would rather travel to the airstrip in Rommel than in the safari car.

By the time breakfast had been eaten, the baggage had been loaded and William had dispensed tips to the boys, it was already nine and time to leave.

I'd arranged with Mkamba that he would stay in camp to see that our "friendly" lion didn't decide to have one of the boys for his breakfast. It was also a good opportunity for him to check over all our firearms, except the Rigby and one shotgun that I would take with me. I decided just to take Makanyanga with me and tried to work out how I could manage to have a quiet talk with Carol, in the hope of her having a last-minute change of mind about staying with me.

I thought the best thing was to be straight with Helen.

'Helen, Makanyanga will drive to start with, do you mind going in the back so that I can have a word with Carol?'

'No, of course not. I'd like to in any case as it is so much better for seeing any game.'

'Thanks, I appreciate that.'

So, off we went with Carol sitting between Makanyanga and me.

'Carol, won't you change your mind and stay? It will only be a few days before we have packed up William's trophies and are on our way to Nairobi.'

'You're also going after that lion, aren't you?'

'Yes, I have to, but that won't take long.'

'How can you be so sure? He's already been around long enough.'

'But this time I'll be able to concentrate on him.'

'I must admit I was in two minds whether to stay or not, but once I knew that lion was back that was that.'

I was feeling very up-tight and frustrated: here was this

wonderful girl, who seemed to like me almost as much as I liked her, and she was going to walk out on me for someone she didn't even care for. How could she do it?

I balled my hand into a fist and banged the dashboard with it.

'How can you do this? We have a chance of something really good between us and you're just going to float off?'

'I've told you everything about me; you know what I'm doing and why.'

So, it went on and on until we were approaching the airstrip and I still hadn't got anywhere.

What more could I say to stop her from leaving?

'I felt that if you stayed and we continued to get on as well as we have been then, perhaps, we could get married when we got back to Nairobi.'

My God! I'd said it.

Carol turned in her seat and looked at me. She smiled and putting her hand on my knee gave a squeeze.

'Oh, Gavin, if only I thought you meant it I'd be very tempted. I fear, though, that once you're out in your beloved bush with all those wild animals round you you'll soon forget poor little me. No, it was a very nice interlude, but I don't think it would work long term. If we'd met in ten years, when you've sobered down a bit, we might have been right for each other.'

'But we are now. As far as I'm concerned no one could be more right for me than you.'

'So, what would I do while you're on safari screwing all your clients' wives?'

'I'm not as bad as that. Helen was an exception and I am at the moment a single man.'

'All right, even if you're not having it off with all the women you come across, there is still the same question: what do I do while you're away on safari?'

'You could come with me.'

'No, that wouldn't work. How many wives do you know that go on safari with their husbands?'

'I don't know any married white hunters so I can't answer that.'

'You have answered it very well—none of them are married.'

'I could give up hunting and we could live on the farm.'

'I can't see you giving up hunting at the moment. You'd be like a bull with a sore head and that wouldn't be any fun for either of us. Gavin, I'm very flattered that you should feel like that about me but you must admit it's just not on. I shall always remember you and the time we had together. Perhaps we may meet again in the future.'

'I could almost weep. I want you to be with me more than anything in the world and yet you are going to leave me for a lot of uncertain possibilities.'

Makanyanga stopped the truck, we had arrived at the airstrip.

If I hadn't been emotionally affected by Carol, I would have noticed sooner that Philip had three passengers with him. As it was, I didn't see them until the plane came to a standstill.

William and Helen Evans were standing some way from the truck but Carol was still sitting in the cab.

'That's funny,' I said. 'What the devil's going on? Who on earth can those passengers be?'

As the plane came to a stop just near us William called out to me, 'Can you come over here please, Gavin?'

I left the truck and went to join them as the canopy was slid back and one of the passengers stepped out.

He stood on the wing and as he turned towards us I realised he was pointing an AK-47 assault rifle at us. It wasn't a weapon I'd had any experience of but I knew it had recently been introduced for use in the Russian Army.

'Just stay exactly where you are and no one will get hurt,' he said in a heavily accented voice.

Knowing only too well what an AK-47 can do I did as

he said, partly because of Helen and William. I thought, *we must just wait and see what happens next.*

He climbed carefully down the wing, keeping the AK-47 aimed at us all the time; nothing I could do there.

Then the penny dropped: the AK was pointed directly at me and not generally at the three of us.

William and Helen moved away from me and stood by the wing of the plane as first another stranger, and then Philip, came down it. A third man followed them.

All three strangers were armed.

I gave Philip a questioning look and he gave me back a "don't know what's happening" shrug.

William was speaking to them in a language I didn't understand but surmised was Russian. Then one of the three went over to the truck and brought Carol back, at gunpoint.

'William, perhaps you would be so kind as to tell me who these people are and what the hell is going on?'

'Not now. Just do as you're told and I'll tell you later when we get back to camp. We need to move the plane in among those bushes and to camouflage it. Everybody will have to help, let's get to it.'

At that moment Makanyanga came from behind the truck holding my shotgun. I don't know what he thought he could achieve but it was a very valiant try. The man who had come out of the plane last, and who I suspected was the leader, turned and, seeing him, gave him a long burst of fire from his AK. Makanyanga spun round with blood spurting from a dozen wounds and as he went down the shotgun went off harmlessly.

I ran to him as one of the three shouted to me to stop. When I reached him and had cradled him in my arms he smiled at me, tried to say something, and died.

Something cracked against my head and I saw flashing lights.

I don't know how long I was out but when I came to I found my hands were tied behind my back. Struggling up I saw the rest of the party had moved the plane and it was now well hidden among the acacia trees and they were draping a camouflage net over it.

Evans came over to look at me.

'Don't be foolish again,' he said. 'My friends don't like sudden unexpected moves.'

'What the hell is going on? Take this damn rope off my wrists.'

'All in good time. Just stay where you are for the moment.'

As I sat there I could feel blood trickling down the

side of my face. Whichever of the three bastards had hit me, he'd hit me hard. Sometime I would get my revenge for that and as I didn't know which one had done it I would revenge myself on all three. I watched them as they moved boxes that they must have taken from the plane, into the truck.

I looked around for Makanyanga's body and at last spotted it. They had dragged it into some nearby bushes and left it.

Evans and one of the three newcomers came over to me.

'You can get up now, Gavin, but don't try anything silly. We are going to release your wrists, as we want you to drive us back to camp.'

'What about Makanyanga's body? He must be buried first.'

'No time for that, he'll be all right where he is.'

'I won't drive you anywhere until he's been buried.'

They conversed for a minute in Russian.

'All right, if you want to, we will give you fifteen minutes.'

They untied my wrists and I collected a shovel from the truck.

'May I help him?' asked Philip.

'Go on then.'

We dug a narrow, shallow grave and we put Makanyanga in it with as many rocks as we could find over him; not enough I didn't think to keep the hyenas out, but there wasn't much else we could do for him.

While we were digging, we managed to say the odd thing to each other without it being noticeable.

'Who are they Philip? Any idea?'

'KGB'

'KGB! What the hell are they doing here?'

'I can only think organising terrorists.'

'Come on you two that's enough time for that, get into the truck. Gavin, you will drive. Helen you sit next to him and,' turning to the man I had concluded was the leader of the three Russians, 'one of your men in the cab to make sure he doesn't do anything he shouldn't. Gavin, we want to get back to camp as quickly as possible.'

As we went towards the truck I looked at Carol. She looked amazingly calm and collected considering that a man had just been murdered and we had been kidnapped. For a fleeting moment our eyes met and I gave her a half smile and look that I hoped indicated that she was not to worry as everything would eventually be all right. I hoped my look was more confident than I felt.

As I drove the truck away from the airstrip I was trying

to work out what the hell was happening.

Who were these new arrivals?

Were they as Philip said Russian KGB officers?

If they were, how on earth did they fit in with William Evans?

If they were something to do with terrorists were they here to help the Mau Mau rebellion that was taking place in the Kenya White Highlands?

If they were they were a bit late as that was almost over.

'I'm sorry about Makanyanga, it was quite unnecessary, he was very foolish to try to do anything.'

'What the hell do you mean, Helen, "you're sorry" and that he was foolish? He was just trying to protect himself and us from your murderous friends.'

I didn't know if the Russian sitting beside Helen spoke English so I tried him. Leaning forward I turned to him and asked, 'Are you quite comfortable Russki?'

He looked at me with a bewildered expression. So, I asked him again in Swahili.

He turned to Helen and spoke to her in Russian.

She answered him and then said to me, 'It's no good speaking to him he doesn't understand you.'

So, now I knew that at least this ugly, tough-looking guy didn't understand either of those two languages.

Just to keep me in my place he stretched his arm along the back of the seat behind Helen and pushed the muzzle of a Colt .45 automatic pistol against the side of my head. Then he gave me what I suppose he thought was a grin and said something unintelligible, which I felt sure, was both Russian and insulting. If only I'd been able to get my hands on my Rigby, which unfortunately had been "confiscated", I'd have not only taken the smile off his face but his head off as well. Now I knew why Evans had insisted on my bringing the truck rather than the safari car, with three additional people and the boxes they'd brought with them, the extra space was needed.

I considered my options and decided that there wasn't anything I could do about my predicament at the moment. I must just bide my time.

I thought about some of the things that Helen had said to me the day before and it sent a cold chill through me. Of course, no one would ever know who had fathered any child she might have from our liaison. There wouldn't be anyone alive to talk about it. When they had finished doing whatever they intended to do, and we were no longer of any use to them, they would dispose of Carol, Philip and me, and probably all the rest of my safari team as well.

I was not going to let that happen but what I was going

to do to stop them I just didn't know. I must start by trying to find out as much as I could from Helen, who shouldn't mind telling me as she believed that I would be disposed of.

'Tell me, Helen, are these three goons that have joined us Russian KGB?'

'You are a clever boy, go to the top of the class.'

'What on earth are you two doing with them? They are enemies of Britain.'

'They may be enemies of Britain but they are friends of ours.'

'How come?'

'I suppose I might as well tell you as by the time you can do anything about it we'll be gone.'

Like hell, I thought, *you mean I'll be dead.*

'Well,' she continued, 'it all started long before the war when William was at Cambridge. He was pretty fed up with things that were happening in the UK when he was approached and asked if he would like to work undercover for the Russian intelligence service. It suited his political feelings very well and also it would give him some extra funds. His family were poor and he was always short of money. Shortly after that he was also approached by the British and asked if he would like to work for the SIS. His

Russian masters were delighted and told him to go ahead as it would be ideal for them to have a "mole" in British Intelligence. He has worked for the Russians ever since and he recruited me when I became involved with him. Now it is time for him to retire from field service and we can go to Moscow where he will be a full KGB colonel. Coming to Africa like this was the ideal way for us to disappear behind the "iron curtain" after we have carried out this last job for them.'

'The mind boggles it sounds more like something from an adventure book.'

'You know what they say? Life is stranger than fiction.'

Then she had the affront to laugh explosively. Bloody cow, I'd do for her before my time was up, but for the time being I must remain calm and passive.

'So, what are you and these cut-throats doing in Africa?'

'We are helping the local people to get rid of their tyrannical overlords. Unfortunately, the Kikuyu of Kenya didn't wait, as we had told them to, but struck too soon before we had time to organise and arm them. If they had followed their instructions, instead of being beaten as they now are, they would have killed every white person in the colony and by now be in charge of their own destiny.'

'So, if it's too late, why are you and your friends here?'

'Because we are setting up an arms supply and helping to organise the people of other territories like Uganda, Tanganyika, Rhodesia, Mozambique and even the Republic of South Africa.'

My God! What I had stumbled on here. My own life now became of secondary importance, I must stop these people whatever the cost.

I thought it was time to give them a small taste of things that can happen when you're on safari so I let the truck run into an ant bear hole. There was the usual crashing noise as the truck swerved, dropped into the hole and stopped.

Helen and my guard were thrown against the dashboard and I could hear everyone in the back falling about. I only hoped that Carol and Philip were not hurt.

For a split second I had the chance of taking the pistol off my Russki friend but I desisted, as there was not much to be gained by it.

The Russian leader appeared at my window with his AK pointing at my head.

'What are you trying to do?' he said in his heavily accented English.

'Sorry, old chap, just a hole I didn't see in time. Something that often happens in the bush.'

'Get out.'

As I got out and stood beside the truck he hit me with the barrel of the AK and down I went for the second time that day. As I tried to get up he kicked me in the ribs.

'You drive more carefully in future or you will suffer.'

I saw William Evans come round the side of the truck and he spoke to my assailant in Russian and they argued for a few minutes. I guessed Evans was telling him to go easy for the moment, as they needed me, at any rate, until they had someone else who could guide them.

Everyone was now out of the truck and Carol started to come towards me even though she was told to stay where she was.

'Stay there, Carol, just do what they tell you. These jokers are not gentlemen. I'm okay, don't worry.'

I could see Philip in the background with the third Russian pointing another AK at his ribs.

They'd certainly got us tied down at the moment, but hopefully our turn would come.

After we'd all sweated away for about twenty minutes or so we finally got the truck back on the road and were ready to proceed.

This time the Russian leader, who I'd heard Evans call Kalashnikov, told Helen and the other goon to get into the back of the truck so that he could ride with me in the front.

'No more tricks,' he said. 'Get us to the camp without any further delay.'

I had a feeling he meant what he said and in any case I wanted to get back as soon as possible as then there might be an opportunity to turn the tables. I particularly wanted to have Mkamba with me and only hoped I would get an opportunity to say something to him before he took any action off his own bat.

CHAPTER 14

t was late afternoon by the time we drove into the camp.

When I'd stopped the truck, Mkamba and Kidogo came towards us, but luckily neither was carrying a rifle. They looked surprised to see not only Sir William and Lady Evans back but also Philip Ryland and three strangers. Having put Kalashnikov to the test during our drive I knew that he didn't understand Swahili so I guessed that neither did the third Russian. Anyway, I had to take a chance.

'Be very careful these men are bad enemies, do nothing until I tell you. Mkamba, pretend you speak very little English,' I said, knowing that only Philip and Carol realised that Mkamba spoke near-perfect English.

'What are you saying? Stop speaking in that language

and speak English at all times,' said an enraged Kalashnikov.

'I'm extremely sorry, old chap, but I'm sure everyone must be hungry and unless I give instructions, we won't get any food.'

'Give the instructions in English.'

'As, except for Mkamba who does understand a little, none of my staff speak English, giving them instructions in that language won't achieve much.'

He turned and shouted to Evans in Russian and I imagined that he was asking him if what I'd told him was true. The answer he got must have been in the affirmative as he turned back to me and said, 'All right but keep it short and be very careful.'

I went over to Mkamba and Kidogo. 'These men are terrorists as are Bwana and Memsaab Sir. They have killed Makanyanga and intend to kill all of us when they have finished with us. We will play their game for the time being, so do nothing until I tell you. Do not tell the others what is happening but give instructions for supper to be prepared.'

'Are you all right, Bwana, your head is bleeding and your jacket is covered in blood stains?'

'My head wound is only minor, Mkamba, and the

blood on my clothes is from Makanyanga.'

Then in English I called out to everyone that food would be ready in about an hour. I turned again to Kalashnikov. 'What sleeping arrangements do you want? Who is to go where and in which tents?'

William Evans had now come over to where we were standing.

'May I suggest, Kalashnikov, that the two women share the tent that was Helen's and mine, I sleep in the gun tent and you three have beds made up in the mess tent. I've no doubt you'll want McKenzie and Ryland chained to a post by the fire where we can all see them.'

'Yes, that is good. McKenzie, you heard what Sir William said, get it done, but before you start, give me the key to your gun rack.'

I handed him my key and was glad to remember that Mkamba always carried a duplicate.

I got the accommodation arrangements organised as best I could, but as we didn't have a lot of extra bedding it looked as if Philip and I were going to be sleeping on the ground. While I was seeing to the arrangements I managed to say a few words to Carol, which was merely: 'Keep your chin up, don't let on Mkamba can speak good English, don't argue with them and, never fear, it will be all right in the end.'

She gave me a nervous smile but wasn't able to reply as Russki number two came up to see what was going on.

When everything was organised as well as it could be, I asked if I could have a shower, change my clothes and have my head wound attended to.

The answer was 'no'. All very jolly, I thought.

A meal was served by Opio and Juma, both looking very nervous and upset. I thought how different it was to the dinner we had the first night Carol joined us. I must do my best to see that she was all right but at the moment I couldn't think how.

Hardly a word was spoken in English as we sat round the table eating,

I made a point of stuffing as much food down as I could, who knew when I'd get another meal.

While we were eating they were jabbering away together in Russian and at times seemed to be arguing. I tried to make some sense of what they were saying but it was not possible. All I did know was that the Ulianoffs were mentioned several times. This had obviously been a well-planned operation and planned well in advance. I decided that I could not really blame myself for not having been suspicious before the event as it all seemed too absurd to contemplate.

At the end of the meal Philip, unthinking, got up and wandered away from the table. Russki number two, who by now I'd realised was the strong-arm member of their team, was up in a flash and knocked Philip to the ground and held a pistol to his head.

'Don't do anything unless you're told to or it may have drastic results. And,' continued Kalashnikov, 'don't think you're indispensable because you are a pilot. We have our own with us.'

So, that's what the third Russian was—a pilot.

With the information that Helen had stupidly given me, and my own deductions, I now felt I, more or less, knew what was what.

After the meal we were allowed, one at a time and escorted by "strong-arm", to go to the shower and lavatory tent. At last, I felt clean again having also been allowed to get a change of clothes from what, a million years ago, had been my tent.

When I got back to the fire Kalashnikov called me over to the mess tent.

'McKenzie, we are going to move the camp down to the coast to a spot near Jardini. Do you know it?'

'Yes.'

'Can you guide us there without going through any townships?'

'Yes.'

'Is there anything we need for the journey?'

'Fuel and more supplies.'

'Can we get what is needed locally?'

'We can get them from the local store.'

'How long will that take?'

'The round trip, about three to four hours.'

'Good. We will do that first thing in the morning and then we can start our journey to the coast in the afternoon.'

I had not told him the truth. We had enough fuel to get us to a supply depot where we could call on our journey but doing it this way I thought there might be a chance of making some sort of contact with the District Commissioner or, at least, the game ranger. If not, then perhaps I would get a chance to pass a message to Mr Patel at the store.

Our Russian friends decided that the best way of securing Philip and me was to take one of the gun rack chains, pass it through a steel hoop hammered into a large immovable log placed near the fire, and then to padlock one end round one of Philip's ankles and the other round one of mine. Not a very comfortable way to spend a night.

Mkamba came over, ostensibly to make up the fire, and grunted to me in Swahili that he had attached his hunting knife under the driver's side of the hunting car's dashboard. Well, that wasn't much, I would have preferred it if it had been my Webley .45 revolver, but at least it was a start.

At last, the camp settled down and I was able to have a whispered conversation with Philip.

'By now they should have started a search for you and your plane.'

'No, they won't do that for at least a week.'

'A week! Of course, they won't wait that long.'

'Yes, they will. I haven't had a chance to tell you yet but those Russians arrived at the office with a letter and cheque from Sir William. In the letter it said that if the three of them managed to get to Nairobi before the safari returned then I was to fly them down to join you. It also said that he would like me to stay on for a week so that I could fly people around as required. The cheque he enclosed covered a full week's hire plus some extra for, as he put it, personal expenses. So, the plane and I are booked out for a week and everybody has been told. No one is going to think it at all odd that I haven't returned and because of my being booked they won't worry about you either. That is unless you've got another safari booked right away, you haven't have you?'

'No, I haven't, damn it! I'd been banking on a search party out looking for us. That's a bit of a sod to say the least of it. We really are on our own.'

It appeared that the three Russians were taking it in turns to mount guard so there was not much we could do during the night except get some sleep in preparation for the events of the next day.

CHAPTER 15

Poor old Philip hadn't had much sleep during the night and was stiff from sleeping on the ground and being chained to a log hadn't helped a lot. I wasn't too bad as I was used to sleeping more or less anywhere when I was hunting on my own and was not like Philip who was used to sleeping on a soft bed—or something even softer!

We were herded like a lot of school kids to do our morning ablutions and then sat round the table for a "jolly" breakfast.

The three "jailers" and Evans looked their usual charming selves, Helen didn't look happy, and Carol looked scared.

The conversation was restricted to asking for something to be passed and saying a curt "thank you" when it was. When we'd finished eating, Kalashnikov rose to his feet.

'The plan for today is that the truck will go to the stores to fill the fuel drums and to fetch any further supplies that are required. Lady Evans, will you check what is required for the kitchen?'

'Well, I'll try, but as I don't speak the lingo it may be difficult.'

'Don't any of those blacks speak English?'

'Only one speaks a little, I think. Isn't that right, Gavin?'

'Yes, quite right; Mkamba speaks a few words.'

'Then, Lady Evans, you will have to use Ryland as your interpreter. Please get on with it without delay.'

He nodded to the "pilot" to go with Philip; which he did, carrying an AK at the ready.

'You, McKenzie, will drive the truck to a spot near the store where you will be left, with one of my men, while Sir William and another of my men goes to the store for the supplies. When they have collected everything that is required they will pick you up on their way back.'

'Wouldn't it be better if I went to the store with them to make sure we get everything we require?'

'What and have a talk to the storeman or leave little

notes for him? No, McKenzie, just you follow instructions if you want to stay in one piece. Now show me on the map where the store is and where you propose waiting for them.'

I showed him where the store was situated and then I had a little idea so I marked the spot by the river, where Carol and I had got to know each other so well, as the place where I and my escort would wait.

'Why there?'

'Because, my dear Kalashnikov, it will be easy for Evans to get to the store and back as all he has to do is to follow the river.'

'Yes, that is good. I don't want the truck lost or to lose the pleasure of your company McKenzie.'

'Neither me yours, Kalashnikov.'

When Philip and Helen had completed their lists and the fuel drums had been loaded onto the truck it was time to go. I was taking with me: Evans, the *pilot* and the *hard one*.

It was decided that the *hard one* would go to the store with Evans while the other Russian looked after me.

I wished we'd been using the safari car, as then I would have had a chance of collecting the hunting knife Mkamba had put in it for me.

It was another great African morning, with lots of game on the plains, as we drove towards the river and Carol's and my pool. It now seemed as if all the fun we'd had was part of a different lifetime.

Would we ever be able to enjoy ourselves together again?

Yes, I felt sure things would come right in the end, but the end might be a long, uncomfortable way off.

When we finally reached the pool the sun was beating down and it was a really hot day. It was good to get out of the truck, which had turned into an oven. The other three, not being used to it as I was, were almost steaming with heat.

'You stay here and don't try anything, Gavin. This man has been given instructions to shoot you at the least sign of trouble.'

'I really go for you in a big way, Evans. I thought what a creepy little cur you were when I first met you and now I know my first impression was right.'

'Say what you like, it makes no difference to me. Helen and I won't have to put up with you much longer.'

'That may be as it is but I'm sure Helen will miss me ... Well, part of me anyway.'

He looked angry, that usually bland, impassive face

went even redder than it already was with the heat. So, he had got some feelings after all.

He started to say something, then changed his mind. Turning to the other two he spoke to them in Russian and then climbed into the passenger seat of the truck.

As the truck disappeared my mind was exploring all the possibilities. I had about an hour or so before they returned.

I was glad Evans had left the *pilot* and not the other Russian as I felt I had more chance with this one.

I walked to the edge of the pool and looked along the river. Across the river, on the edge of the bank, inconspicuously sunning themselves, I could see three crocodiles. Just what I wanted.

I turned to the Russian and pointed to the pool, and then to myself, and then made swimming motions with my arms.

He shook his head in the negative.

I stood and smiled at him and in an exaggerated manner wiped the sweat off my brow. He grinned. Then I did the swimming motion again.

He looked at me for a moment, then nodded in agreement but at the same time holding up his AK made it quite clear that if I tried to swim away he would shoot me.

'No intention of doing that, old chap,' I grinned at him.

Pulling off my sweat-soaked clothes I took another look to make sure the crocs were still on the bank then in I went. I just stood for a few minutes up to my neck in the cool water. Looking across the river I could see the opposite bank where the crocs were sunbathing—or had been sunbathing! Time to get out.

As I climbed onto the bank I looked back and could see the ripple on the water made by the crocs as they swam, practically submerged, into the pool to investigate whether there was a meal waiting for them.

I walked past my Russian friend so that he turned away from the water.

With gestures and signs I made it clear how good the cool water had been.

Then I made further signs to indicate that he should also enjoy the cool water.

He kept nodding his head from side to side to indicate that he couldn't go in because of me.

I moved further away from the river and sitting on a log, lit my pipe. I then indicated that I would stay where I was.

I could see he was weakening and the thought of the water was almost too much for him.

It was a really hot day and seemed to be getting hotter by the minute. My Russian friend was soaked with sweat.

Suddenly, he said something that was quite unidentifiable and sitting down with the AK beside him took off his shoes, socks and trousers.

Grinning at me he stood up, picked up the AK, which he held across his chest, and walking backwards he went towards the river.

He watched me all the time as he reached the bank and stretched back with one leg to lower himself onto the first *step*. From where I was sitting I couldn't see the surface of the water, only the bank and the Russian.

He had a sickly grin of anticipation on his face at the thought of the cool water that he was about to lower his genitals into.

Then I saw the croc. With their immense power they are able to propel themselves out of the water to a height of some six feet and, that is what this one did. He came into sight as he launched himself into the air and at his prey. He closed his jaws on the Russian's upper thigh and took him back into the water. The Russian's face was contorted with horror and fear and he emitted agonised screams.

I jumped up and ran to the bank where, looking down

at the water, I could see my Russian friend, still with the AK in his hands, being dragged under the water.

As the croc pulled him into deeper water it started to turn over and over. Crocs don't bite bits off people or animals they tear them apart by whirling them round and round as they turn over and over.

After a few seconds the croc let go and the Russian frantically struggled towards the bank. When he was in shallow water he stood up but only momentary as he immediately overbalanced, only having one leg left to stand on. At that moment he was hit by a second croc that took hold of his abdomen, and the third one came up from under the Russian and had him by his shoulder. Then the two crocs started to fight over him, and the water was churned to foam—a foam coloured red from the Russian's blood. He came up once more but by this time he was silent and I could not see his face as there was not much left to see. Then he was gone and they were fighting over his remains. It was a horrifying sight and, even though the man was an enemy and probably responsible for the torture and death of dozens of people, I could not help having a feeling of pity for him. Still, looking on the bright side, that was one less to worry about.

Damn and blast where was the AK? I desperately needed it.

As the water settled, the three crocs having each got a piece of meat to chew on, I saw the glint of the barrel under the water five or six feet from the bank.

I waited until I thought the crocodiles were busy digesting the bits they had torn off the Russian then I slid into the water and made for the AK. Immediately, one of the crocs spun round in the water and made for me. I was still near the bank so I was up it in a jiffy but only just in the nick of time. His jaws closed and his front most teeth actually gripped the bottom of my trouser leg. I thought I was a goner as I started to slip back towards the water. He opened his jaws to get a better grip and I was onto the bank rolling away from him. He tried to climb out after me but it was too difficult for him to climb the rocks so he fell back and swam away.

I sat for a few minutes gasping with exertion and fear. If there is one thing I'm really frightened of it's crocodiles.

When I'd regained my composure, I went to the edge of the bank again to see if I could have another go at getting my hands that AK. As I was staring down at it there was a roar and the truck drove out from the trees. I had lost all count of time and discretion and now I was back in the bag.

William got out of the truck and came towards me with the Russian just behind him, both were pointing AKs at me.

I was cursing myself, I could have been away from here, and even if I'd had to go without the AK, it would have been better than being a prisoner again.

'What the devil has been going on here?' shouted Evans.

'Something rather awful,' I said playing for time as I thought up a plausible story. 'The chap you left with me was so hot he wanted to stand in the river to cool down. I tried to tell him, but he didn't understand English, that there were crocodiles in there but he just thought I was trying to be difficult. I even tried to get hold of him to stop him and he nearly shot me. In the end there was nothing I could do, as you can see he took off his shoes and trousers, he got into the river and they got him. I tried to rescue him, look at where one of the crocs actually tore my trouser leg, but it was no good. I'm afraid he is dead and eaten.'

William Evans looked at me, trying to figure out if I was telling the truth or not. Then the Russian spoke to him and he replied in Russian telling him, I supposed what I'd told him. From his attitude I thought the Russian was going to shoot me but Evans restrained him.

They spoke to each other for a few more minutes when Evans turned back to me.

'Where is the assault rifle our man had?'

'I don't know, there was too much going on to worry about that.'

'Where do you think it is?'

'It must be on the bottom of the river.'

They went to the riverbank and looking into the water saw the AK on the riverbed. Only one of the crocodiles was still in the pool.

'You'd better go in and get it, McKenzie.'

'If I go into that water I'm croc meat.'

'I don't know if that matters to me very much,' Evans said.

'Okay, so how do you get back to camp and how does your fucking leader get himself and your party to the coast?'

I was ruffled, I was sure that for a moment he really meant it, and I could imagine what would happen if I got into the river.

He stood looking at me and then said something to his companion.

'See if you can find something that we can drag it in with.'

I decided that it didn't make a lot of difference to my situation if they got the AK back so I might as well tell them how to do it.

'Two of the crocs have gone back upstream, so if you shoot at this one you will scare him away and then your goon can pop in and get the gun for you.'

'We'll do that, but you can pop in and get it instead of my companion.'

'Fine,' I said. This was great, once I'd got my hands on that AK I could take them out, two to one in a shooting battle wouldn't be too bad for someone of my experience and expertise, as long as I could be out of the water before any crocs came back.

William Evans looked at me and smiled.

'On second thoughts, you're right, my companion can go in and get it.'

They fired a few rounds at the croc and it made off up river to join its friends. Then the Russian jumped into the river grabbed the assault rifle and scrambled up the bank again at record speed. I can't say I blamed him.

'Right, get behind the wheel, McKenzie, and drive us back to camp without any further delay.'

CHAPTER 16

We arrived back at the camp long after we should have done as not only had we been delayed at the river but we also had a puncture and the wheel had been devilish difficult to get off.

The three of us had travelled in the cab together but hardly a word had been spoken either in English or in Russian.

On our arrival, Kalashnikov made up for the lack of dialogue on the journey. He shouted and ranted and raved in Russian for a good ten minutes and I now knew something else about this bunch, Kalashnikov was definitely senior to Evans. This meant that if Evans really was going to Moscow as a KGB colonel then this man, Kalashnikov, must be a really big fish.

At last, Kalashnikov turned to me.

'What did you do to my man? I think you killed him and threw him into the river so that the crocodiles would eat him.'

'Come on, Kalashnikov, be your age. If I'd managed to catch out your goon and kill him why the hell would I have thrown his gun away; the only point of killing him would have been to arm myself against you bastards.'

He punched me in the face and I staggered back against the truck. As I came forward to take him, the other Russian stuck the barrel of his AK into my ribs and Evans shouted, 'Stand still or he'll shoot you.'

I stood where I was and, even though my nose was bleeding, I was feeling better. These guys were getting nervous, they were starting to do things out of emotion and not from cold logic, and anyway they were now one down and three to go.

I came to the conclusion that there was more to Kalashnikov's temper than the fact that he had lost one of his men, but I couldn't imagine what it could be. However, I didn't have to wait long to find out.

'There are some important documents in the plane that will have to be collected,' Sir William Evans said. From the look on his face, and from the obviously hard things that had been said, I came to the conclusion that he was being held responsible for them having been left behind. 'We will be staying here another night so that you can go back to the plane to collect them.'

'You want me to go in the morning?'

'No, as soon as you have had some food. You will have to travel back in the dark.'

'Will you be coming with me?'

'No, Pavlov will.'

So, that was the chap's name. The first time anyone had mentioned it.

'That'll be fun.'

'Be very careful, McKenzie, that man is a professional killer and he enjoys his work.'

'I'm sure that compared to you he has hardly started in the killing game.'

'What, may I ask, do you mean by that?'

God, this man was still prissy, even now.

'I mean that as a traitor you must have caused the death of countless people and all from the safety of your desk in some Whitehall office.'

'How dare you call me a traitor?'

'You're weird man, just weird.'

I turned on my heel and walked towards the mess tent.

Carol and Helen were there and Carol came over to me, to look at my bloody face.

'I'm going to get something to bath it with. How could they do that to you? They're vile people.' And then looking at Helen, she added, 'All of them.'

When she came back, she had a bowl of water and a cloth and she knelt beside me and washed the blood from my face. The punch hadn't meant much to me, but it was nice having Carol fuss over me. Helen stood in the background watching us and so did, whatever his name was, Pavlov.

'Are you all right, Carol? Are you being treated properly?'

'Yes, but I want to get away from here, I don't like it.'

'Nor me, but our time will come.'

'What happened to the Russian that was with you?'

'He took a little swim in the pool where we swam but, unfortunately, the crocs didn't like him as much as they did you and me. Perhaps I said that wrongly, perhaps I should have said that they liked him better than they did you and me.'

'They didn't eat him?'

'I'm afraid to say that they did.'

'Ugh. How awful. What a way to die.'

I put my arm round her shoulder and gave it a squeeze, she looked up at me and managed a small smile.

'Don't worry, Carol, everything will come out okay in the end.'

Kalashnikov strutted into the mess tent.

'Enough of that, McKenzie, eat your food and be on your way. Lady Evans, please take this young lady back to your tent and keep her there until this man has left camp.'

I gave Carol another squeeze and kissed her cheek.

'See you later and don't forget what I told you.'

I watched her as she went away with Helen and wished that we were somewhere together and away from all these dangerous people.

'Shall I take the hunting car?' I asked Kalashnikov after Pavlov and I had had a quick snack.

'Yes, I want you there and back as quickly as possible.'

'Can we take one of my staff with me?'

'No.'

'But what happens if we bog-down or something?'

'The two of you will be able to manage.'

'That may be so but it could take us hours if we went in a pig hole or something.'

'Didn't I make myself clear? The two of you go and no one else.'

'Okay, if that's the way you want it but don't blame me if it takes ages to get back.'

'That is the point, McKenzie, I will blame you.'

'I don't think that——'

The roar of Rommel being started stopped me in mid-speech. The three of us went out of the mess tent to see what was happening. The truck was moving away from where I'd left it parked and as it crossed the clearing, making for the track down the hill, I could see Philip crouched over the steering wheel.

My God! He was making a run for it.

To my left I saw Pavlov bringing up his AK but as I started to move towards him I was stopped by Kalashnikov pointing a pistol at me.

'Stay where you are, McKenzie, or I'll blow your head off.'

I had no alternative other than to do what he said.

The AK jumped in Pavlov's hands, and I could see Philip slump forward; his foot must have come off the throttle as, although the truck continued for a few yards, it slowed to a crawl and then stalled. Pavlov ran over to it, opened the door, and pulled out the unconscious figure. Then he did something I was quite unprepared for; he placed the muzzle of his AK against the back of Philip's head and fired a shot.

I left Kalashnikov, at that moment I didn't care if he shot me or not, and rushed to where Philip lay. The top of his head had been blown away and he was dead.

Mkamba came up beside me.

'Do you know what he was doing?' I asked him in Swahili.

'He saw the keys were still in the truck and he thought everyone was occupied so he told me to stay here to tell you where he was making for if he managed to get away.'

I was devastated. Philip was an old, old friend and to see him shot down like a wild dog knocked me for six.

Carol came up to us, she was weeping.

'Poor Philip,' she cried. 'He hadn't a chance. They're going to have to kill us all now, aren't they?'

'Hold on, Carol, they won't do it yet. If we're clever we still have a chance. They need me and the rest of you more than ever now. There is only one way out of here, as both the pilots have been killed, and that's by road. They don't stand a chance without me to guide them. Play it cool, cause no trouble and nobody try anything until I give the word.'

I walked over to the three Russians, okay one was meant to be an Englishman, but I no longer counted him as one, and keeping as calm as I could, I stopped in front of them.

'What did that murderous little son-of-a-bitch do that for? It would have been just as easy for him to stop the truck.'

'I and Sir William are annoyed he did it, not that we lament Mr Ryland very much as he deserved what he got, but we are upset to lose our pilot.'

'You and your compatriots are nothing more nor less than fucking pigs.'

I thought he was going to hit me again but he changed his mind, perhaps I'd become too valuable.

'You had better bury your friend before you go to the plane, unless you want to leave him to the hyenas.'

It took a great deal of will power to stop me just having a go right then and there regardless of the outcome, but I remembered Carol, Mkamba and the rest, and managed to restrain myself. I could see by the look in their eyes that they knew that I had almost reached the point of no return.

We buried Philip with as much dignity as we could muster.

After we'd placed him in the grave we'd dug we covered him with lots of bits of rock, to keep out the scavengers, and then covered the whole thing over with earth.

Boculy, who was a Christian, had made a cross that we placed at the head of the grave.

Then Carol, Mkamba, Kidogo, and all the remaining boys and I gathered round his grave and I said a few words in English, and Swahili, about what a good friend he'd been and how we'd all miss him. Carol held my hand as she wept, and none of the rest of us had a completely dry eye.

The bloody Russians had the good sense to keep well clear and not to try to hurry us or anything like that, although, out of the corner of my eye, I could see Pavlov, with his AK-47, watching our every move.

I knew that without a doubt I was going to kill Pavlov, somehow, sometime.

I had killed a lot of opposing solders during the war and, unlike some of the guys serving with me, had never enjoyed it and had always felt a sense of guilt. This time it would be different, I wanted to kill Pavlov, and I would enjoy doing it.

CHAPTER 17

ate the meal that was prepared for me, alone in the mess tent.

What was I going to do next?

I didn't know, I would just have to wait and see what happened and what opportunities occurred.

I could see Pavlov over by the hunting car checking that it had fuel and that everything was in order.

As it was now almost dusk it would mean that the whole journey, both ways, would have to be driven in the dark. Not an easy task but perhaps it would give me more opportunity to take some sort of positive action. Something had got to be done, and done soon, as we were running out of time.

Mkamba came into the tent carrying a cup of coffee.

'You're turning into a very good mess steward,' I joked with him in order to ease the tension. 'Now, don't forget, don't start anything while I'm away. If, however, anything happens to me then you must do what you can to get yourself and the others away. You've still got the gun chain key, haven't you?'

Before he could answer Evans came into the mess tent.

'What are you two talking about? You can just cut it out and be on your way, McKenzie.'

I desperately wanted to see Carol before I left but I knew it wasn't possible.

When I got into the driving seat of the safari car Pavlov climbed in after me, not beside me, but in the row of seats behind me. Clever stuff, I thought, now his AK could point directly at me all the time and also he could see every move I made.

When the car bumped away from the camp it was already dark and I was going to have to pay attention to the track or we could quite easily get lost. The moon would be up soon and that would at least make driving a little easier.

As I drove, I was racking my brains for an idea on how to trick my guard and to take control of the situation. I decided that the best chance was going to be when we were driving up a dry ravine that was situated close to the landing strip. The incline was quite steep and the going very rough. Pavlov would be hanging on for dear life the way I intended to drive up it. The track there was overhung by vegetation that would shade it from the moon and make it dark. But I still hadn't any real idea what I going to do, anything was going to be difficult with him being so well placed to see my every move. If I did anything suspicious I didn't think he'd kill me, he needed me too much, but he would be very nasty and I could do without that.

The first hour-and-a-half went without incident and I reckoned it would be the best part of another hour before we reached the ravine.

Pavlov signalled that he wanted me to stop the car. With signs he indicated he wanted a drink. I handed him the water bottle. Would this be my chance?

He made me stay in the car while he got out and standing a few feet away, where he could see me and I couldn't get at him, he took a drink. Then he got back into the car and, without offering me a drink, indicated that I should drive on.

It was now cold and clear with bright moonlight; a great evening to take a drive with someone you loved but not with some Russki pig you intended to kill.

It wouldn't be long before we reached the ravine and that was, I was now certain, the most likely place for me to take some sort of action.

I dropped down another gear as we climbed up the beginning of the ravine. It seemed quite dark with all the overhanging foliage screening the moon and the going was very rough. As the hunting car climbed out and over the top we had a rock face to one side of the car and a steep, rocky, short incline on the other. It was, I decided, now or never.

I waited until we were passing under some stunted trees that overhung the track from the rock face and blacked out the moon then I spun the wheel hard over towards the incline.

It was like being on a roller coaster, the car bucked and slurred for a couple of seconds then the near side wheels dropped into a crevice and over we went. Being prepared, and having the steering wheel to hang onto, I remained in the car and went with it but my Russian friend was thrown out of the open side and disappeared from sight.

I'm not sure how many times the car rolled over, but I think it was three, before it came to a standstill at a crazy angle on its side.

I was fine, hardly even bruised. The first thing I did

was to feel under the dash. Yes, there it was, good old Mkamba. I pulled the eight-inch blade hunting knife from the place Mkamba had hidden it and felt a bit better. At least I was now armed, even if a knife wasn't much of an answer to an AK.

Where was that Russian pig? He might even have been killed when he was thrown out of the car.

As I looked around there was a flash from back up the slope, a crack and then a thump as a bullet hit the side of the car.

I scrambled out and slid down the opposite side, ending up under the bottom of the car which was at an angle of forty-five degrees with the two wheels on one side resting on the ground and the other two in the air. Then there was a bam-bam-bam as Pavlov fired a burst from his AK at the car. It was harmless as far as I was concerned as the shots either embedded themselves in the car body or hit the steel sides and, in a shower of sparks, ricocheted off.

I could hear him swearing in Russian as he fired some more shots and then I heard him change the magazine and fire another short burst. This man was meant to be a professional but he certainly wasn't behaving like one.

All went quiet.

I thought about moving but decided I was better where

I was as at least here I had some steel round me and, lying snugly into the corner where the ground and the upended car met, I was partially concealed.

I lay there and waited.

After a short time I heard a dislodged stone roll down the incline past the car.

So, he was moving down towards me for the kill.

I was in the shadow so I would at least have the advantage that he would be coming in from the bright moonlight.

What would he do?

If he had any sense, he would go down the slope past the car and then turn back, and standing below, blast hell out of me.

Another stone rolled past the car.

He must be close now.

Should I make a run for it?

No, no point, I'd be dead before I'd run twenty yards.

Suddenly, there he was. He came round the car holding onto it with one hand to stop him from sliding down the incline and in the other hand he held his AK, which was pointing into the air.

I took immediate action: I leant forward and grabbed his testicles with my left hand. He let out a yell and involuntarily fired a short burst into the air. Then he tried to bring the AK round to bear on me but he was having difficulties because the upended car wheel was in his way.

Leaning forward I stabbed him in the thigh with the hunting knife. By now he was screaming blue murder.

I pulled the knife out and then plunged it into his thigh again.

Then I heard a great sound: it was the clatter of his AK as it bounced down the car as he let go in order to try and release his testicles from the grinding my left hand was giving them.

I tried to get my knife into a position for a body blow but I was too restricted in my movements. He was trying desperately to pull away from me so, quite suddenly, I pulled the knife out of his leg and at the same time released my hold on his balls and he overbalanced and cart-wheeled backwards down the slope.

In a flash, I was after him.

When I reached him, he was lying on his back just beginning to try to get to his feet.

I straddled him and forced him back down.

I placed the point of the razor-sharp hunting knife on his throat, just below his Adam's apple.

He said something in Russian, in a pleading voice.

In the moonlight I could see his fear-crazed eyes looking up at me as he lay there not daring to move.

I hesitated for one second then I said to him in a quiet, calm voice, 'My dear Pavlov, you have just cold-bloodily killed a very good friend of mine and for him, and for the many others that I suspect you have done the same to, I am going to execute you.'

He gave me a sort of relieved smile, he must have thought I was saying something nice to him.

If I waited any longer I knew I'd relent so I leant forward onto the knife hilt and plunged the blade into his throat. His eyes clouded and his body arched under me as he gave a gurgling cough. Blood gushed out of his mouth and with a long shudder, he died.

I had been judge, jury and executioner. I had no regrets or feelings of guilt. When he'd killed Philip I'd made my decision and now I'd carried it out.

I rested for a few minutes to compose myself and then I examined the car.

It had had it and there was no way I was going to be able to right it on my own and, even if I could have done, I would never have been able to get it back up the slope.

Then I found the AK and checked it over. It was okay except for one thing, he had fired all but two rounds.

I checked his pockets for a spare magazine but there wasn't one. Then I checked the ground round about in case he had dropped one. Except for the empty one he had thrown down, no luck.

Damn and blast! If only the idiot hadn't been so trigger happy I would have had at least one full magazine.

I opened the back compartment of the hunting car where I always carried a few clothes and things in case a client needed a change. The clothes I was wearing were blood soaked, luckily Pavlov's and not mine, I was pleased to be able to change them.

I reviewed my situation. I was at least free, and it was now two down and two to go. However, it was going to take me a long time to get back to camp on foot.

My biggest worry was what they would do to Carol and co when Pavlov and I didn't arrive back by morning.

Thinking about it, I came to the conclusion that probably they would not be too worried until evening as they would consider that we must have been delayed by a bog-down or breakdown.

If I went hard I could be back at camp by the next afternoon but I would have to hang around as there was no way I could just walk in and take over. That would have been possible if only I'd got a better supply of ammunition. It was, in the circumstances, going to be a "catch-as-catch-can" situation, which would have a better chance of success once it was dark.

It looked as if I myself was now going to become a 'Moonlight Predator'.

CHAPTER 18

gathered the few things I'd got and prepared to set off on my march back to camp and God knows what.

The hyenas had arrived. I could hear them giggling and crunching Pavlov's bones. Jolly good luck to them. It was no more than he deserved.

It was already dawn and another beautiful African morning. I stepped out at my best pace, wanting to cover as much ground before it got really hot.

All I had with me were: a half-full water bottle, a pipe and tin of tobacco that had been in the hunting car's locker, a box of matches, the AK with two rounds of ammunition, Mkamba's hunting knife, a pocket compass, a map that was meant to show the area but didn't, and a stub of pencil.

I came to the conclusion that perhaps I was not perfectly equipped to be going after two heavily armed, unscrupulous foreign agents. But what choice did I have? I couldn't waste time going to try to find assistance. I must get back as quickly as possible and do what I could to save Carol and the rest of them, or die in the attempt.

I stopped and took a drink. I hadn't covered many miles and it was already getting hot. Still, I would reach a stream in an hour or so where I could refill my water bottle and I would soon be going through the forest as it would be a shortcut and also be cooler.

As I trudged along I couldn't help thinking about Carol and how beautiful she was and what a wonderful lover she had turned out to be. What a day that had been by the river and what I'd have given to be there with her again now instead of trudging along towards what could well turn out to be disaster.

I wondered how Mkamba was getting on and only hoped that he didn't do anything silly. I certainly didn't want him killed.

What was I going to do when I got to the camp? I still didn't have a plan or see how I could make one. I only had two rounds in my AK and two people to deal with, that is if one disregarded Helen Evans. Was she any sort of threat? Yes, I thought, she probably was to a certain extent. It could be dangerous if she was given the job of guarding Carol and disposing of her should any emergency arise.

The more I thought about it the more I became convinced that I must get into the camp, somehow, and release Carol, and as many of the others as I could, before I tried to deal with the two Russians.

So, it was definitely an after-dark operation and, probably, one for the middle of the night. I would, however, try to get to within sight of the camp during the afternoon so that I could observe what was happening, and where everyone was placed, while it was still light.

I had reached the forest and was walking through it with my mind fully occupied with my thoughts and plans.

Then two things happened: firstly, I got a sudden whiff of wood smoke, secondly, I heard a rasping sawing snarl.

I stopped in my tracks.

A measly fifteen to twenty yards to my left front was a large leopard standing astride a prostrate baboon. I should have seen him long before this but my mind had been fully occupied with my problems.

Under my breath I cursed myself for a fool. How could I have been so stupid?

A leopard is a very dangerous animal. In fact, he is

considered by a lot of hunters to be the most dangerous. He is very fast, very powerful, aggressive and, unlike nearly all other animals, kills just for the joy of it. He is also used to attacking an upright target. Lions, for instance, prey on four-legged beasts so an animal that stands upright on two legs is a bit of a problem, he's not quite sure what is the best method to attack and kill. A leopard's favourite diet is, however, baboon and a baboon stands on its hind legs so to a leopard a man is just another baboon. When attacking, a leopard springs at you and attempts to get a good hold on your shoulders with its front paws while it buries its fangs into your neck. Then it brings its rear legs as high up your body as it can get them and, inserting its claws into your abdomen, straightens out and disembowels you with one fell swoop. Not very pleasant! Even if you are lucky enough to get away from him after the attack and haven't been disembowelled, you are likely to die from the infection carried on his talons unless you are able to get immediate medical attention.

This leopard was very angry, he thought I was after his kill. He kept letting off his terrifying growl and swishing his tail as he crouched low over his prey. Then, to add to his irritation, the baboon, which was still alive, started to move. It was funny, in a way, I could see the perplexed look on the leopard's face: what should he do now? He knew he had to finish the baboon off or get out of his way, baboons have very powerful jaws and the leopard wouldn't want to risk being bitten, but he didn't want to take his eyes off me.

He made a choice and moved off the baboon and with his body almost flat on the ground started to move towards me. His jaws were gaping and his tail was swishing from side to side.

I stood with the AK at the ready but the last thing I wanted to do was to shoot him. I didn't want to kill him, and I certainly didn't want to use one of my precious bullets.

Sometimes you can shoo an animal away, I've often done it with lions, buff and even elephants, but not this chap. He intended to have me.

There was nothing for it, as he started to come across the ground, I brought up the AK, it felt very strange after my hunting rifles, and walloped him. He went up in the air completed a somersault and dropped to the ground dead.

I stood and waited for a minute to make sure he was finished, I couldn't use my one remaining bullet, and I didn't want to get close enough to use my hunting knife, just in case.

The baboon, in the meantime, was making a lot of noise and dragging itself away from me. He was badly mauled and would obviously die in pain but there nothing I could do for him.

Once he'd disappeared, I sat on a convenient fallen tree and filled and lit my pipe. I felt I deserved a short rest and I was beginning to feel the pangs of hunger.

As I puffed away, I was suddenly aware of three sets of eyes looking at me from among the bushes. They were human eyes.

I stood up and shouted, '*Jambo.*'

The bushes parted and out came an old friend of mine, Katunga, accompanied by two of his sons.

Katunga was a very likeable old rogue who had at one time, many years before, been my father's number two gun bearer. He had then been approached by another professional hunter, who was not a great friend of my father's, to become his number one gun bearer. My father, Mkamba and I, although I was only a boy at the time, hadn't wanted him to go and also were rather worried that, although he was an excellent number two, he was not up to the job of a number one. Anyway, much to our regret, in the end he decided to go. Some months later he was thrown and stamped on by a wounded buff and that was the end of his gun bearer days. His leg was badly smashed but my father, because Katunga was an old friend, arranged and paid for him to have medical treatment. Katunga ended up with a leg that was good enough to get him around but not good enough to get him a job with a professional safari team. After hanging around for a while he turned poacher. Not a big time ivory or rhino horn poacher, but just killing a few beasts for meat. We all knew about it but turned a blind eye. He was a good man of the old school and we could all have done with a lot more like him.

I shook hands with the three of them and they laughed about the funny *bonduki* I was carrying and wanted to know what I was doing out here on foot and on my own.

I explained briefly what had happened and told Katunga that I would need him to carry a message for me to 'Bwana DC.'

He answered that he would of course do that or anything I wanted him to do, but first shouldn't we have some food.

Then I knew what the faint wisp of smoke I had smelt just before I encountered the leopard was, it was Katunga and his sons cooking.

We went further in among the trees and where there was a small fire burning with Thompson gazelle chops sizzling over it. Quite made my mouth water.

After we'd had a good feed, I lit my pipe and using the back of the map I'd brought with me, I wrote a note to the District Commissioner. I told him briefly what had happened, where my camp was situated and where on the coast I considered there would be a gathering of local terrorists. I stressed that the rest of my party was in extreme danger and that unless something was done very quickly I didn't think that any of them would still be alive.

Katunga said the boys could take the message and he would come with me to help me. I declined because firstly, I didn't want to be responsible for any more people being killed and secondly, as he was only armed with a spear and bow and arrows, I didn't see what help he could be. He was very upset but after I explained to him the great importance of the message he was carrying and that he was the only person I would want to trust it with he was more than happy to take it and not to accompany me.

As I left them and walked on, I worked out that if they were lucky and the DC was at home then he would have my message by the next morning. If, however, he was away on safari somewhere in his district then it might be several days before he received it.

One thing was certain: I couldn't wait, I had to get on with it and to do the best I could for Carol and the rest of my team.

By late afternoon I was pretty exhausted and feeling the strain, but I was not too far from the camp. I had covered a lot of miles in very good time.

Although I was desperate to get back and see what had happened during my absence I knew I must slow down and cover the last few miles of the journey with a great deal of caution. I was in no position to burst in and take over. If I was going to come out as the victor of this situation it was going to be through stealth and cunning and not brute force.

CHAPTER 19

peered cautiously at the camp from among the bordering wait-a-bit thorn bushes and wished I had a pair of binoculars, as I was too far away to pick out details. I wanted to see everything before it got dark.

I must get nearer.

It meant I would have to crawl through one of the tunnels made in the thick scrub by various animals.

It was hard, uncomfortable going but at last I reached a small clearing where I was able to stand upright; it felt great.

I breathed in. I could smell lion.

So, this was where my old friend the Moonlight Predator had been hiding away.

I got down on my hands and knees and continued through the next section of bushes.

When I came to the end of it I was only fifty or so yards from the back of the camp but couldn't see much at the angle I was at. I would have to chance it and move along a short distance in front of the scrub and hope to find another inlet where I could secrete myself.

I was in luck. After thirty or forty feet I found just the perfect place that would camouflage me yet allow me to see a large part of the camp area.

The first thing I saw was Mkamba and Kidogo chained to the same log that Philip and I had been.

As I would have expected, Mkamba had already spotted me. He made no sign except to look away from me but at the same time to hold up his left arm above his head. This was a sign we had between us, when we were hunting, to tell the other, without having to speak, that we had seen something. He put his arm down and turning his head in my direction pointed with his lips to the main sleeping tent.

From that I knew that that was where they were.

I held up three fingers.

Mkamba held up two.

So, there were only two of them there. Which one was the missing one and where was he?

I held up three fingers again and pointing to the third

one with my other hand I then held up both hands as if to say, where is he?

Mkamba held up his two hands and gestured upwards with his palms. Another of our hunting signs meaning the quarry had moved off, or gone away.

I then pretended to turn a key and pointed at him.

He nodded.

The crafty old so-and-so still had his key to the padlock but had, as instructed, not used it or done anything, pending my return.

I nodded to him, made a display of turning the key again and then pointed to a position behind the mess tent.

I had thought there was something a bit different about the camp layout and suddenly I realised what it was. Rommel wasn't parked where it usually was. I moved slightly so that I could see further round the kitchen tent, but it wasn't there either or anywhere to be seen. It had gone.

I could see Mkamba whispering to Kidogo and then unlocking the padlocks. The two of them moved like shadows in the growing dusk and disappeared behind the mess tent.

I just sat and waited. I wanted it to get darker before I made my move.

Where, I wondered, were the rest of the team? There didn't seem to be anyone else in camp. Most importantly, who was in the tent with Carol? If there were, as Mkamba had indicated, only two then it must surely be the Evans couple, so where was Carol? My heart sank as I thought of the various scenarios. Why hadn't I got back sooner? But I knew I was being absurd. There was no way I could have got back quicker than I did.

After I had waited a few more impatient minutes the tent flap was raised and out came William Evans followed by his wife. They walked towards the mess tent, but being engrossed in their conversation, they didn't notice that Mkamba and Kidogo were no longer chained to the log.

After a few minutes they emerged from the mess tent, presumably, to look at their prisoners.

I brought up the AK deciding just to disable Evans with a leg shot but then thought better of it. I must take this opportunity to even things as much as possible. He was carrying an AK, which obviously was fully loaded and I only had one shot to do as much damage with as I could. I changed my aim to the centre of his face, just between the eyes, and moving out into the open, I wanted him to see me and know where the bullet that killed him had come from, I squeezed off. There was no explosion just a metallic click. Bloody hell! A misfire.

He had seen me and had realised what had happened.

He raised his AK and pointing it at me, started to walk towards me with Helen following him. When he was a few yards from me he stopped and looked me up and down as though I was something that had crawled out from under a stone.

'Not so clever this time, McKenzie. I think I'm going to have a great deal of pleasure killing you. Nothing too quick, mind you. We must enjoy it, mustn't we? Where is the hunting car? I didn't hear you arrive.'

'No, you wouldn't have done, I have hidden it a short distance from here.'

'I think that you're going to have to show me where it is, that is if you want to die quickly and relatively painlessly.'

'Evans, you certainly are one of the most unpleasant little impotent runts I have ever had the misfortune to meet. No wonder your wife has to get someone else to screw her in order to get a bit of action and to try to blot you out of her mind.'

I thought for a moment that I'd gone too far, I could see his finger tightening on the trigger of the AK.

'Don't take any notice of him, William. We both know

what he says is not true and what the real reason for my going to his bed was.'

'Quite right, my dear. Now then, McKenzie, are you going to show me where the car is?'

This was a good one. As soon as I got amongst the undergrowth there would be a chance to turn the tables and also it would give Mkamba an opportunity to do something.

'Okay,' I said. 'Follow me.'

As I turned to lead them across the clearing, the bushes on the far side of the camp parted and out charged a dirty, thin, bedraggled lion running on three legs. He was charging straight for Evans when Helen, panicked at the sight of this fearsome object, turned and ran towards the mess tent. The lion immediately switched its attention to the moving object, passed Evans, and knocked down Helen, burying his fangs into her neck.

She screamed once, just once, as her neck was broken.

Evans ran to the gory heap and fired his AK into the lion as it mauled Helen. The mortally wounded beast turned and with his last bit of strength took a swipe at Evans. His claws struck him and, taking away half his face, knocked him across the clearing.

Mkamba and Kidogo came running from the scrub

where they had been hiding and the three of us examined Helen, Evans and the Moonlight Predator. Helen was dead, the Moonlight Predator was dead and Evans, though still alive, was so seriously injured I concluded he would not last long.

I felt sorry for the poor old lion, he was so thin you could see his ribs practically sticking through his flesh and he was filthy and had almost lost his mane. He may have done a lot of damage in the last few weeks of his life, but however you looked at it, I owed him my life.

There wasn't much we could do for Evans and anyway I reckoned he would be dead before morning. He lay on the bed where we put him, moaning and calling for Helen. I gave him a heavy shot of morphine, which was all I could do for him.

While I'd been doing what I could for Evans, I'd asked Mkamba where Carol was and he'd told me she'd been taken away from the camp by Kalashnikov.

We buried Helen in a shallow grave and then I was able to ask for full details about what had happened while I was away.

From what Mkamba reported, my assumptions had been correct. No one had been too surprised when Pavlov and I hadn't returned during the night, but by mid-morning they were beginning to worry. After lunch there had been a big argument among the three conspirators in Russian and then, Mkamba assumed, Kalashnikov had decided to take the truck to look for Pavlov and me. As they were obviously suspicious of Mkamba and Kidogo they chained them to the log and then made Carol and the remainder of my staff get into the truck. Mkamba got the impression that Kalashnikov thought that any African would be able to guide him to wherever he wanted to go. He was very wrong in that assumption so by now they could be well and truly lost. It was going to make it more difficult for me to follow as they might be going in any direction. I certainly hadn't seen any sign of them on my way back to the camp, but they could have passed along the track when I was taking my shortcut through the forest. No, on second thoughts, it couldn't have happened then, that would have been too early. They must have even started from the camp in the wrong direction.

I told the other two that we would have a good meal, some sleep, and an early breakfast and then go out and track down our Russian.

I didn't feel much like eating or sleeping, I was too worried about Carol, but I forced myself as it was important to be as on the ball as possible.

Sometime during the night William Evans died, as befitted a traitor, on his own and unmourned. Before breakfast we dug him a grave beside Helen.

I thought we'd better take plenty of supplies with us, as I wasn't at all sure how long it was going to take us to catch up with Rommel. We took two backpacks with food and water and one with ammunition for two AKs and one HH .375.

I began to feel as if it was years since I'd had a normal day's hunting, but in fact it was just that so much had happened so quickly and unexpectedly.

I wrote out a long message to leave for the DC's party, if they ever arrived, telling him what had happened since I got back and what we now intended to do.

As soon as it was light enough, the three of us scouted around for signs of which way Kalashnikov had gone. Although he had used the truck, it was not easy as the truck and hunting car had been in and out of the camp so many times during the last three weeks that the ground was all cut up and criss-crossed with tyre tracks. Still, in Mkamba I had one of the most experienced trackers in Africa and I knew that sooner or later he would be able to work it all out. As it happened, Kidogo eventually found the tyre marks we wanted, and we were able to see the direction the truck had taken.

It was as I'd thought. They'd set off in exactly the wrong direction, that is if they were trying to follow me. They were heading for the swamp and not the plane.

Perhaps Mkamba hadn't got the story right; after all, it was pure conjecture. He didn't understand Russian any more than I did. Maybe Kalashnikov was up to something quite different, something we knew nothing at all about.

I didn't like it. I didn't like it at all. I was now even more frightened than ever about Carol's safety.

CHAPTER 20

We pressed on as fast as we could following the tracks made by Rommel.

Although we were travelling under a hot, blazing sun, I had noticed a build-up of cloud which could mean a tropical storm was brewing. This was the last thing we wanted as it would wipe out all trace of the tracks we were following.

Rommel's tracks were still leading us straight towards the swamp area. What the devil was Kalashnikov up to? He certainly was not looking for Pavlov and me.

By now the clouds overhead had become a dense, threatening mass, so much so that I expected the storm to break at any moment. We struggled on under the weight of our packs and weapons. I was carrying one of the AKs and Mkamba the other, while Kidogo had the HH.375. Before we left camp, I'd given Mkamba some instruction on how to operate the assault rifle so now, with his reasonably proficient handling of it, between us we had quite a bit of firepower.

Mkamba, who was taking his turn in the lead following the tracks, suddenly stopped. Standing still, he pointed to a spot some two hundred yards in front of us. There was an animal, or some object, just to one side of the track.

'What is it?' I quietly asked.

At that moment several vultures landed near the object and waddled towards it.

'Whatever it is it's edible. Let's approach slowly and have a look.'

With our weapons at the ready we moved cautiously towards the object.

'It's a man's body,' Mkamba said.

We moved forward at a run and chased off the vultures that had started to tear at it.

He was lying face down.

I leant over him and turned him onto his back; it was Opio.

He was dead.

He had been shot several times through the chest.

Poor old Opio. He'd been on safari with me and been a good friend for many years. I was shocked and saddened to find him like this.

'Why did that man do this? Opio was not a warrior. He would not have been a threat.'

'I don't know Mkamba. Perhaps Opio had enough of whatever was going on. Whatever happened Kalashnikov must pay for this and everything else he's done. How are we going to bury him as we've no shovels or anything?'

'We must cover him with large rocks, that's all we can do, *Bwana*,' Kidogo said, as practical as ever.

There was a small hollow a few yards away and this seemed the ideal place to lay Opio's body.

As we moved him, I noticed there was something in his clenched hand, on examination I could see it was a piece of paper looking like the inside of a cigarette pack. It took quite a bit of effort to prize his hand open—as rigour mortis had set in—without tearing the paper.

At last, we got it out. I unrolled it and on it were some words written with what I imagined to be lipstick.

It simply said: Going Memba for pick-up by associates.

So, now I could see what must have happened to poor old Opio. Carol obviously slipped the note to him to try to get it to me. I surmised Kalashnikov saw him trying to make a run for it and had shot him out of hand.

Memba! That was down on the Mozambique coast, quite a journey by truck with only enemies as your companions. Kalashnikov would have to drive the whole length of Tanganyika, which was nearly five hundred miles, and then a further two or three hundred miles into Mozambique. He was also going to have to find some more fuel for the truck, even though he had several drums of spare with him.

As I stood looking at the message the first large drop of rain landed on it. The storm was almost upon us. What a bit of luck we'd found Opio with his note, otherwise we'd have lost all trace of our quarry but now, as we knew where they were heading, we could follow without too much difficulty.

By the time we'd covered Opio's corpse as well as we could, the rain was deluging down upon us. We made a run for some thick scrub and sheltered under it.

As we sheltered I considered what lay ahead. I'd only ever been to Memba once before and Mkamba had been with me on that occasion as well.

*   *   *

It had been some two or three years before when we had been hunting in the same area as now, using the same camp. We had come across some poachers who were slaughtering animals in the area and when we had tried to apprehend them they had fired on us and made off. As my client at that time I had a really great guy who was an ex-WWII SAS colonel who was all for following them and arresting them however long it took. So, off we went and eventually, almost a week later, we caught up with them near Memba. We had already gone down through Tanganyika without any authority, and we finished up in Portuguese territory without so much as a "by-your-leave" from the authorities. To add to the embarrassment, when we eventually caught up with the poachers they surrendered without a fight. So, there we were with five prisoners and their loot in a country we shouldn't have been in. We went into Memba, found the local police chief and handed over the prisoners and their ivory. Luckily for us the police chief turned out to be a very keen big-game hunter, who, by chance, already knew my name, having heard about some of my hunting exploits, so he was delighted to take over the responsibility for our captives. He then gave us a good feed, bed for the night and escorted us back to the border in the morning. A very good outcome to that little adventure, but I feared it was too much to hope that the same man was still in charge in Memba.

*   *   *

'Well, it looks as if we've got to go to Memba unless we can catch up with them before that. Do you remember the last time we went there, Mkamba?'

'Ndiyo, Bwana.'

'I thought you would, that was a lot of fun, wasn't it?'

We moved on again.

This time we were able to go at a faster pace as we knew where we were going and did not have to bother about tracks—which was lucky as now there weren't any anyway!

We cut straight through the swamp, heading in a direct line for the Tanganyika border. We passed a lot of game: a large herd of buffalo, a pair of rhino, giraffe, wildebeest, a small pride of lion, and a large mixture of antelopes.

By late afternoon I estimated we were into Tanganyika and we were beginning to slow down as we tired but, in any case, we would have to stop when it got dark.

'Within the next hour we ought to find a spot to spend the night. We can't be far from that small river we used to camp by. Either of you got any idea where it is?'

'We are going towards it now; another half hour or so.'

'Let's keep going until we reach it. You all right, Kidogo?'

'*Ndiyo, asante sana, Bwana.*'

'Good.'

Dusk was now falling fast and as we approached where Mkamba was sure the river was, we suddenly saw ahead of us three campfires burning brightly.

'What the hell! Who can that be? Surely it can't be Kalashnikov and his friends? They wouldn't have had time to get down to Memba and back. You'd better sneak up and have a look Mkamba, we'll wait here for you.'

Kidogo and I crouched down, watching the camp as Mkamba disappeared into the glum.

After a few minutes we heard shouting and could see Mkamba and another figure on the edge of the camp waving to us.

It was Harry. My God, what a bit of luck to come upon good old Harry. It was the first bit of luck I'd had for some time.

Kidogo and I hurried to the camp where Harry and I warmly shook hands.

'It's good to see you, Harry. You don't know how good.'

'Well, I must say, you lads look a bit dishevelled and worn. Let's go to the kitchen tent and have a mug of tea with a drop of scotch in it then you can tell me what the hell's going on, and why you're carrying those military weapons.'

It was good to sit down and the tea, with a very large dollop of scotch in it, went down extremely well.

'I suggested coming over here so that we can have a bit of a chat before the prince meets you. Now come on, Gavin, tell me what's going on.'

I told him as briefly as I could all that had happened from the time that Philip Ryland had brought the Russians to join us. Harry was very perturbed and upset to hear how Philip and the others had been killed but thought the last endeavours of the Moonlight Predator great stuff. He didn't like the idea of Carol having been abducted and, like me, didn't think she'd survive unless she was rescued before the Russians were ready to leave Africa.

'So, what do you want me to do, Gavin? Shall I come with you?'

'What about your client, would he agree to your coming? He may want to join in; after all Carol is meant to be his girlfriend.'

'I shouldn't bank on it. In the first place the man's a

real prick. I don't think he considers Carol a girlfriend as he made me avoid your camp on the way through as he didn't want to meet her.'

'Didn't want to meet her! I thought he couldn't wait to get his hands on her.'

'That may have been so at one time but then he met someone else. Do you remember little Mary, the Goanese train driver's daughter?'

'Yes, I most certainly do.'

Mary was a gorgeous girl with dark golden-coloured skin and long, thick black hair. Her body was a temptation to any full-blooded male she met. She always wore brightly coloured, sleeveless cotton dresses which accentuated her perfectly shaped breasts and the curve of her hip. Her family lived in Nakuru, but she had moved to Nairobi where she was completely spoilt by all the European men, or the ones who had plenty of money, and ignored and hated, without exception, by all the European women.

'Well, she's here with the prince. He met her in Nairobi, just before we were due to leave, and that was that. He fell for her hook-line-and-sinker and, obviously for a lot of shilling-i, she agreed to accompany him on safari. That's why I had to avoid your camp as word had got to us that Carol was waiting for him there.'

'Well, I'm damned, he sounds like a real old sod.'

'You've no idea. He's hardly fired a shot since we've been here. He isn't even interested in my going out and getting the trophies for him. Consequently, we've just sat around in camp most of the time while he and Mary usually only come out of his tent for drinks and meals. He's a really unpleasant fellow, so I'm quite pleased to be shot of him. The general boredom has just about killed me. I'm the opposite to you, as from what you've told me you've had a bit too much excitement. Incidentally, why on earth did Carol want to get mixed up with him?'

'She told me quite candidly that she wouldn't let him do anything unless he married her when she would have been prepared to put up with him until she could arrange a divorce with a really big financial settlement.'

'I only met her once in Nairobi before she went up-country on her modelling job, but she didn't give me the impression she was that sort of girl.'

'I don't think she really is. It's just that she's so worried about her financial future.'

'Is she more to you than just a friend, Gavin?'

'Yes, I think I'd like her to be.'

'Then we'd better do something about getting her back.'

'That's great, Harry, but I don't want you to do anything without your client's approval.'

'Okay, let's go and talk to him, if we can prise him off the nest.'

As we walked towards the sleeping tents, Mary emerged from one of them and started towards the mess tent when she caught sight of us.

'Hello, Gavin,' she said smiling. 'I didn't know you were here.'

'I've only just arrived. How are you?'

'Getting very tired,' she replied, smiling broadly. 'I think it's time I got back to Nairobi before I'm a shadow of my former self.'

I laughed. She was a good sort and didn't seem to take the way she earned her living too seriously.

The tent flap opened and out stepped Gianne looking ruffled and bad tempered.

'Who are you?'

'I'm Gavin McKenzie, another white hunter.'

'Aren't you the one that Carol is with? I hope you haven't been stupid enough to bring her here.'

'No, she's not here,' and then I told him briefly what had happened to her.

He was not very concerned or interested. I looked at

Harry and he raised his eyes towards the sky in despair.

'Prince,' Harry said. 'I think we should assist Gavin to rescue Carol.'

'And how do you think we can do that?'

'We could leave the camp and go with him to find these people.'

'We most certainly could not. In any case I'm ready to go back to Nairobi as I want to take Mary to see Rome.'

'You mean you're not prepared to do anything to help rescue Carol who will almost certainly be murdered if we don't do something.'

'It's no concern of mine she got herself into this mess and, anyway, it would seem McKenzie is going to rescue her.'

'You amaze me, Prince, I really must do something to help Gavin rescue her.'

'No, Harry,' I said. 'Don't get involved, you must put your client's safety first. What I could really do with is the loan of a vehicle. Is that possible?'

'I've got two Land Rovers with me, take one of them.'

'Doesn't that mean that we'll be rather cramped and uncomfortable on the journey back to Nairobi if we are only left with one Land Rover?' said Prince Gianne, looking even more bad tempered.

Suddenly Mary, who had been standing quietly listening to all that was said, broke in, 'For God's sake, let Gavin have it. That's much more important than our being a bit squashed, after all, we've been squashed together ever since we've been here.'

Harry and I laughed, we couldn't help it.

Prince Gianne scowled.

'All right, I agree,' he said and walked back to his tent.

I smiled at Mary and said in an undertone, 'Thanks, I'll remember that.'

She grinned, gave me a wicked wink and went off to the prince's tent.

'Right,' Harry said. 'We'll load up the Land Rover with food and supplies. I suggest that the three of you have a good meal and then get some sleep. You wouldn't gain a lot by leaving before dawn.'

'Thanks, that sounds great. I think we have a sporting chance now of sorting this little old lot out. Can you update the DC on your way back either by seeing him or by sending him a message?'

'Don't worry, I'll make sure he gets the latest news. Would you also like me to go into your camp and leave one of my chaps to look after it for you until you get back?'

'Yes please, that would be a great idea.'

Harry and I went to the mess tent and I tucked into a good meal while he sat and talked to me and then I went to his tent, where a bed had been made up for me. As I drifted off to sleep I was thinking about Carol and hoping against hope that I would get to her in time.

CHAPTER 21

The next morning Mkamba, Kidogo and I set off refreshed from a good night's sleep. Harry had insisted on giving us a large quantity of supplies, so we were well set up for all eventualities. It took me a short while to get used to the Land Rover with its four-wheel drive as I had never used one before, even though they were becoming very popular in East Africa.

I drove hard all morning and we covered a lot of miles before we stopped for a midday break. I had decided to risk it and go direct to Memba and just hope the message we'd found on Opio's body was correct.

Everything went well for us that first day and by dusk we had covered nearly two hundred miles, very good going indeed under the prevailing conditions. If only one of the other two had been drivers we could have continued after dark, but with only me driving it was more sensible to have a good night's rest.

At the crack of dawn we were off again and during the morning we went at a cracking pace, by midday we had already covered more than a hundred miles so we stopped for a short break and some food. Then we were on our way again.

That's when things started to go wrong.

The first happening was a puncture. Not in itself a major disaster, but there was an added complication; one of the wheel nuts had a crossed thread. I just didn't think for a while that we were ever going to get it off. After the three of us had taken turns at trying to move it, and torn our hands etc, it at last moved and we were able to get the wheel off. Then we found that the spare wheel that we had put on had very little pressure in it so we had to change that for the second spare. I decided that before we moved on, we'd better blow up the spare in case we needed to use it in a hurry. This took considerable time because the foot pump wasn't working very well.

At last we were on our way but we'd lost nearly two hours because of our problems.

But our troubles for the afternoon hadn't finished.

We now found our path blocked by an elephant herd. I tried to nose my way through but a big enraged bull, obviously kingpin of the herd, decided he didn't like us. He charged the back of the Land Rover and got his tusks partly under the rear bumper, the vehicle lifted a foot or two off the ground, swayed and damn nearly went over onto its side. At the last moment the bull disengaged his tusks and we crashed back onto all four wheels. He was still right behind us roaring and stamping the ground with his massive feet. The engine of the Land Rover had stalled but I managed to restart it and to drive away from our tormentor at full speed. By this time the rest of the herd had been panicked by all the noise and had started to charge round in more or less a large circle while they tried to decide which direction they should be going in. The noise and dust created by them was phenomenal and mind blowing. We were then actually struck a glancing blow by a cow as she chased her calf away. The Land Rover rocked again and Kidogo, who was sitting on the outside of the front seat, was nearly thrown out onto the ground which would have been the end of him.

Then, as suddenly as it had all started, it all stopped. The elephants that were one minute charging all round us had disappeared and the only sound was that of the over-revved Land Rover engine. I drove under the shade of a tree and stopped. The three of us looked at each other and then we roared with laughter. It had been an exciting few minutes and we had been very close to disaster.

'That was a big bull. Those tusks he was carrying must be almost a record for today. Pity we haven't got time to go after him. That's put us well off the track. Which way do we need to go now, Mkamba? Would you say out through there? Yes ... I'm sure that must be right.'

We were on our way once again, but not for long.

Another puncture, another wheel change and as soon as we reached some water we would need to repair the two punctured tyres.

Towards evening we came to a small river where I thought we might as well stop for the night as we could deal with the tyres before we ate and slept. I calculated we had another day or two before we reached our destination and I didn't think we could be too far behind Kalashnikov, especially, if he'd had any of the problems we'd had. In fact, I thought, it quite possible that he was stuck somewhere but it still seemed that our most sensible plan was to go to his supposed destination and then to backtrack if he hadn't arrived. I said a little silent prayer for Carol and any of the others who were still alive.

When we set off the next morning I felt happier now that we had two repaired spare wheels and we had also been able to make sure that we were able to get all the wheels off with ease. It was lucky that we had taken care of these matters as we had hardly travelled ten miles before I missed seeing an ant bear hole and a back wheel dropped into it and, when we got the Rover out again, we found we had a buckled wheel. That was soon changed but now we were back to one spare wheel.

Then we had a bit of luck. We came to a small native village. In the village there was an Indian-owned store where we were able to buy the supplies we needed, including, amazingly, a spare wheel.

During conversation the storekeeper told me that a Mercedes truck had stopped there the day before and that a very nervous young lady had called out of the window and ordered some things from him. He said he hadn't seen who else there was in the truck, except for a man sitting in the cab beside her, because as soon as he'd handed her what she'd ordered she'd paid for the goods and they had driven off without further conversation.

So, Carol was at any rate still alive, and relatively well,

yesterday. I felt cheered, we were definitely catching up with them and it seemed we were both taking the same route.

When I thought about Carol's safety I came to the conclusion that, as Kalashnikov must have taken her with him as a hostage to bargain with if necessary, he would want to keep her alive, at any rate, for the time being. This didn't mean that he might not treat her brutally, or even molest her sexually, but I felt sure he wouldn't kill her until he was ready to leave Africa. He would kill her then, as he would all the others if he hadn't already disposed of them, in order to protect William Evans, as he couldn't know that he was already dead.

As we drove away from the village, I had my foot hard down on the throttle—I wanted to catch up with Kalashnikov—and I wanted to do it as quickly as possible.

CHAPTER 22

pushed on all afternoon with the old Land Rover bucking and grinding its way through the never-ending African bush.

When the sun was already disappearing below the horizon, and I was thinking it was about time to stop for the night, we saw some distance ahead of us the red flickering of a dying fire.

I stopped the Rover.

Kidogo got out and handed me the binoculars.

Looking through them I could see that it was some sort of vehicle that was now almost burnt out.

I swept the glasses round the area but couldn't see any movement or sign of life.

'I'm going to drive slowly up to whatever it is so keep

your guns at the ready, just in case.'

We bumped, at a few miles per hour, towards the fire.

I stopped the Land Rover when we were still several hundred yards away from it and we remained where we were for a few minutes surveying the surrounding area.

Nothing moved.

I engaged gear and we rolled slowly forward until we were so near we could feel the heat from the fire.

'You know what that is Mkamba, don't you?'

'Yes, *Bwana*, it is Rommel.'

'You mean what is left of Rommel. Let's have a look round. Kidogo, you stay in the car and guard it with your life. Mkamba, you circle from left to right and I'll go in the opposite direction. Keep well back from what's left of the truck and when we meet on the far side we'll go in close and see if there's anything there.'

I managed to keep my voice cheerful even though I was scared stiff that we might find the remains of Carol.

When Mkamba and I met on the far side of the burning truck neither of us had found anything.

Then together we approached Rommel.

When we were so close that it was getting too hot for comfort we came across a body, or what was left of it.

It was Juma.

His remains were scorched by the fire but that was not what had killed him, he had been stabbed to death before he was burnt.

Between us, Mkamba and I managed to drag his body away from the flames.

Then we worked our way round the fire getting as close to it as we could stand.

We found badly burnt remains of another person, an African male. But we couldn't tell who it was as there wasn't enough left for identification. We moved those remains away as well.

When we got back to the Land Rover we told Kidogo what we had found.

'We'll have to bury Juma and the other body, who I suppose must be either Boculy or Laboso. I wonder what on earth can have happened here and where the others are. I think we could all do with a strong mug of tea before we start the graves. We can boil a kettle on the burning remains of poor old Rommel.'

As we drank our tea I puffed my pipe and my mind was racing around trying to work out what on earth had happened and where Carol was. At least her body wasn't here so I could only guess that she was still alive. But in what state and was she with anyone or was she wandering through the bush on her own?

There was not much we could do to find out where the others had gone until it was light and we were able to look for signs and any trails that had been left.

We buried Juma, another good loyal friend gone, and with him whomever else the other remains belonged to.

Then I said we must eat something, although we didn't feel like it, and get some sleep ready to start tracking at the earliest possible moment.

We split the night into three shifts so that there would always be one of us on guard. I drew the first shift, Kidogo the second and Mkamba the third.

I had a job to keep awake during my stint, as, although I was extremely worried about Carol, I was deadbeat. As soon as Kidogo took over from me I curled up by the remains of the fire and went straight to sleep.

I hadn't the faintest idea how long I'd been asleep when I was woken as a hand was put over my mouth and my shoulder was gently shaken.

Opening my eyes I looked straight into those of Kidogo. He held a finger to his lips then took his hand away from my mouth.

I slowly sat up and saw Kidogo was now doing the same to Mkamba.

I took hold of my AK and silently got to my feet.

Mkamba was now also standing, holding the other AK. We both looked at Kidogo with raised eyebrows.

He held a finger to his lips again and then pointed away from our camp towards a just discernible clump of small trees and bushes.

We stood silently and listened.

Then we heard it.

Someone, or something, was moving in among the bushes.

Through gestures I made it clear to the other two that I intended to switch on the lights of the Land Rover which, very conveniently, was pointing in the right direction. Then I pointed to Mkamba and showed him I wanted him on one side of the Rover and to Kidogo that I wanted him on the other. Then we stood there all looking towards the trees where the noise had come from.

I turned the headlights on full.

For a second, I didn't see anything among the trees, and then I saw a crouched figure.

I started to bring up my AK when Mkamba shouted, 'Boculy, it's Boculy.'

Boculy, who was turning to run away from us, at the sound of Mkamba's voice stopped in his tracks. Then he turned and ran towards us. Even at that distance and in the poor light I could see that his face was distorted with fear.

As he came up to us I turned the headlights off. He hugged Mkamba and hung onto him for dear life.

He was gibbering away, but I couldn't understand what he was saying as, not only was he incoherent, but he was talking a mixture of Swahili and some tribal language.

I let him burble on for a few minutes then I took him gently by the shoulder and told him that now he was among friends and should calm down.

It seemed as though it was the first time he had realised that I was present and turning he took my hand and shook it warmly, still jabbering away.

Kidogo and Mkamba were grinning, obviously pleased to find him still alive.

I spoke to Boculy again and this time he listened and quietened down.

'I want to hear what happened here and where the others have gone, but you just sit quietly for a minute, Boculy, while we make sure there isn't anyone following you.'

We all stood quietly listening but apart from the normal African night noises there was nothing.

'I'll just have a look, *Bwana*,' Mkamba said as he silently glided into the darkness.

The three of us stood where we were and listened. It was good for Boculy as during this few quiet minutes his breathing, which had consisted of huge gulps, gradually returned to normal and his face became more relaxed.

Mkamba was suddenly with us again.

'No one there, it's all clear.'

'Well done, Mkamba. Now then, Boculy, let's hear what happened. We know you stopped at the village for supplies, you can start from there.'

'*Bwana*, I didn't see much, I was tied up in the back of the truck, but I heard the storekeeper talking and then we drove out of the village again. We seemed to be going for a long time, it was very uncomfortable bumping on the floor with my hands and feet tied, then we stopped for one of our short breaks. During these stops *Bwana mbwa mwitu* would untie us one at a time and let us relieve ourselves and have a drink and sometimes something to eat. When we stopped here I was the first one to be released and I went into the trees to relieve myself. While I was there I heard a lot of shouting and a shot being fired. I thought that you must have caught up with us but luckily, I didn't rush straight out. I came back to the edge of the trees and had a look. Then I saw it was not you but a large gang of Africans who, as I watched, killed Juma and dragged the *Memsaab* and *Bwana* out of the truck. Then they took everything out of the truck, except Laboso, and set fire to it. I could hear Laboso screaming as it got hotter and hotter and all they did was to laugh. Their leader was a very large and frightening figure and they all did what he told them. From the way he was pointing I knew he thought I was in among the trees but decided not to waste time looking for me. I was very lucky. They loaded up all the kit on the women they had with them and then they left dragging the *Bwana* and *Memsaab* with them. When you arrived I thought some of them had come back for me as I didn't recognise the truck and couldn't see who was in it. I kept very still until I thought whoever it was had gone to sleep and then I was trying to make my escape when you spotted me. Oh, I am glad to see you all, *Bwana*.'

Boculy had told his story well and I could picture the scene when the raiders arrived. Boculy had been very lucky. I hadn't heard the boys' nickname for Kalashnikov before but '*Bwana* wild dog' was very apt.

'You told it well, Boculy, but there are one or two questions I would like to ask you. How many men do you think there were?'

'About forty men and five or six women.'

'Had they got firearms?'

'Very few but they took the ones from the truck.'

'Did they hurt the *Memsaab* in any way?'

'No, they just tied her wrists and I heard their leader shout at them that they were not to harm her as he wanted her for himself.'

'Did you get any idea who they were?'

'I think they are a Mau Mau gang on the run.'

'Did you get any idea of where they were going?'

'No, but I think they are just trying to find somewhere, anywhere, to hide from Kingi Georgi's soldiers.'

'Which way did they go when they left here?'

'That way, *Bwana*, I heard their leader say they would camp for the night on the other side of that hillock.'

'Well done, Boculy. Mkamba, Kidogo how do you feel about going after them? It is very heavy odds against us.'

'What would you do if we didn't go, *Bwana*?' Kidogo asked.

'I will go anyway but you must decide for yourselves.'

'You don't have to ask me, you know I go where you go,' Mkamba said.

I grinned at him and gave him a wink of appreciation.

'Of course, I come too, *Bwana*,' Kidogo said.

'What about me?' asked Boculy. 'I want to help and anyway you might want the leader skinned and I'm the only one that could do that.'

We all laughed.

'Good, we all go then. We'll start now as we still have two hours of darkness and I would like to be able to hit them before it's light. We'll take a chance and go straight over that hill and hope Boculy heard right. I intend to get as near to them as I can in the car, without disturbing them, and then do the last bit on foot.'

We carefully checked our weapons, making sure that they were fully loaded and that we had plenty of spare ammunition ready for use.

We filled the Land Rover's tank with fuel from the extra drums we were carrying and made sure the tyres on all wheels, including the spare ones, were fully inflated. I even checked the wheel nuts to make sure we could do a quick wheel change. Most of these precautions were so that if we were able to snatch Carol away from these brigands, and to make a run for it, we would not be held up by any mishaps with the vehicle.

As we climbed aboard the Land Rover I felt very apprehensive. I felt it more than likely that Carol was already dead and, if not, how were the four of us ever going to snatch her away from this gang?

CHAPTER 23

Twenty minutes later, as we came over the crest of the hillock, we could see in the distance a large campfire burning and, when I turned off the Rover's engine, we could hear the beat of drums and wild shouting.

We had found our quarry.

They were either drunk or high on some drug, or maybe both. The odds against finding Carol alive and unharmed seemed to be getting longer and longer.

'I think I can drive a bit nearer as with all that noise they're not going to hear us. Keep your eyes open for any sentries, though by the way they're behaving I don't expect them to have taken any precautions.'

I let the Land Rover coast down the hill towards the fire and commotion. We didn't have long to spare, it would soon be dawn.

We were soon within a few hundred yards and we were able to vaguely see figures through the scrub.

Then Kidogo put a hand on my shoulder and I instinctively stopped the car. He pointed towards a tree, twenty or thirty feet to our right.

There was a figure hanging from the branches.

I took a deep breath. Would it be Carol?

'Stay here,' I said. 'I'll have a look.'

Easing myself out of the driving seat, I took the AK Mkamba held out to me and cautiously moved towards the tree.

It was Kalashnikov's body hanging upside down. He was suspended, naked, from a branch of the tree by a rope that was tied round his ankles. I wasn't sure whether he was actually dead or not, but if not, he hadn't got long to go. He had been severally beaten but that was not his worst injury. Where his testicles and penis should have been there was just a gaping wound. From past experience I knew these were taken to be used in some evil rites ceremony. It seemed poetic justice that Kalashnikov had been tortured and killed by the very people he had come to organise and help. Because of the evil things he had done he deserved to die—but not like this—no one deserved that. I moved back to the car and whispered to the others what I'd found.

It was time to move nearer and to see what was happening and to get Carol out, if she was still alive.

I told Boculy to stay and look after the Rover.

Then Mkamba, Kidogo and I moved off through the small trees and scrub that separated us from our enemy's camp. The noise coming from them was terrific. They must be nearing the climax of their ceremony, or whatever it was.

I'd seen this sort of thing before and gradually all the participants just flaked out and slept for several hours or, sometimes, even days.

As we approached the edge of our cover we were moving very cautiously. I signalled to the others to stay hidden while I got closer to see exactly what was happening and to make a plan of attack.

I completed the last bit on my hands and knees then, lying flat, I parted the grass and bushes and was able to look straight into the camp.

What a sight!

It looked like some monstrously evil painting.

In the middle of the clearing there was a huge fire with yellow and red flames dancing above it. To one side of the fire were two drummers who were frantically beating their drums. All over the place were contorted bodies lying on the ground, those were the ones who had already flaked out.

The five or six women Boculy had seen were being kept busy as men lined up to take their turn at enjoying them and, judging by what I could see, their ideas of enjoyment had many variations.

Everyone was naked including a big ugly fellow who was sitting on an old packing case and whom I took must be the leader.

But where was Carol? I frantically looked all round the camp.

Then I saw her. Until he moved slightly, she had been hidden by the figure of the leader. She was lying on the ground beside him, she was naked and was trussed up like a chicken.

While I watched, I saw him put his hand down and feel between her thighs and then he laughed and shouted something to some of the others. Two or three of them went over to join him and they all stood swaying and laughing looking down at Carol. Then, to my horror, two of them masturbated onto her.

The chief convulsed with laughter and shouted some further instructions.

They picked Carol up and started to cut the ropes that tied her.

My God, we had to do something without delay.

I crawled back to the other two.

'We have to attack right now. Kidogo, I want you to stay on the edge of the clearing with the H&H and cover the *Memsaab*. Kill anyone that tries to get near her. Mkamba, we will walk into the camp together, you to the right of Kidogo's line of fire and me to the left of it. Kill as many of them as you can, and I will do the same, making the leader a special target. As soon as we get to the *Memsaab* I will grab her and we'll make a run for it back to the Land Rover. All right? Then let's go.'

As we came out of the scrub, I could see that four men had hold of Carol, spread-eagling her on the ground and their leader, sporting a monstrous erection, was above her preparing to plunge himself into her. Before I had time to even aim my AK at him his head turned into pulp as Kidogo blew it off with a soft-nosed bullet from the .375.

Then I opened up with my AK and saw bodies being pushed aside by the bullets. When I stopped to change magazines, I could hear the bam bam bam of Mkamba's AK.

We had come in so quickly and unexpectedly that we

didn't meet any resistance.

Mkamba and I reached Carol at the same moment.

I reached down with my left hand and took hold of one of her arms and pulled her to her feet. She was hardly conscious. Crouching forward I was able to get her onto my shoulder.

'Okay, Mkamba, time to say farewell to these bastards.'

We backed out the first few yards towards Kidogo, then we turned and ran. As we were leaving the clearing I could hear the crack of the H&H as Kidogo gave us covering fire.

Then we were in among the trees and the three of us were running for dear life.

It seemed like a hundred miles to the Land Rover but at last we were there. I stripped off my bush jacket and put it on Carol before helping her into the back of the Land Rover.

As I got into the driving seat someone fired a shot at us from among the trees. So, they were after us already.

Mkamba ran round the car, back towards the trees, and fired his AK at our pursuers. They fired another shot and Mkamba went down on his knees, but he was up again firing short bursts to keep them back.

'Come on, Mkamba, in the car, we're off.'

As soon as he was in I drove like hell not caring, at that moment, where we going as long as it was away from our enemies.

I drove hard for twenty or so minutes, by which time I considered we had covered enough miles to be safe for the moment, then I stopped, as I wanted to check on how Carol was.

When I got her out of the car she was still very scared and shocked but didn't seem to have received any serious physical injuries. I gave her a spare bush shirt and trousers to wear.

'*Bwana*,' Kidogo called out in a voice that was far from his usual rather stolid tone.

He was standing beside Mkamba who was still sitting in the front passenger seat of the Land Rover.

'Yes, what is it?'

He held up his hand; it was covered in blood.

'Mkamba is hurt.'

When I reached Mkamba he was having difficulty in breathing. When Kidogo and I lifted him out of the car we found the back of his shirt was soaked in blood. That last shot from our enemies must have hit him and he'd never said a word even though he must have been in a great deal of pain as I drove hell for leather. We gently lowered him to the ground and removed his shirt. I felt as if I'd been hit by a sledgehammer. I'd seen enough shot men to know that this was a mortal wound.

'Get him some water,' I said as I plugged the wound with a strip of shirt and laid him gently on the ground.

'You'll be all right, old lad, just lie still and don't you worry.'

'No, *Bwana*, this is the end. I know it.'

'Don't talk like that, you'll be as right as rain in a week or two.'

'No, this is where I'll finish my days and it is a fitting ending for me. I wouldn't want to end my days sitting outside my hut being nagged by women and then being put out for the hyenas when it was thought I was about to die. Now, I am dying like a warrior in the company of a great warrior. I am well satisfied, my only regret is that I will not be able to serve you any longer. *Bwana*, take Kidogo into your heart, as you have taken me, I know he will serve you well.'

'How will I ever hunt without you? You have always been my hunting companion and my eyes and ears.'

'You will manage, *Bwana*. There is one thing I must ask of you, as I am nearly gone now, please don't let the hyenas eat my body.'

'Have no fear, old friend, no hyena will get anywhere near you.'

He half sat up and putting out his hand, he took hold of my arm and squeezed it affectionately, smiled into my eyes and died.

As I put my hand down to close his eyes, my mind was in turmoil. I wondered why his face was wet and then I realised that it was because my tears were falling on it. This good and courageous man had been my friend for as long as I could remember. He had saved my life on several occasions, as I had his.

Kidogo and I wrapped Mkamba's body in a blanket and placed him in the back of the Land Rover as I was not going to bury him until I could make sure that his body was one hundred per cent safe from hyenas or any other scavengers.

I put Boculy in the back next to Mkamba, to look after him, and Carol, now enveloped in one of my spare shirts and pairs of trousers, in the other corner. She was still pretty shattered.

As Kidogo was about to climb into the seat beside me he stopped and pointed back the way we had just come.

'They're following us. Can you see them, *Bwana*?'

'Umm, yes. Not as many as there were; we did quite a

good job. What do you think, fourteen or fifteen of them? Good. We must have just about halved their numbers. As long as the old Land Rover keeps going and we don't have a breakdown they won't catch us now. We'll head back to that village store, pick up some materials to bury Mkamba, and then report this lot as soon as we can. What do you think Kidogo, am I going in the right direction?'

CHAPTER 24

Our journey to the village was uneventful and on our arrival I went straight to the village shop. I was able to purchase six sheets of corrugated iron and six strong, six-foot long, wooden posts.

Kidogo, Boculy and I managed to strap these onto the rear of the Land Rover and then we were off again.

This time I was heading back towards our own camp, as it was also in the direction where we should find the DC or some government authority.

After we had been travelling for nearly an hour we saw a cloud of dust on the horizon in front of us.

We came to the conclusion that it must be a vehicle coming in our direction.

Twenty minutes or so later we could see it was a large

truck and fifteen minutes after that we met.

It was an army vehicle filled with men of the KAR (King's African Rifles). There was a young officer in charge who turned out to be Andy Robinson, the son of one of my father's old friends.

'What are you doing out here, Andy?' I asked after we had greeted each other.

'We're tracking a Mau Mau gang of about fifty people that are on the run from Kenya.'

'We've just had a dust-up with them and I think there is only about half that number now.'

Then very briefly, I told him the whole story.

'Phew, that sounds like some adventure. Trust you, Gavin, you always seem to be where the excitement is.'

'Not too good this time, I've lost too many friends, including Mkamba.'

'Not old Mkamba? I've heard lots of stories about his hunting escapades on safari with both you and your father. My God, you're going to miss him. What about the young lady? She doesn't look too good.'

'She's still in shock. I don't think there is anything fundamentally wrong with her, but I want to get her back to civilisation as quickly as possible.'

'I think that would be a good idea. In the meantime,

Gavin, I'll radio a message back to my company commander and get him to let the authorities know about that Russian ship and what has happened to the gang we're after.'

We decided that we would all have a meal together and then the soldiers could go their way and we could go on ours.

Carol got out of the Land Rover when food was ready but sat apart from the rest of us and just played with her food.

When the troops had gone and we were about to get into the Land Rover, I tried to put my arm round Carol's shoulder and to say a few comforting words to her. She pushed me away.

'Please leave me alone,' she said.

'I'm sorry, I was only trying to be nice to you.'

'Maybe, but at the moment I don't want to have anything to do with any man. I've had my fill for the moment. I don't think there's much to choose between any of you, under the surface you're all basically animals and only after one thing. Just get me back to Nairobi so that I can get away from this ghastly country and its ghastly people.'

'Come on, Carol, I think you're rather overreacting.'

'Overreacting! You must be mad. After all I've gone through.'

'You can't really take it out on my country and its people. None of this would have happened if it wasn't for those Russians.'

'That terrible man that kept fiddling with my body and was just about to rape me, and God knows what else, was one of your so-called people.'

'Yes, agreed, but all countries have monsters, don't they?'

'Maybe, but I don't want to discuss it, I just want to get home to England.'

'I thought I was beginning to mean something to you?'

'Yes, I must admit I had fallen for you, but I shall just have to get over it—unless you want to come to England with me.'

'What on earth would I do there?'

'I'm sure there's lots of things you could do. You could work in the city or something.'

'Can you honestly see me wearing a bowler hat and carrying an umbrella?'

'Yes, why not? That is if you love me enough to want to start a fresh life.'

'It's not the time or place to discuss it, we must move on.

I want to find a good place to bury Mkamba and then we will head back to our old camp and on to Nairobi.'

*   *   *

That evening we were back in the country that I had hunted many times with Mkamba when we had used, as our base, the camp that Harry had just vacated.

I knew just the spot where Mkamba would be happy. It was a grassy hillock, with outcrops of rock, from which you could look way out across the open grass plains. There was a mass of game in the area and, in fact, we had to move on a pride of lions that were snoozing in just the spot I wanted for Mkamba.

Kidogo, Boculy and I between us dug a deep grave. Then, using the corrugated iron sheets and wooden posts we lined it and laid Mkamba in it. We covered him with the last corrugated sheet and secured that with two of the posts. On top of that we placed a layer of rocks and then filled the remainder of the grave with earth. Then we formed a cross with large chunks of rock. He was well and truly away from any scavengers and I would always be able to find the spot again.

By the time we had finished it was quite dark, so I

decided we should camp there for the night.

We were all extremely tired so after a quick meal we stacked the fire up and settled round it to sleep.

The next morning we were up at dawn for a quick breakfast. Before we left to continue our journey, I went and stood for a few minutes by Mkamba's grave and said a silent farewell to him.

Carol seemed to have profited by a good night's sleep and, although not her old self, she was a bit more cheerful. I couldn't help noticing, though, how suspicious she was of both Kidogo and Boculy. It was going to take her some time to get over her experience. She was also still treating me in a very cool manner, even though she had the previous evening invited me to go to the UK with her. I wondered if she'd meant it or, as she must realise that I would never leave Africa on a permanent basis, she was just using it as a "pleasant" way to get rid of me.

*　*　*

After we had been driving for a couple of hours, Kidogo, from the back seat where he was now sitting as Carol had decided that she would sit in front again, shouted to me that there was another cloud of dust on the horizon—another vehicle approaching.

'This place is getting as busy as the centre of Nairobi. Who on earth can that be?'

Twenty minutes later we could make out another Land Rover and then Kidogo shouted, 'It's *Bwana* Harry.'

So, it was. Good old Harry and a couple of his chaps.

When the Land Rovers were abreast of each other we stopped and both Harry and I jumped out of our respective cars and shook hands warmly. God, I was glad to see him.

'Dr Livingstone, I presume,' he said with a laugh. 'I was beginning to get very worried about you lot. Hello, Carol. *Jambo*, Kidogo. *Jambo*, Boculy. Where's Mkamba?'

'Dead. Killed by a shot from a Mau Mau gang we tangled with.'

'Bloody hell! I can't believe it. You must be devastated.'

'Yes, I am. I'm trying to reconcile myself to it by remembering that he said, just before he died, that it was the way he wanted to go. He was, you know, very old; none of us knew exactly what age he was but my father says that when he first employed him, which was well before I was born, he was already a mature man.'

'Your father won't half be upset.'

'Yes, he will. Still, enough of that. What on earth are

you doing down here?'

'After you'd left we packed up camp and I tried to persuade the prince to follow you, but he wouldn't agree. Anyway, to cut a long story short I got more and more worried about you all until I decided I just had to come after you. So, I arranged everything for the prince's journey back to Nairobi and told him to sod off. He wasn't very pleased, because, as I was taking the only Land Rover left, he and his lady friend had to travel in one of the trucks.'

'I hope it's not going to cause you a lot of trouble.'

'It may or it may not, but I can't worry about it. Friends are more important than that. Now tell me what happened after you left my camp.'

As Carol joined us, and tea was brewed, I recounted a blow-by-blow account of what had happened.

When I'd finished talking, they both sat for a minute in silence and then Carol cleared her throat. 'Gavin, I've been very unfair and churlish. I only saw what had happened through my own eyes and had not given any thought to what you had done. I just didn't appreciate the effort and risks you must have taken on my behalf. To have followed us as you did and then to actually attack that gang the way you did just shows what an honourable and courageous man you are. I'm going to say now, what I should have said at the time you rescued me, thank you from the bottom of my heart, and I can only hope that you will forgive me for being the cause of Mkamba being killed. I should have known better than to behave the way I did as between you, regardless of personal risk, you and Mkamba had already saved my life once.'

I didn't know what to say. I would have liked to take her in my arms and to tell her I'd do it all over again if she'd just love me and want to be with me, but I didn't think it the right time or place. Then Harry came to my rescue.

'You don't want to say too much of that sort of thing to Gavin, he's already big-headed enough.'

The three of us laughed together and as my eyes met Carol's, she gave me a warm smile.

'Thank you, Carol. Don't listen to Harry, he only says these things out of jealousy. Now you're feeling a bit better would you like to tell me what happened to you after I'd left camp with Pavlov?'

'Yes, of course. I'd quite forgotten that you weren't in on any of that. When you didn't come back, they weren't too worried as they thought you'd had a breakdown or something like that. Kalashnikov was quite confident that Pavlov was more than capable of taking care of you. Incidentally, did you know why you had to go back to the plane? No, I thought perhaps you didn't. Hidden on board is a fortune in local currency and gold. Pavlov had also been instructed to set fire to the plane to make it look as if it had crashed and everyone on board had perished. Because so much had gone wrong they had decided to abort their plans and to go down to Memba where, off the coast, they had an undercover Russian ship waiting in case they needed picking up in an emergency. They decided to split the party and for us to go on first with the rest following when you and Pavlov returned. Helen Evans told me most of this. I think she was beginning to regret being involved in wholesale murder and treason, and I could tell she was not happy with my being taken off by Kalashnikov. When we left I was not tied up like the others, but he kept a pretty good eye on me. However, when he was supervising the others I did manage to get hold of an old cigarette packet from the truck's glove compartment and to write a message on it for you. I slipped it to Opio and just said your name. He took it and instead of waiting for a better opportunity, tried to make a run for it straight away. It was awful. Kalashnikov shouted at him and when Opio stopped and turned he shot him several times. He was already dead when I got to him and Kalashnikov just left him where he was. Luckily, he didn't notice that Opio was holding a message so, even though you didn't get it, he didn't know I had tried to send you one.'

'I did get it.'

'How on earth did that happen?'

'We found Opio's body and when we were moving him to bury him we noticed the piece of paper in his hand. It was because of that message that we were able to catch up with you so quickly.'

'So, Opio didn't die in vain and he got a proper burial after all?'

'That's right. Go on with your story.'

'Not much more to tell really. I lost track of time, but it didn't seem to be long after that we were attacked by that fearsome gang which did the things you know about. Then you arrived and rescued me.'

'My God, Carol, you've had a pretty hair-raising time; bit of luck you had Gavin batting for you. What are you going to do now, stay for a while in Nairobi or going to go on safari with Gavin?'

'Neither.'

'Well, if you want to see other parts of Kenya, and

Gavin is tied up, I'd be pleased to show you round as I've got two weeks before my next safari,' Harry said, grinning at me.

'Thank you for the offer, but all I want to do is to get back to England as quickly as possible.'

Damn, I thought, her nice little speech didn't mean anything, she was still going to leave me high and dry.

CHAPTER 25

When we eventually arrived back at camp everything was just as we had left it and Harry's chap was waiting to greet us.

We decided to start to get things packed up, stay the night and set off for Nairobi the next morning. Harry had already told me that he had arranged for his truck to come back from Nairobi as, at that time, he hadn't known whether I'd get Rommel back or not.

The plan was that Carol, Harry and I would take one of the Land Rovers back to Nairobi via the abandoned aeroplane. The others, with Kidogo in charge, would stay behind and wait for the truck to arrive and when they had loaded all the gear they would go direct to Nairobi. One of Harry's other men, also being a driver, would be able to drive the second Land Rover.

We left camp just after dawn and had a pleasant morning's drive—no punctures, breakdowns or getting stuck—and stopped for a drink in the shade of some acacia trees.

We drank warm beer and relaxed, in a somnolent mood while I contentedly puffed my pipe.

'What are you going to do about the money and gold that Carol says is hidden in the plane?' Harry asked.

'Take it to Nairobi and hand it back.'

'Back to who—sorry, to whom?'

'To the rightful owners, of course.'

'What, to the KGB?'

'I see what you mean. I suppose it would have to be to the police then.'

'And then it will just disappear into some fund or other, or even someone's pocket, never to be heard of again.'

'You're not suggesting that we should take it, are you, Harry?'

'No, I'm not, but I don't think we should just hand it over to some bureaucrat to do what he likes with. After all, it's certainly no more theirs than it is anybody else's, that is, except for the KGB and I'm sure nobody wants them to have it.'

'I agree with all that but I still don't see what you're suggesting.'

'I have two suggestions. As I understand it, there is cash and gold involved.'

'Yes, I believe so. That's what they told you, isn't it, Carol?'

'That's right.'

'But we don't know how much cash there is or what the gold is worth do we, Gavin?'

'No, we don't, but come on, Harry, for God's sake get to the point before I nod off.'

'He's an awfully rude fellow, Carol, isn't he? I sometimes wonder how I put up with him. So, what I'm proposing is as follows: we give the cash to Carol as compensation from the KGB for all the hassle they caused her, and the gold we just leave in the plane when we return it. No one will know where it has come from, no one is going to claim it, so everyone will think it was Philip's and his parents will be able to keep it, again, although they won't know it, as some small compensation for losing their one and only son.'

'I think that's an excellent idea but, as we don't know how much is involved, it may be so small as not to be worth worrying about.'

'It's a lovely idea,' Carol said. 'But I don't think I could accept it however small or large the amount. It should, in my opinion, go to the descendants of people like Opio and Mkamba.'

'I'd thought about that but it wouldn't be possible. If any of them suddenly received a large sum of money, and with them you must appreciate I'm talking of anything over a few hundred pounds, everyone would want to know where it had come from. This other way, when you'd got the money, you could quite openly give a few "rewards" without causing any suspicion.'

'Not bad thinking, Harry, I like it. I do think you deserve it, Carol, and it would, as Harry says, then allow you to give the others a bit as well.'

'I'm not sure that I'd be too happy about it, even though I would like to be able to help the others.'

'Let's just wait and see. Harry has these fine plans, but we don't even know if the money is still there and, if it is, how much is involved. If we start now we should reach the plane in time for an early lunch and then we can see what we're talking about.'

*   *   *

When we arrived at the airstrip we found the aeroplane still hidden as we had left it, what now seemed like, an age ago.

We had a warm beer before we started our search.

We found the cash straight away. It had just been stuffed, in large brown envelopes, under the rear seats.

We took it out of the plane and had another warm beer each as we started to unpack and count it.

The notes were of different denominations and there were a lot of them.

As we counted the contents of each envelope we wrote down the total enclosed. When they had all been counted I added up the overall total.

'How much do you guess there is, Carol?'

'What, do you mean the English equivalent?'

'Yes, in pounds sterling.'

'It seems like rather a lot. Five thousand pounds.'

'No, I think much more than that,' Harry said. 'I'm going to say at least twelve thousand.'

'Neither of you is right. Hang onto your hats: thirty thousand pounds.'

'My God! That is one hell of a lot of money. Even today, in the over-priced fifties, you can still do a lot with a pile like that. Come on, let's have a look for the gold.'

With that Harry got up and went back to the plane.

I looked at Carol. She had looked so much better this morning with her colour back, but now it had gone again, she looked quite pale.

'You aren't seriously thinking of giving me that money?'

'That's what has been suggested. I can't see why not.'

'But it doesn't really belong to you and Harry. It's not yours to give.'

'Quite right, but I think Harry's reasoning was right. There is no way that money is going to find its way back to the KGB and why should it? They brought that money to Africa illegally to be used to support terrorists in their plans to disrupt governments and to kill anyone that stood in their way. I have lost several good and loyal friends through it and, but for the grace of God, we would have lost you as well. I think Harry is right you should have the money as compensation from the KGB.'

'Yes, but I——'

'Come on you two, cut the chat and come and give me a hand. I think I've found the gold.'

There were two boxes in the luggage compartment and, although they were not very big, they were so heavy it took both Harry and me to lift them out.

We prised the lid off one of them, pulled open some

waxy paper and there it was: small bars of dull-coloured gold.

We took the lid off the second box and found it contained the same.

'Phew! Don't ask Carol and me to guess how much that little lot is worth, but one thing I can tell you, Gavin, it's a small fortune.'

We checked to make sure there were not any identifying marks anywhere to be found on the boxes and then, with some difficulty, put them back into the aeroplane's hold.

We had a somewhat silent lunch, each with their thoughts, and then we moved off again.

Having two competent drivers, we were able to reach Nairobi by late the next afternoon where we went straight to Harry's house, in preference to my tiny city centre flat. Harry's house, a spacious three bed-roomed affair with a large veranda and all mod cons, is in one of the best parts of the city, near the Mutheiga Club.

Carol was still not her old self and hadn't spoken much during our journey.

Anyway, it was good to be somewhere where we could have a proper bath again and to get into clean clothes. We sent one of Harry's servants to the New Stanley Hotel to pick up the rest of Carol's luggage, which she had left there pending her return, and arranged that we would get together at nine to go out for a real "blow-out" dinner.

When I'd bathed, I considered going into Carol's room but, in the present circumstances, decided against it.

Recent events had certainly changed her. I wondered if it was a temporary phase or if she might never be quite the same again. She had certainly gone through a very traumatic experience, but I would have thought she would have been able to come to terms with it.

I still felt the same. Thinking back on it, I decided it must be what they call "love at first sight". At the beginning I'd thought I was in with a sporting chance, but now my chances of it coming to anything seemed to be getting less and less.

I couldn't believe I'd only known her such a short time. It seemed like forever.

It was going to take me a long time to get over the events of the last few days. I'd lost so much in such a short time. If I was now going to lose Carol as well, I began to think the anger and frustration would drive me round the bend.

After dinner, which had been a fantastic meal with lots of amusing conversation between the three of us, we went back into the bar for a nightcap.

'Gavin, when you were having your bath and resting, Harry and I got onto the travel agents he knows and booked me a flight to London.'

'I see, when are you going?'

'Tomorrow afternoon.'

'Tomorrow afternoon!'

'Yes, I want to get home as soon as I can.'

'But that doesn't give us any time to sort anything out.'

'Excuse me you two, but there's an old friend of mine over there who I'd like to pop over and say *jambo* to.'

Good old Harry, as discreet as ever.

'Gavin, there isn't anything for us to sort out. You know how I feel.'

'No, I don't think I'm too sure. I thought I did a few days ago but not now.'

'Don't be silly. You know I'm fond of you, very fond of you, but I can't stay in Kenya, I wouldn't be happy here.'

'Is there no answer?'

'You could come to England.'

'We talked of that. I'd be like a fish out of water.'

'There is no answer then.'

'I suppose not but it makes me feel so frustrated I could smash something.'

'Don't be like that, you'll soon forget me what with all

your other women and safaris etc.'

'I don't want any other women. I want you.'

'Oh, Gavin, don't make it any harder for me, I don't want you to be upset.'

'So, basically, what you're saying is that you don't give a damn about me.'

'Of course, I'm not saying that. I've already told you I'm very fond of you.'

'If you stayed for a while perhaps that fondness would turn into something more.'

'It might, but I just want to get out of here without any delay. In any case, my mind is too confused at the moment to think clearly. Every time I close my eyes I see that horrific scene with that monstrous man leaning over me. I feel unclean and still frightened.'

I leant forward and took her hand.

'I'm sorry if I'm being unfair to you but it's just that I can't bear to see you go. I want to be with you.'

'Perhaps when I've gone you may feel differently.'

'No, I won't. Have you thought that you, might miss me?'

'I know I'll miss you.'

The next afternoon Harry and I took Carol to the airport. I felt almost suicidal with frustration. Here was a girl I'd really fallen for from the minute I first saw her, and she said she was very fond of me, but she wasn't prepared to stay on and give things a chance.

At the airport she was very cool, calm and collected. When I'd gone to her room, the night before, she'd made me welcome but only to hold her in my arms and nothing more. She had said again that it was going to take her time to get over her experience and, until then, she couldn't face the thought of anything physical.

'Carol,' I said as we were sitting in the airport lounge, 'Harry and I have been able to arrange the transfer of the money we discussed. We'll keep back fifteen hundred pounds to pass onto the families of the others and the remainder will be deposited in the account you gave me details of. It should be there within seven or eight days.'

'That's very kind of you both, but I'm still not sure you should do it.'

'Can't think of any reason why not. Can you, Harry?'

'None at all.'

'There you are then, that's all settled.'

When, a few minutes later, her flight was called, she kissed Harry goodbye and then turned to me.

'I shall be thinking of you, Gavin. Don't be too hard on me; I can't help it. I've just got to get away.'

'I know, darling, I understand. I will think of you, and miss you, all the time until we're together again.'

She kissed me on the cheek and went towards the exit gate. Then she stopped, turned and ran back into my arms.

Tears were running down her cheeks as we kissed and hung on to each other. After a minute or two she pulled herself away from me and with a backward, wan smile, went through the exit gate and out of my life but not, I desperately hoped, forever.

Harry and I waited to see the plane take off and then drove back into Nairobi.

I moved out of Harry's house and back into my own

little three-room flat in the centre of Nairobi. I usually enjoyed being there when I got back from safari as it looked down onto Delamere Avenue and there was always plenty going on. But not this evening. I felt lonely and unhappy.

By eight I was feeling very miserable and, unlike my usual self, very pessimistic. I desperately needed some diversion. I couldn't think of anyone I wanted to call, I didn't feel like seeing any of the old gang, so I decided to go down the road to the New Stanley Hotel to see who was there and to have a few drinks.

When I was having my third large scotch, another white hunter, John Bradbury, came into the bar with three people.

'*Jambo*, Gavin, nice to see you. May I introduce Mr and Mrs Blundell and their daughter Jackie, who come from Charleston in the USA. This is Gavin McKenzie who is not only one of our best-known white hunters, but also one of our most highly decorated soldiers.'

I said my "how-do-you-do" and looked at the threesome. Mr Blundell looked very pleased with himself, Mrs Blundell was an attractive, middle-aged women, but obviously rather subdued by her lord and master. Jackie Blundell was another matter. She was very good looking and had, what can only be described as, a rather full and voluptuous body.

I bought them all a drink while John told me that they'd just returned from a four-week safari.

'Say, if you've got nothing better to do, Gavin, why don't you join us for a few drinks and dinner?' Mr Blundell said.

'Yes, that sure would be nice,' interjected Jackie as she moved a few inches along the bar until her hip touched mine.

'That's awfully kind of you, I'd like that.'

We sat at one of the tables in the bar and drinks came fast and furiously as Jackie's legs, under the table, got themselves more and more entangled with mine.

When it was time to go into dinner John Bradbury asked if he could be excused as he had a lot to sort out before the Blundells left the next afternoon. This was regretfully agreed to by the Blundells as the remaining four of us went into the dining room.

During dinner we talked about their safari and safaris in general.

'I've had a real nice time,' Brad Blundell said. 'We're going to come again next year, but it'll just be the two of us. Jackie will be married by then.'

'Oh, that's a pity,' I said in what I hoped was a gallant,

rather than an alcoholic-sounding voice.

'Why is it a pity?' Jackie asked as her hand stroked my thigh under the cover of the tablecloth.

'For two reasons. Firstly, because if you'd come back to Kenya, I might have been lucky enough to see you again. Secondly, as a bachelor, I never like to see a beautiful girl getting married.'

They laughed uproariously. They were, I decided, now rather the worse for wear.

'Jackie came over with us to sort of have her last fling, didn't you honey? She's marrying a very successful, straitlaced lawyer who, once they are married, won't want his wife to go gallivanting off with her Ma and Pa. So, I reckon this is the last bit of fun we'll have together,' Brad said, leaning over and patting Jackie's arm.

'He's not that bad, Pa, but I sure as hell won't be able to do anything like this.'

I wondered to myself, if the other two had any idea what their daughter's left hand was doing, to my anatomy, as she was saying this.

Just before we finished dinner a hotel messenger came over to the table with a note for me. I excused myself and opened it. It simply said: We would be grateful if you would come to Government House at 11am tomorrow.

What was all that about? I didn't really care. I was doing what I was doing to try and blank out my sorrow about Carol going and the death of Mkamba and my other friends, so, why should I worry about a little thing like a summons to Government House?

When we eventually left the table in the dining room, we went into one of the lounges where Brad insisted on our having a last bottle of champagne. Not that he had to do much insisting.

At last, it was time to break up as Brad and his wife wanted to get some sleep.

'Gavin,' Jackie murmured, 'could you be an angel and get my key from reception for me, I just don't think I could walk all the way there and back. It's room forty-eight.'

Brad and his wife got up to leave and when they said goodbye, Brad gave me a big wink. Was this, I wondered, father's approval to have a bit of slap and tickle with his soon-to-be-married daughter?

Ah well, it takes all types.

When Jackie and I reached her room, I unlocked the door for her and stood aside to let her enter. She turned to look at me and as I was about to say my farewells, she grabbed my arm and, pulling me after her, closed the door. Then we were in each other's arms and her lips were seeking mine. Wow! What a kiss. I'd always found American girls were good kissers and imagined it was because of the experience they'd gained during their college snogging parties. But this girl was something else. It was almost like being attached to a soft, voluptuous suction pump!

The room was dimly lit as a small table light had been left on. It gave a romantic, cosy glow.

I swung her round and pushed her back against the closed door and our lips re-engaged. By this time, I was feeling just about as randy as it was possible to feel! After all, I'd been drinking all evening, mostly champagne, and I hadn't had any real good hard physical sex for some time.

She parted and bent her legs slightly so that I was pressed hard against her fanny. I brought my right hand back from the door and caressed her left breast. It was rounded and voluptuous and her nipple was extremely large and hard. My breath was now coming in spasmodic gasps and my stomach was contorted with lust. She was moaning and almost sobbing. I had to remove my lips from hers for a minute to get some breath into my lungs.

Leaning slightly sideways and lowering myself I was able to get my hands under her skirt and to run them up her plump firm thighs until they reached her microscopic knickers. I started to push them down and her hand joined mine to help me; then she bent one leg followed by the other and before I knew what had happened her knickers were gone.

She was now really making quite a noise with her moans and sobs.

Her hands moved to my trouser tops as she tried to undo them. I did it for her.

We leant back against the door again and although only partially undressed the most important parts were bare and pressed together.

I put my hand back between her thighs again and caressed her fanny. It was hot and sticky. I ran my fingers along it and then inside it and she let out a frenzied cry and pressed herself hard against me.

I was rock hard and had been for some time. It was time to penetrate this noble fanny.

As soon as I was inside her she brought her legs up behind me and clasped them together round my waist.

My hands were against the door and my arms were supporting her under her armpits. I didn't waste any time, this was not a long-drawn love match of niceties and seduction, this was just raw animal sex wanted and required by both of us.

I rammed into her and it felt good. Her fanny was all consuming.

She let out a cry and seemed to vibrate. She had reached her zenith!

I started to shudder and came in no uncertain manner.

Phew! It had been hot and good.

We moved away from the door.

'Gee, Gavin, that was real good. I'd been waiting for something like that for a long, long time.'

As she was saying this she was throwing off the rest of her clothes. She then said, 'I think it's time to go to bed.'

I wondered what on earth she meant by that. Did she mean it was time for bye byes?

It quickly became obvious what she meant as she climbed onto the bed and, pushing the pillows to one side, she knelt forward with her face resting on the bedclothes, her bottom high in the air and her knees slightly parted.

It would have been difficult for her to do anything more sexually stimulating than this. I felt quite intoxicated with lust for the second time within the last half hour. Her bottom was delicious but the creme de la crème was her fanny. Now I could clearly see it. No wonder it had felt so good to be inside. It was plump and its lips were pouting and now slightly parted.

This invitation was too good to be true. I was rock hard again and, throwing off the rest of my kit, I climbed onto the bed and moved up behind her.

Using my thumbs, I parted the lips of her fanny and implanted a kiss on them before tickling her clitoris with my tongue. She was making a rasping noise and her juices had started to run. She couldn't wait any longer and neither could I. My dick was practically bursting as I slammed into her and took her "doggie" fashion. Leaning forward, I caressed her breasts and rolled those magnificent nipples. This seemed to give her an extra kick because she started crying out again.

*   *   *

When I awoke light was filtering through the curtains. My watch showed me it was five thirty. That had been quite a night! Jackie was still in a deep sleep, not surprising! She looked good lying there. She was certainly a very attractive, voluptuous-looking woman. I resolutely looked away or all would have been lost and I would never have got to Government House!

As I struggled into my somewhat crumpled clothes, I had a slight feeling of guilt. I was incorrigible even in my own eyes. But in all fairness, Carol had left me feeling devastated, tremendously hurt and utterly frustrated. Also, she had made no promise of ever seeing me again, a real letdown.

Anyway, the evening had been like a sort of safety valve going off and, I had to admit, rather enjoyable!

CHAPTER 27

Even though the next morning I arrived at Government House a few minutes early, I wasn't kept waiting in reception, I was shown straight into a small conference room and offered coffee.

As I sat there sipping black coffee, and feeling pretty hung over, I was cursing myself. Why had I been so weak the evening before, getting drunk and then getting into that American girl? God damn it! I'd only said goodbye to Carol yesterday afternoon and I'd already been unfaithful to her. I'd made a complete fool of myself. I hadn't really wanted to spend the evening with those people, and I'd only gone to bed with the nymphomaniac daughter to try to numb my brain—what little there was of it!

Still, it proved something. It wasn't like me to have any

regrets like that, and it just showed how much Carol really meant to me. I decided I wouldn't have anything to do with any other women until I'd given Carol long enough to decide whether she wanted me or not.

The door opened and in came two men, both strangers to me.

The younger of the two came forward and held out his hand.

'Mr McKenzie, I'm Bill Anderson and this is my colleague, John Smith.'

As I shook hands I looked Bill Anderson up and down. Dressed in a well pressed KD safari suit he was of medium height with a very sun-tanned face under a head of fair hair. He looked fit and tough.

His companion didn't come forward to shake hands, but just gave me a nod from where he was standing. He was quite a different type to Anderson. He was tall, almost my height, and very slim. His face was olive complexioned and he had almost black hair. He was dressed in an immaculate, and obviously very expensive, beige-coloured linen suit. With it he wore a cream-coloured silk shirt and an old school tie. His shoes I noticed, which were lightweight brown brogues, were polished until they were mirror-like.

Bill Anderson motioned me to sit down at the conference table and he took the chair opposite me while John Smith, if that was his real name, sat further down the table.

'Thank you very much for coming to see us this morning, Mr McKenzie, as there are one or two points we would like to talk to you about,' Bill Anderson said in a modulated, relaxed voice. 'We are mainly interested in the demise of Sir William and Lady Evans. You see, we work for the Foreign Office, as did Sir William, so we are obviously interested in what happened to him. We understand that both he and his wife were killed by a lion, is that correct?'

'Yes.'

'We also understand that you could not be blamed for not having protected them, as their professional hunter, as you were being hounded by terrorists at the time.'

'You've got that a bit wrong. William Evans was one of the terrorists.'

'I don't think that can be correct. Sir William was a member of the Foreign Office.'

'Sir William "Bloody" Evans was about to defect to Russia having been a double agent ever since before the war. He was about to kill me when the "Moonlight

Predator", as we had nicknamed the lion, attacked. If it hadn't been for that lion I wouldn't be sitting here now and Evans and his wife would probably be in Moscow.'

'Mr McKenzie,' John Smith spoke for the first time. He had a quiet, refined voice but one that indicated that he was used to being listened to. 'I think that perhaps there has been a misunderstanding somewhere along the line. Mr Anderson and I have come out here to discuss with you the service you have done your country by being instrumental in the breaking up of a large local terrorist gang and, even more to the point, of a group of KGB agents who had entered this Crown Colony to help undermine law and order, both here, and in other parts of Africa. If this were the case, then HM Government would have great pleasure in awarding you a CBE for outstanding service in the fight against the KGB and terrorism in general. However, if there is some talk of Sir William having been in some way concerned then the matter becomes more involved and we would not be able to recommend your award but would have to institute an enquiry instead.'

'But surely, Mr Smith, you would like to find out all the facts concerning this case?'

'Mr McKenzie, let me put it bluntly. It would be much

less of an embarrassment, do less harm to the country, and to all concerned, if Sir William had simply died through a hunting accident that was no one's fault except the terrorists who had caused you to leave the camp at the time of the accident.'

'If you had told me that it was in the national interest not to say anything about Evans's KGB connections I would have agreed. There was no need to dangle a CBE in front of my nose as, quite honestly, I don't give a damn if I get one or not and as far as I'm concerned you can stuff it where it hurts most. I feel rather insulted that you should think you could buy my silence with the promise of some medal. However, for my country, Mr John Smith, I would be prepared to do most things including lying.'

'We should have known you would react like that. In any case the CBE recommendation will certainly go forward as you have struck a very great blow for anti-terrorism and must have caused the KGB a big reversal in their plans for an African campaign. Thank you, Mr McKenzie, for your co-operation and, if you will excuse us, we must go now as we have an aeroplane to catch.'

With that he shook me by the hand and left the room.

Bill Anderson handed me a sheet of closely typed paper. 'My thanks, Mr McKenzie. Here is the storyline we would like you to follow. You will see that it is as close as possible to what actually happened with just one or two minor variations.' He shook my hand and left.

I sat down and read the paper I'd been given.

It followed the true story apart from two instances. Firstly, when the Kalashnikov party arrived William and Helen Evans were also meant to have been taken prisoners by them. Secondly, they were reported as having been killed by the "Moonlight Predator" just before I arrived back at camp after I'd dealt with Pavlov. In the circumstances, neither of these variations to the truth worried me.

After my interview with Anderson and Smith, or whatever his real name was, I had a series of further interviews with administration personnel, and the police, concerning the various things that had happened, and people who had died. They had, however, all been given copies of the same paper I'd been given by Anderson, so the interviews didn't take very long.

I thought I'd have to spend a bit of time in Nairobi, but instead they said I could leave whenever I wanted.

They also told me that a press release had been sent out so I should expect someone from the media to approach me for the story which would, of course, follow on the lines already agreed by us all.

*　　*　　*

The first thing I did when I got back to my flat was to ring the local dealer for Land Rovers and order one for delivery the next day.

The second thing I did was to phone Harry and ask him to arrange for one of his chaps to collect his Land Rover and could he take the safari I was booked to start in two days. He agreed, even though he had intended to take a short break at the coast. He told me he had had a visitor from "Government House" who had informed him of the "true" story concerning the Evanses, which I'd agreed to. He wanted to know if it was okay by me. I confirmed and said I would fill him in when we next met.

Then I had to get onto the clients, who luckily already knew Harry from a previous safari and agreed to the change.

I then went down to the warehouse that several of us shared to keep our safari equipment in and where Kidogo was staying while we were in Nairobi.

He was pleased to see me and even more pleased when I told him we were off the next day for a safari of our own. I discussed with him the matter of a cook to take with us and he said he'd see who he could find. I also said to try to find Boculy, the only other surviving member of my team, and we'd take him as well. I knew I shouldn't be going, there were a lot of people I should see, and arrangements I should make, but I just wanted to be back out in the bush for a while.

Then I phoned Philip's parents for a quick word. I'd already spoken to them about his death and told them where he was buried. I arranged to take a pilot down to the abandoned aeroplane so that he could fly it back to base.

The rest of the day I spent getting my gear ready and planning where we should go. The first part of the journey I didn't have to think much about as it was straight to where the plane was and then we could get rid of the pilot. After that I wanted to have a look at my stranded hunting car and see if I could salvage it. Then I thought we might as well go on down to our old camp and look for the monster elephant we'd seen.

It was a long time since I'd been on a safari of my own and it would be a lot of fun not to have clients to worry about. It was also going to be an opportunity to see how Kidogo made out as my number one gun bearer and how we got on together. I was sure he would be as fine as Mkamba had said, but it would be good to have the chance to prove the point when we were on our own.

As the day wore on my depression gradually left me and, by evening, I was beginning to feel as excited about the coming safari as a schoolboy about to set out on his first adventure.

I didn't feel like getting myself a meal, so I decided to pop along to the New Stanley for a drink and a sandwich.

When I walked into the hotel reception area Pam, the reception manager, called out to me that several people had been looking for me. I asked who they were but she only knew one, Bob Bates. Bob was the local contact man for several international daily papers.

'I wonder what the devil he wants,' I grunted.

'I think he wants to know what our local hero has been up to now,' she said, giving me a very nice smile.

Suddenly Bob was by my side and a crowd of other people was surrounding me.

'Well done, Gavin, we hear you're a hero once again. These are members of the international press and we all want to hear how you kicked the Russians up the arse. Please tell us what it's all about.'

'Okay, Bob, briefly this is what happened.' Then I told them the story that I had agreed with the government boys. When they asked me questions, I was able to embellish because they were not really interested in William and

Helen. Once they had ascertained that Helen had not been raped in any vile, but front page worthy, fashion they just wanted to know about my attack on the KGB and the local terrorists.

Word must have got around the hotel as when I walked into the bar for my sandwiches everyone stood up and clapped, and people who knew me kept coming up and patting me on the shoulder as they said things like well done, jolly good show.

Well, I thought, *all that for knocking off my client's wife and chasing a gang to save the love of my life.*

I finished my food as quickly as I could and made my way back to my flat still as excited as ever at the prospect of getting away with my team.

CHAPTER 28

t was early afternoon before we eventually left Nairobi in the new Land Rover. It seemed a very good vehicle but certainly hadn't got the room of my old hunting car. Kidogo had found Boculy and a new cook, so with them, the pilot Hugh Beresford and all our kit, we were pretty crammed in.

Starting so late, because of various delays, we were not all that far from Nairobi when we stopped for the night.

The new cook, known as George, produced a good meal for us before we fell into our camp beds under the stars. It was good to hear the night noises of the bush again.

Next day we were off at the crack of dawn and went hard all day, with Hugh and I sharing the driving. We reached the aeroplane in the late afternoon. It brought a lot of memories flooding back and made me very sad to think of those friends who had perished during those dramatic weeks.

Everything was in order, and we soon had it out on our airstrip.

Opening the luggage locker I looked in. The two small boxes were still there.

'Looks as if Philip left some of his kit in the plane, Hugh. Better let his parents have it so that they can sort everything out.'

Within half an hour or so Hugh took off and circling came back over the top of us when, with a wave, he banked and headed for Nairobi.

I had to admit to myself that I was pleased to see him go, now I could get on with my safari.

'Kidogo, we'll make for the place where I abandoned the hunting car and camp there for the night.'

It was dusk when we reached the small escarpment where I had turned the car over and disposed of Pavlov. It was still there lying on its side. When we climbed down to it and had a good look I realised how lucky I'd been. The bodywork was badly smashed from rolling over and then it was literally peppered with bullet holes. Looking at the wreck, and that's what it was, I wondered how I had survived; it was nothing short of a miracle.

'I don't think that is going to be worth getting back to Nairobi, do you, Kidogo?'

'No, *Bwana*, he's finished.'

'Agreed. We will move a bit further along the track and camp.'

We had another good night in the bush and moved on again at dawn the next morning and were back at the old campsite in time for an early lunch.

Later in the afternoon I shot a gazelle for the meat and a brace of guinea fowl for supper. Then, leaving Boculy and George in camp, Kidogo and I set off to look round to see what game was in the area. Shortly after we'd left camp I stopped the Land Rover.

'Kidogo, there was only one thing that Mkamba couldn't do and that was drive. I want you to be able to drive, if at all possible. So, let's make a start right now.'

We changed places and I explained the basics to him and away we went. He was a natural, most unusual for Africans who are generally known as being notoriously bad drivers.

As Kidogo drove us around I wondered if we could stay in this area. It had too many recent memories for comfort.

Then we picked up the trail of an elephant herd travelling in the direction of the swamp. We drove to the edge of the swamp and could make out the herd foraging among the trees.

'No closer, Kidogo. Back to camp. We'll come after them in the morning.'

That evening we sat round the fire Boculy had built and ate food cooked by George. I made a mental note to congratulate Kidogo on finding George. He had certainly found a winner.

After we'd eaten, Kidogo and I spent some time checking the rifles ready for a dawn start, and then the camp turned in as I wanted to be off by four am.

We had an enormous breakfast at three-thirty and moved out before four leaving the camp as it was. I let Kidogo drive and sat beside him with Boculy and George, who we didn't need with us but I had brought along for the fun, in the back.

As we approached the swamp area the sun was just coming up.

I heard the elephants before I actually saw them.

They had left the swamp and were in among the trees at the edge of the forest.

'Stop here, Kidogo.'

I got out of the Land Rover and took my Rigby from the gun rack.

'Kidogo, take the Holland and Holland .500. And plenty of cartridges.'

I filled my bush jacket pockets with spare cartridges for the Rigby.

I was feeling very excited.

'Boculy and George, you stay here with the Land Rover. We'll see you later. Come on, Kidogo, let's get on with it.'

We moved towards the trees and Kidogo picked up some dust and let it run through his fingers to test the breeze. There was very little but what there was, was in our favour. It was blowing from the herd to us.

As we entered the edge of the forest, I could see the bulky bodies of elephants spread out among the trees. They were enjoying a good feed as they tore down branches and munched them. Kidogo and I moved slowly and cautiously forward until we were in among the main body of the herd, but I still couldn't spot a big male with good tusks. It appeared females and youngsters surrounded us.

We came to a large clearing that was empty of elephants. I stopped. Kidogo came up to me and I leant towards him and whispered in his ear, 'Let's go across the clearing and into the trees on the far side and see if there's anything big over there.'

He nodded his agreement.

It was some two hundred and fifty yards across the clearing and when we were about halfway a baby elephant, must have been only months old, ran from among the trees, saw us and stopped in its tracks screaming blue murder.

Immediately—and why we hadn't spotted him standing under the trees on the edge of the clearing I'll never know— an old bull with tusks which, I reckoned, were at least two hundred pounds per side, came to its rescue.

He stopped by the calf and with his trunk propelled it towards the trees, and its mother, then he turned and came for us.

He was roaring and shrieking in rage as he approached at an alarming rate with his trunk held high and his ears spread out.

I had a pretty good idea he was only demonstrating as otherwise he would have tucked his trunk across his body and his ears would have been flat.

The Rigby was already tucked into my shoulder with the safety catch off and I had two extra cartridges between the fingers of my left hand ready for super quick reloading.

I aimed at his gaping mouth; a shot there from my

Rigby would drop him in his tracks. But I didn't squeeze the trigger, I held my aim and just stood and watched him. He was magnificent, awe inspiring.

He thundered up to within about twenty feet of me and then stopped. He stood there bellowing, waving his trunk, flapping his ears and stamping his huge feet.

He backed away ten or fifteen feet and then ran in towards me again. The noise, dust and size of him were enough to strike terror even into the bravest of men.

I had decided that after all I didn't want to kill him, so I just stood my ground.

He backed off yet again and then charged at me, this time I nearly shot him because I thought he was going to have me, but at the last minute he stopped. He was a mere fourteen or fifteen feet from me. He towered over me, the smell from him was almost overpowering and I was splattered by his saliva.

For a few seconds it was as if we were looking into each other's minds, assessing the other's worth and capability, and then he quietened, lowered his trunk, spun round in his own length and thundered off into the forest.

All was quiet—the whole herd had gone.

I stood for a minute then I lowered the Rigby and let out my breath, which I realised I had been holding for some considerable time.

I wondered where Kidogo was. I turned to find him slightly behind me and to one side, his rifle still at the aim. My God, Mkamba had been right, this was a good man. There were not many who would have stood and faced that.

We slapped palms and laughed together.

'I'm sorry, at the last minute I just didn't want to kill him even though he had a lot of ivory. I'm not even sure whether or not I ever want to shoot another elephant.'

'You are right, *Bwana*. They are great and wonderful animals and soon there will not be any left.'

'We're a fine pair! We both earn our living by hunting and here we are saying we shouldn't be killing them.'

'We only do it because we have to. It is the way we live.'

'Perhaps it's time we found some other way.'

'It's all right for you, you are a rich powerful *Bwana*, but I have to earn my living however I can.'

'Don't you worry, if you want it, I'll always have a job for you whatever I do.'

'That is good, *Bwana*, because Mkamba told me that if anything happened to him, I must take his place and look after you.'

It seemed strange that I no longer had the urge to

shoot elephant. I wondered if I was going to feel the same about other big game. I was also pleased to hear Kidogo say what he did. There was even more to him than I had thought. In time he would certainly be as important to me as Mkamba had been.

When we got back to the Land Rover Boculy and George were fast asleep and hadn't seen anything of the elephants or, for that matter, anything else.

We drove back to camp and had another good evening eating round our fire.

The next morning, I told the others that we were going to have a few days' holiday and forget about shooting, and that's just what we did. The only animals we shot were for food and we spent the days driving about and camping where we wanted. Kidogo and I tracked rhino, buff, lion and even some more elephants, getting as close as we could without panicking them or having to shoot anything. We had a lot of fun, including one or two very scary moments, and got to know each other that much better.

On the last day before we were to start back to Nairobi, I suggested we spend a day at the pool, the pool where Carol and I had spent that heavenly day together.

When we were swimming we took turns at croc watching and had a real laugh.

We were all naked as we splashed in and out of the water. It didn't matter about colour, financial or educational differences, we were just a bunch of friends having a lot of fun together.

In the evening we set up camp on the elevated rocks above the river to make it impossible for the crocodiles to come out after us as we slept.

As we sat round the campfire, I felt rather sad for a few minutes as I thought of the time I'd spent, in that same spot, with Carol.

Then I cheered up as I made a decision that I would go to London, see her, and carry her back to Kenya with me. If I could be based in Nairobi for more of my time I felt sure she could be happy as the social scene was returning now that the Mau Mau rebellion was virtually over.

When I lay under my mosquito net, looking at the stars through it, I was already making plans of how this could be achieved.

*   *   *

It took us two days, with Kidogo and I sharing the driving, for us to get back to Nairobi.

Once in the city we went to the warehouse to unload

our camping kit and to lock away the rifles in the strong room. While the other two put the tents and beds away, Kidogo and I cleaned and oiled all the firearms. When we had finished I took off the hunting knife that I'd carried ever since Mkamba had hidden it for me in the hunting car the day I killed Pavlov with it. I handed it to Kidogo.

'I want you to have this knife. It was left for me by Mkamba and saved my life. It came to me from a good, strong man that I could trust and I want to give it to another man that I think will be his equal.'

He looked at me and for a minute, he didn't know what to say, then he gave me a big appreciative smile.

'Asante, bwana. Asante sana.'

I could see how pleased he was and I felt sure it was because of what I'd said about his going to be a match for Mkamba more than the receiving of the knife.

After we'd finished the unpacking I took Boculy and George to their houses and drove on into the city with Kidogo who was going to help me get the rest of my gear into my flat before I took him back to the warehouse where he would be sleeping again.

As we pulled up in front of the flat there was a government car just pulling away, which stopped when the driver saw me. A young chap that I knew by sight but not by name, who worked at Government House, jumped out and came round to my window.

'Hello, sir, I've been trying to track you down. The Governor would be pleased if you could come to Government House immediately as there is someone from London he wants you to meet.'

'Can't I change first? I've only just come in from safari.'

'No, sir, he just wants you as you are as quickly as you can make it. I think it's because this big wig from London is very short of time.'

'Okay, we'll follow along.'

As he drove off I turned to Kidogo.

'You'd better come with me and then we can come back and deal with the kit etc. and afterwards I'll take you back to the warehouse. I don't know what it's all about but if this man from London is in such a hurry I shouldn't be too long.'

CHAPTER 29

As soon as I arrived at Government House I was ushered into the Governor's private office.

'Hello, Gavin, thank you for coming so promptly. Sir John let me introduce Gavin McKenzie. Gavin, Sir John Gainer of the Colonial Office.'

I remembered seeing this man's name in the papers, and hearing people talking about him. He was a prime mover in anything to do with the British Colonies.

He was a big gruff man with silver grey hair and a weather-beaten face.

'How do you do, sir. Please excuse my appearance but I've just arrived back from safari and I was asked to get here without delay.'

'Quite all right. I'm only sorry we've had to interfere

with your evening.'

'I'm going to leave you two to it,' the Governor said. 'I'll be in the room through that door so when you've finished talking, if you'd like to come through, we can have a drink together. Had lunch with your parents last Sunday, Gavin. They both looked remarkably well. I'll see you two later.' With that he left us.

'Let's sit down over there, shall we, McKenzie?'

We sat opposite each other in deep leather armchairs at one end of the room. Sir John leant forward.

'Everything I'm going to say to you is, at any rate for the time being, off the record. I've recently read a rather full report concerning you because of your being put forward to receive a CBE for your anti-terrorist work. I've read about how you won your VC and MC. You have, if I may say so, led a very adventurous and courageous life. I am now about to make a proposition to you that, if you decide to decline, we must both forget was ever discussed between us. Things are changing in East Africa and it will not be long before our territories here are given self-rule, so we are trying to prepare for that. The interest we have in you is twofold: game preservation and tourism. Now that the terrorist activities in Kenya have been more or less defeated, the economy of the colony must be looked at with an eye to the future when these people will have to stand on their own feet. The animals of British East Africa, and in particular Kenya, can be an enormous tourist attraction. It is very important, therefore, that proper game management is put into effect without delay. This is where you come in. We need a man who will not be in the Game Department but will have an overall responsibility for co-ordinating game preservation throughout the three territories concerned. He will report, until independence takes place, directly to the Governor or even to Whitehall. It does mean, McKenzie, if you took the job that you would have to give up killing game as you do at present and also, if you will excuse the presumption, have a slightly less raffish life. What is your first reaction? Is there any point in our continuing this conversation?'

'My first question must be—why me? There must be many other men who are more suitably qualified.'

'You have a lot of experience that is relevant and you have something more. Africans, and this is very important, would be willing to follow you because of your reputation as one of Africa's leading white hunters and because you have the highest rewards for military valour.'

'I see. I must admit that I'm extremely interested, more so than you would believe. I had, in just the last few days, been thinking that I might give up professional hunting. Both I, and surprisingly enough my gun bearer, have become worried as to how long the big game can last. Just as important to me as that is that there is a girl I want to marry and she would not come and live out here if I was going to be away on hunting safaris all the time.'

'Well, well. It would seem that, for different reasons, we are heading in the same direction. I must admit that I thought we would have to talk you into giving up your present lifestyle as you have always lived such an adventurous one. Is there anything else you want to ask?'

'One question: what happens to my job when these countries obtain independence?'

'That I can't answer, who knows? If the new governments have any sense they'll continue with the policy of game conservation, but whether they will want a white man running it or not I couldn't say. But, in any case, that's a few years off yet. We will definitely go ahead with an appointment of this nature and as soon as possible. When can you give your decision of whether you will accept the job?'

'I can give you my decision now, with one proviso. I will go to England as soon as I can get a seat on a plane and tell all this, with your permission, to the girl I want to marry and if she'll accept me, and come out here to live, I'll agree to your offer.'

'That's very good. Let me tell you a couple of other things now that we are agreed. Salary will be whatever you want that is reasonable for the responsibilities and status. Do you know Sir James Robertson's house, that large white Moorish place, up near the Mutheiga Club? ... Yes, well the Government has bought that house and it will be your official residence. The only other point is that the CBE you have been put up for, if you take this appointment, will be changed to a KBE. Much more status and authority as Sir Gavin, what!'

I sat back and grinned, I couldn't help it.

'What's amusing you, Mr McKenzie?'

'I was just thinking a CBE was dangled in front of my nose in order to get me to do something for the nation, which I would have done regardless of any reward. Now a knighthood is being proffered in order to make me take the sort of job that couldn't, in my opinion, be more perfect for me.'

'Well, there you are, just shows that things can go well at times. But please don't think the KBE is a bribe. We know too much about you to think that that would be the right way to approach you. Can we take it as settled then, subject to your young lady saying yes to your proposal?'

'You most certainly can.'

'If you could come and see me at the Colonial Office in London when you have seen her we could get everything moving without any further delay.'

'Yes, I'll do that. I'll see when I can get a seat on a plane.'

'If you can be ready by tomorrow evening you can come back with me on an RAF Transport Command aircraft.'

'That would be fine.'

'Good, ring here tomorrow, early afternoon, and they'll give you flight times etc. Shall we go through now and have that drink with the Governor?'

After a quick drink I excused myself, as I didn't want to leave poor old Kidogo waiting in the Land Rover any longer.

When I was sitting in the driving seat I leant back and laughed and laughed. It didn't seem possible. I'd been racking my brains on how I could spend more time in Nairobi so that Carol would be willing to come out to Kenya to live, and now this.

Kidogo sat looking at me but not saying anything.

'Don't worry, Kidogo, I'm not going mad. I've got to go to England tomorrow. Do you want to stay on at the warehouse or do you want to go back to your village for a few days? If only you'd got your driving licence you could have taken the Land Rover.'

'I would like to go back to my village if you're going to be away. How long will you be?'

'Maybe one week.'

'Then I will go after you have gone, *Bwana*.'

'Okay, you've got plenty of money coming as you haven't had your pay yet and I'll give you your train fare etc. We must remember to put you in for a driving test when I get back.'

As I was driving towards the flat my mind was absorbed by my incredible luck, all this and I wasn't even thirty yet. The best thing of the lot being that I felt sure Carol would say yes to my proposal when I told her I was going to be based in Nairobi, working for the Government. As I pulled up outside the flat I decided I must try to phone Carol, no matter what the time was in London, to tell her I was on my way over to see her.

'Kidogo, can you start to sort the stuff out while I go in and make a telephone call. If I'm not back in a few minutes you can start to bring it up.'

'*Ndio, Bwana.*'

I bounced up the stairs my spirits high.

The door was difficult to unlock. I'd have to get the

lock changed, there seemed to be something wrong with it, perhaps someone had been trying to force it. At last, it opened, and I rushed into the dark flat, making for the phone.

I'd only taken a couple of steps when a rope went round my throat and tightened. It was a garrotte, the large knot was trying to push my Adam's apple back through my throat. I struggled for breath and tried to get hold of my assailant but another person came up in front of me and hit me hard in the stomach. What little breath I had was gone.

I was hit several more times and my knees buckled.

They released the rope round my neck and let me drop to the floor where they took turns at kicking me. I felt a couple of ribs go and could feel blood running down my face.

They rolled me onto my back and one of them shone a torch onto my face.

'Where is our gold and money?' he said in English, with a heavy Russian accent.

I didn't say anything.

The torch went out and in the gloom they started to kick me again. I felt another rib go.

'Tell us what we want to know, it will save us all a lot of trouble.'

One of them put his boot on my face and pushed down hard and then, lifting it a few inches, stamped the heel down, breaking my nose.

Then lowering himself, he kneeled on my chest and, leaning forward, he forced the muzzle of a pistol into my mouth. I waited for the blast but it didn't come.

After what seemed like eternity the one holding the pistol removed it and turned towards his companion.

'Go into the kitchen and get a kettle of boiling water, that may help him to remember,' he said in his broken English obviously so that I could understand what was in store for me next.

This had got to be my chance while there was only one of them in the room and because he would not expect anything from me, thinking I was done for.

I rolled to my left and he wobbled as his knees started to slip. He righted himself by leaning the other way when I instantly rolled to the right and he overbalanced. I managed to get my right arm free and hit him in the throat and although there wasn't much strength in it he brought up his hands to defend himself and in the confusion dropped the pistol.

At that moment the second man came back into the room to see what was happening. Just as I was thinking my last minute had come the front door opened and in came Kidogo carrying an armful of kit. He hesitated, for just a split second, then dropping the kit, he stepped forward and as he did so I saw the light from the open door glint on old Mkamba's hunting knife just before it was buried into the Russian.

My Russian was trying to get up when my hand found his pistol. Hoping it was cocked I stuffed it into his ear and pulled the trigger. There was a loud bang and he fell sideways onto the floor. He was dead.

I staggered to my feet, I must make sure the other one was dead as well, no one, from the Government down, could afford to have a KGB agent telling his story about the events of the last few weeks.

I got to him and felt his pulse.

He was dead.

'Well done, Kidogo, *santa sana*,' I said as the room started to spin and I felt myself falling into a never-ending black pit.

CHAPTER 30

became conscious that I was lying in a bed in strange surroundings. I didn't immediately open my eyes, I just remained still and listened and tried to concentrate.

There was a smell that was familiar. It must be a hospital. Was I still in a military hospital after being wounded behind the German lines?

At last, I opened my eyes. Everything was a blur, then a mass of dazzling lights. As my eyes gradually focused, I could see the white ceiling and walls and then I became aware of tubes that hung down and seemed to be attached to various parts of my body.

My memory came floating back—those bloody KGB agents.

'Hello, Mr McKenzie,' a voice said to my left. I turned

my eyes towards it and there was a nurse in her crisp white uniform.

'Just stay still while I fetch a doctor.'

I lay there wondering how long I'd been unconscious and if I'd missed my aircraft to go and see Carol. My mind felt fuzzy and I couldn't focus my eyes for any length of time, I had to keep blinking them.

The nurse was back and there was a man in a white coat with her.

'Hello, Gavin, how are you feeling?'

I looked at him but my mind was so fuddled that it was a minute before I could make out who he was.

It was Bunny Marshall, a right "lad" whom I often saw when he was on the town with someone or other's wife but was known to be one of the best doctors in East Africa.

'I must admit I'm feeling a bit fragile. How long have I been here?'

'No more talking for the moment. I'm just going to give you a little something to make you sleep for a while.'

*   *   *

The next time I opened my eyes I was feeling much more with it.

It was a few minutes before a passing nurse noticed I was awake.

'Good morning,' she said. 'I'll just go and tell Dr Marshall that you're awake.'

Morning, I thought, perhaps I'd still be able to make this evening's flight with Sir John.

In came Bunny followed by a couple of rather nice looking nurses. I must be feeling better!

'Gavin, old son, you're looking a bit better. Let's just take your temperature and blood pressure etc. and then we can talk for a few minutes.'

As they were doing various things I noticed that the tubes that had been hanging around me had now gone. After a few minutes the nurses departed and Bunny squatted on the end of the bed.

'Have I been here all night, Bunny?'

'All night! My dear chap you've been here for four days.'

'For four days! I don't believe you, I can't have been.'

He laughed.

'I'm afraid it's true. You've been a bit poorly. In fact, when you first arrived, we had our doubts that we could save you. It's only because you have such a tough constitution, and determined mind, that you've survived. Your parents came down to Nairobi and spent much of the first few days by your bed. People from Government House have been in and out and the Chief of Police says he wants to talk to you as soon as you can manage it. We have also had a bit of a problem with your gun bearer who has refused to leave the hospital until he has seen you. He's been camping in the grounds. Still, we let him, he obviously means well, and from what I hear he saved your life. So, Gavin, as usual, your presence has created absolute pandemonium.'

'I think that's a bit unfair as all I've done is to lie here quietly sleeping.'

'Ah, here are your parents to see you.'

'Good morning, Colonel. I'd be grateful if you and Mrs McKenzie would make this just a short visit as I want Gavin to get some more sleep.'

My parents were not very demonstrative people, but I could tell they had been worried and concerned about me and my mother took and held my hand.

'You're looking a bit more like your old self, dear,' she said smiling down at me.

'Hope I haven't caused you and Father too much worry.'

'We've certainly been very worried, but it seems you're over the worst now.'

'Anyway, my boy, you certainly seem, according to all

reports, to have done a very good job for the old country and Mother and I are, as always, very proud of you.'

'That's nice of you to say so, Father. I'm desperately upset, as I'm sure you are, about Mkamba. I feel responsible for having taken him into that situation.'

My father cleared his throat, I could tell he had not got over the loss of Mkamba who had been with him for so many years. 'Gavin, we have just got to be philosophical about this. Remember, Mkamba was quite an age and he had had a pretty good life for someone in his circumstances. I think that if he had been able to choose the circumstances of his demise they would have been pretty near what happened. You know what a warrior he was and he would have wanted to finish his days in an action of some sort and not slowly dying in a mud hut. Also, to be with you would have been the finest thing. He looked up to you so much. He considered that you were a great warrior, a great hunter and that you stood in the place of his now non-existent tribal chief. You must have realised that his greatest joy was to be with you and to serve you.'

I just lay silent for a few minutes as I was really touched by what my father had said. He usually was a man of few words and, therefore, one knew that he meant what he had said.

We chatted for a few more minutes then I asked my father if he'd give Kidogo a message for me, to the effect that I was recovering fast, and then take him back to the farm to stay until I got out of hospital and came up there myself.

When they'd gone, I was given another draft of some description that made me feel sleepy. As I drifted off, I was thinking about Carol, and how desperately I wanted to be with her.

*　*　*

As I came out of a deep sleep, lying with my eyes closed, I could feel a nurse straightening my sheets and then taking hold of my hand. Hers was a nice warm slender hand and it didn't let go, it remained holding mine.

Was this some new way of taking my pulse?

No, it couldn't be, that hand was gently caressing mine.

I was going to have to open my eyes, I couldn't lie possum much longer. With an effort I opened them and turned my head to look at the nurse.

My God, I was hallucinating—she looked exactly like Carol.

I closed my eyes firmly and squeezed the lids down, even though it made my broken nose hurt.

Then I flashed them open again.

It was Carol—it wasn't a nurse—it was Carol.

'Carol, oh my darling, darling Carol.'

She leant forward over the bed and very gently kissed my torn, bruised lips.

'Dearest Gavin, what did they do to you?'

'You think I look a mess, you should see the other guy.'

She laughed one of her wonderful laughs.

'You're just as incorrigible as ever.'

'How long have you been back in Kenya?'

'I flew in this afternoon and came straight here.'

'How did you know I'd been injured? Did Harry phone you?'

'No, Harry doesn't know anything about it, he's on safari.'

'Yes, of course he is, I'd quite forgotten, he's taking one for me. Who told you then?'

'A friend of yours, a John Gainer.'

'Sir John Gainer?'

'Yes, I suppose so. He phoned me and said that you'd been on your way to see me when you'd been seriously injured. He asked me if I was fond enough of you to want to make the journey to Nairobi to see you even though you might be dead by the time I arrived. When I said yes, of course, and that I'd realised that I loved you more than anyone or anything else in the world and only wished I'd never left you, he said he'd book me on the next flight to Nairobi; and here I am.'

'Kiss me again, darling, and then just sit and hold my hand for a minute while I enjoy the thought of your being with me again.'

After a few minutes I felt strong enough to talk. I told her how much I loved her and asked her if she would marry me and said that if she didn't want to live in Kenya I was prepared to go somewhere else, anywhere she wanted, just as long as we could be together.

'Yes, I'll marry you and I'll live here in Kenya with you. This country is part of you.'

Then I told her about the appointment I'd been offered and how I'd accept it if it were what she wanted for us.

'It sounds wonderful. It's what you've worked for. It's just you.'

'Oh, Carol, it's all too good to be true and the best part is that we'll be together. I shall settle down and be the quietest, best-behaved man in East Africa.'

'You quiet and well behaved! That will be the day,' she said, followed by another of her delicious laughs.

9 781922 958488